HOOD by T. Rogers

Published by T. Rogers/Barnsdale County Publishing

realtrogers@gmail.com

www.realtrogers.com

HOOD was written by T. Rogers

HOOD by: T. Rogers/Barnsdale County Publishing

1st edition, 2026

Hardback ISBN: 979-8-9943276-0-9

Paperback ISBN: 979-8-9943276-1-6

Ebook ISBN: 979-8-9943276-2-3

HOOD

A Novel

T. Rogers

Barnsdale County Publishing

For Helen Lee Burt (1933-2000), beloved grandmother, who planted a seed the moment she put To Kill a Mockingbird *in my hands as a child.*

"So the police are out," Mom asked, "or did I misunderstand you?"

Dad sighed. "We can try. Unfortunately we're not going to get anywhere."

Mom looked at Loxley. "Do you know for sure who did this?"

"Yes ma'am."

"Tell me."

"I'd rather not."

"Why?"

"Because I don't want you to be a party to what I'm going to do."

"What do you mean?" Dad asked.

"I mean exactly what I said," Loxley replied simply.

"What are you going to do?"

"What the law won't."

"Robin," Mom said gently. "There's nothing you can do."

"I disagree ma'am."

Dad spoke up again. "She's right. We have to figure out how to do this legally."

Loxley raised an eyebrow. "So... what are you going to do?"

Dad didn't respond.

"Robin," Mom said. "Tell me what you're considering."

"What do you think I'm going to do, Mrs. Ellie?"

"I don't know."

"What would you do if you had them sitting here right now?"

Mom's expression darkened. "They wouldn't leave this room alive."

Then it was Loxley's turn to remain silent.

"Never doubt that a small group of thoughtful, committed citizens can change the world: indeed, it's the only thing that ever has."

Margaret Mead

Chapter 1

"BOB? HOW MUCH LONGER, you think?"

Dad glanced down at his phone. "GPS says less than an hour."

Mom nodded and went back to reading the file in her lap.

From my seat behind him, I turned and looked out the window. Ever since we'd gotten through Mobile, the scenery hadn't changed.

There were trees, trees, and more trees.

"It looks like the interstate was cut straight through the forest," I remarked.

"It was" Dad shifted in his seat. "We're traveling through the southwest corner of Sherwood National Forest."

Sighing at the lack of visual stimulation, I rolled my head against the leather seat, glanced at the back of Dad's head, and smiled. Even cruising at highway speeds, he kept his hands at a perfect ten and two o'clock position — one of his many quirks.

We'd been in the car since daylight. After leaving my brother Howard's place in New Orleans, we'd driven through Mississippi into Mobile where we stopped for gas before picking up I-65. Our destination was Barnsdale County, Alabama.

Dad was a former F.B.I. agent. After breaking his leg chasing a suspect, he took early retirement. Before that, his specialty was organized crime.

After he healed, he became a private consultant to law enforcement agencies all over Texas. His reputation was so good the Rangers had him on speed dial.

Alabama's governor had run on a platform of getting tough on crime. From what the news reported, she was holding up her end of the bargain. Funding for law enforcement was up significantly. She'd green-lighted a new gang task force in Montgomery and a sophisticated narcotics squad in Birmingham. The Feds were also involved with Homeland Security and the D.E.A. stepping up their presence at the port of Mobile.

That's what brought us to Barnsdale County, Alabama.

Barnsdale County was in the Black Belt region bordering Florida. Forming a near perfect rectangle, it had a population that wouldn't even fill an NFL stadium. But with its access to Interstate 65, the Sherwood River, the Florida border, and its relative closeness to the ports of Pensacola and Mobile, it was geographically perfect if you were into crime.

From what I'd gathered from overhead conversations, this little county had an overabundance of it, from the petty stuff to rumors of widespread political corruption. The murder rate was astronomical. It was to be Dad's biggest challenge.

"Is this our exit?" Mom asked.

Dad glanced at the sign. "Yep. This is it."

He flipped his blinker and changed lanes. Mom began packing up her papers.

Dad eased us onto the off ramp and made an easy right. I caught a sign that said "NOTTINGHAM- 15 MILES".

The exit looked nearly abandoned. A truck stop had a convenience store and diner, with few visible cars. My guess was it didn't get many tourists.

After a few miles, the view changed — from woods to farmland. Rows upon rows of green plants extended into the distance.

"What are they growing?" I asked.

"Cotton," Dad replied. "They grow a lot of it here."

"I thought cotton was white?"

"It is when it's ready. That'll be later in the year."

Mom changed the subject. "When do you have your meeting with the A.B.I.?"

"Monday."

"Where at?" I asked.

"I think they're coming over to the house."

Mom sighed. "Bob, we're not ready for guests. We haven't unpacked anything."

"Don't worry about it," he assured her. "I've already told them. We'll pick up some sandwich fixings and they can eat off paper plates. They're not coming to be entertained. They just want somewhere private to meet."

"Private?"

"Private," he repeated. "You know how it is — little town, big ears and bigger mouths."

Mom sighed again.

Then it was Dad's turn to change the subject. "You ready for school to start, Kitten?"

"Not really..."

He picked up the tone in my voice. "You sure you're okay with going to public school?"

Since kindergarten, Mom and Dad had put me in private school to avoid the increasing crime rate in Dallas. This would be my first time mingling with the "unwashed masses," as Mom jokingly said.

"I guess," I grumbled. "It's more the fact there's nothing to freaking do."

He looked at me in the rearview mirror and raised his eyebrow at my choice of language.

"Sorry," I said quickly, "but seriously, no soccer team?"

"They got football," he offered jokingly.

I rolled my eyes.

"You could play basketball or softball."

I blanched. I was decent at softball, but I sucked at basketball and wasn't interested in playing either.

Dad's phone started ringing. He stuck his earpiece in and answered. "Hello?"

There was a pause and he said, "Calm down, Mrs. Sadie. What's the problem?"

He sighed. "Great."

There was another pause and his tone lightened. "Really? He can?"

The muffled voice said something else and Dad replied, "Okay... great! Yes ma'am, tell him to go ahead. Can he get parts today?"

Her answer must've been 'yes' because he then replied, "Very good. We're on Highway 311 now. We'll see you soon. Bye."

He hung up and removed his earpiece before he let us in on the conversation. "One of the movers was washing his hands and broke the handle on the faucet. Mrs. Sadie called to give me a heads up."

"Who's Mrs. Sadie?" I asked.

"One of the locals. She's retired and sort of does odd jobs for extra money. She cleaned the house for us and was trying to make sure the movers didn't break anything. I guess she didn't figure they could mess up a sink."

"Oh, dear," Mom sighed.

"It's no problem. She said she knew a guy who was going to get right on it."

"That's good," I replied as my eyes caught sight of a large object in the road up ahead.

Dad noticed it too and slowed down. It turned out to be a tractor doing all of ten miles per hour. He grunted and settled deeper into his seat as we moved at a crawl. The driver was oblivious we were behind him.

"Should I honk?" Dad asked.

"You're asking me about tractor etiquette?" Mom teased.

"So this is Nottingham?" Mom remarked. "Quaint."

I giggled. Dad snorted and shook his head.

Unlike Dad, Mom came from money. Her father had been in the oil business and her mom was a textbook socialite. I didn't remember them, but I'd heard stories.

Whenever Grandma saw something she didn't exactly approve of, she used the word "quaint" — usually with a sniff and her nose pointing towards the ceiling. That represented her code for "falling short of my expectations." It was a running joke between my parents. They used the word "quaint" for anything they believed Grandma wouldn't have approved of.

"York is bigger," he informed us. "It's where most people shop since there's really only a small grocery store and a few Mom-and-Pop places here. Nottingham is the county seat and where the Sheriff's department is, so I was glad to find a house here."

We drove into the town square that was an actual square. Dad made the slow circle around and we passed the courthouse. There were shops on each side. I caught sight of a few: a barber shop, a pawnshop, a café, and a tattoo parlor. More than a few buildings appeared abandoned. The center of the square had a small park with a large fountain and benches strategically placed under mature oak trees. On the south side of the square, opposite the courthouse, was a two-story building with "Barnsdale County Sheriff's Office" on the sign.

I felt like we'd landed in Mayberry.

Dad drove west through a residential neighborhood. Watching as he maneuvered slowly down the street, I admired the aged yet well-maintained houses. They all had well-tended lawns and an array of flowers lining each walkway.

I didn't know how I was going to get along here. I was a city girl, used to bright lights and traffic and having my pick of things to do on the weekends. I was used to Cowboys games and malls. This place wasn't me.

Then again, Dallas wasn't me either — at least not anymore.

I paused that thought as Dad pulled into a driveway.

"Wow!" Mom breathed.

'Wow' was right. The house was beautiful.

It was a two story with white siding and green shutters. The property featured a large porch, a chain-linked fence, and a side door directly facing a two-car, two-story garage. Only a moving van was parked on the street, with no other vehicles in sight. Lush green grass, flanked by blooming magnolia trees, adorned the walkway. It wasn't a mansion, but it was impressive regardless.

"You like it?"

"It's lovely, Bob!" Mom gushed, reaching over to squeeze his hand.

"It's got five bedrooms and four bathrooms, a living room, den, dining room, and an office. The lady who sold it to us is recently widowed and is moving to Huntsville to live with one of her daughters. She was motivated to sell. There's also an apartment over the garage." He looked back at me.

I bit my bottom lip. "What are my odds?"

He shrugged, then glanced at Mom who matched him.

"You don't plan on sneaking out or having a boyfriend sneak in, do you?"

I rolled my eyes. "Dad... seriously?"

That earned me a grin. "Cowboy is bunking with you then."

"Great! When will he be here?"

"It'll be a couple of weeks. He's getting some refresher training. If you're going to be outside the main house, I'd feel better if he was with you."

Cowboy was our six-year-old Great Dane. Mom liked him because he was a breeze to housebreak. Dad liked him because he was very well trained and as protective of me as a mother hen.

"Deal!"

"I can't wait to see this house!" Mom said with obvious excitement.

We made our exit and walked up to the porch. Dad handed both of us a key. I gave him a quick grin and slipped it into the pocket of my shorts. I didn't hold that smile for long because yelling from inside the house caused all our heads to turn.

"I don't care!" yelled out a woman's voice with a drawl so thick I wondered if her lips even touched together when she spoke. "Mr. Fitzwalter's paying y'all to put his stuff where he say and that's what you gonna do."

"I ain't haulin' that goddamn heavy thing up them steps!" replied a gruff voice with an equally syrupy twang.

"There some sort of problem?" Dad asked as he purposefully made his entrance.

"Mister Fitzwalter!"

An elderly black woman wearing a one-piece calico dress entered the room. She was shorter and thinner than I was, but I could see fire in her eyes despite the deep wrinkles and glasses. She had to be pushing eighty.

"What's going on, Mrs. Sadie?"

"I told him your safe go upstairs," she replied, her voice sounding both annoyed and frantic. "He say he ain't gonna do it."

Dad looked up at the mover, with Mom and I trailing behind.

He swallowed and went to looking unsure as Dad eyeballed him with his patented F.B.I. stare.

"That so?"

The man glanced at Mrs. Sadie, who put her hands on her hips. Looking back at Dad, he shook his head.

"We didn't want to damage any of the contents," he explained.

"It's empty."

The guy gave a slow nod of acknowledgement.

"Well? What are you waiting for?"

"Yes, sir."

The man dropped his head, turned, and went down the hallway.

"Lord," she sighed. "I wish I'd known you hired one of them Johnson boys. They all shiftless."

'Lord' came out as 'Lawd.'

"Don't worry about it," Dad assured her. "They break anything else?"

"No sir, I made sure they didn't."

Dad smiled as he guided her to us. "Good. Come meet

my family. This is my wife Eleanor and my daughter Marian."

"It's nice to meet you," Mom said, offering her hand.

Mrs. Sadie took it. "Pleasure, ma'am." She then turned to me. "And aren't you just a sight!"

I smiled at the compliment. "Nice to meet you."

She released Mom's hand and took mine. Hers were gnarled, but her grip was much stronger than I expected from someone that appeared so wizened. Her brown eyes sparked once more, but with intelligence instead of anger.

She might not have sounded like she had the best handle on the English language, but I was betting there was nothing dull about her mind.

"Any other problems?" Dad asked.

She released my hand and turned back to him. "No, sir. That safe was the last thing needing moved."

"And the sink?"

"The sink is just fine. I got Max on it. He had to replace the entire faucet."

"They broke it that badly?" Dad asked.

She rolled her eyes, threw her hands onto her hips again, and huffed. "If I'd known they was that clumsy, I'd a told 'em to use the hose pipe."

"You don't worry about it. What do we owe Max?"

She shrugged. "We'll get a receipt for the parts to you. You can give him whatever you like. He was glad to do it."

"I've got some cash in the car," Mom offered.

"Y'all got any luggage with you?"

"There're only a few suitcases. But you don't concern yourself with that."

She snorted. "You hired me to help get this house in order. That's what I plan on doin'."

"Would you care to join us for an early dinner first?" Dad asked. "We missed lunch and we're a bit hungry. Our treat."

"Sure! Let me get my purse out of the kitchen."

"I'll grab it," I offered.

"It's that way," she pointed.

I stepped around a pile of boxes and went in that direction, turning my head towards them. "Is that café on the square any good?"

"It's decent. Their cornbread's too dry for my likin'."

I stepped through the door and slammed into something hard.

"Oof!" I squeaked as I fell backwards.

A large, pale hand grabbed me before I could bruise my backside. Its owner snatched me back to my feet like I didn't weigh anything.

"Thanks," I said before my mouth went dry.

He was huge. Well, big anyway. The man standing over me was just a bit taller than my dad, but younger, broader, and more muscular. He had bleached white hair and wore a t-shirt, overalls, and heavy work boots, with a wrench hanging loose in his right hand.

I stepped back. "I'm sorry..."

He didn't answer. His face reminded me of Michael Myers — expressionless except for his eyes, which seemed to bore holes right into me.

"Max!" Mrs. Sadie exclaimed. "Watch where you goin', son!"

Without a word, he moved so I could pass.

I darted around him into the kitchen. My eyes found the oversized, multi-colored purse on the counter and I grabbed it quickly before hurrying back into the living room. Max stayed put, his gaze following me the entire time.

"You okay, Kitten?" Dad asked when I returned.

"Yes, sir. He just surprised me."

"Don't mind Max," Mrs. Sadie said. "He don't mean no harm. Sometimes he forget how big he is. Max, use your manners and come meet the Fitzwalters."

Max slowly ambled up to us. He faced my father first, swapped the wrench to his left hand, wiped his right on the leg of his overalls, and extended it.

"Bob Fitzwalter," Dad introduced as they shook.

Max didn't respond.

Dad looked a little unnerved. "This is my wife, Eleanor."

"How do you do, Max?"

He released Dad's hand and gave Mom a slow nod but still didn't say anything.

"This is Marian," Mrs. Sadie told him. "She'll be starting school with you and the rest of the crew."

Max's eyes settled back on me, and I tried to steady my nerves. To my surprise, I found myself less afraid at second glance. He didn't look dangerous. In fact, he looked like a toddler with a case of the shies that was about to bury his face against your leg- only much, much bigger.

"Hi, Max."

Just like with Mom, all I got was a nod.

"Max don't talk," Mrs. Sadie explained.

Chapter 2

Mrs. Sadie sent Max off before we went to eat. He only responded with a nod, then left with his toolbox.

The café on the square was your regular greasy spoon. The meatloaf was okay, but I knew I couldn't keep eating like that or I'd gain three dress sizes by Christmas. Once we finished, Mrs. Sadie insisted she come back to the house and help us unpack. Mom and Dad tried to talk her out of it, but she was adamant. Dad had paid her to do a job and she asserted she was allowed to complete it.

"So, Mrs. Sadie," Dad said as he began opening another box. "What can you tell me about crime in the area?"

"What you mean?"

He shrugged and tried to sound like he was making small talk. "It's been my experience that if I want to know what's really going on in a small town, it's best to ask a long-time resident. They've been around and know who's who and what's what."

She nodded along as she wiped one of the picture frames

with a cloth. "That makes sense. What are you wanting to know exactly?"

"You know why I'm here, right?"

"I do."

"So, what can you tell me?"

"I can tell you this whole county has always had a darker side than most. Barnsdale County outdoes itself."

"Who's doing it?"

She snorted and laid the picture aside. "Take your pick."

"Not to sound rude, but gangs tend to segregate themselves. So if you don't mind me asking, what color are they?"

"You right," she agreed. She then pondered the question. "It depends on which rumors you believe."

"I want to hear them all."

"Well, you got the colored folks... Black Fox Family they call themselves... runnin' vice and doin' some robberies."

"I've heard of them."

She nodded and continued. "People have been spreadin' rumors for years that the Injuns are running guns."

"Heard that one too."

"Been seeing more Mexicans around. Them and Fox probably going to be tyin' up over drugs."

Dad nodded along.

"As far as the white folks? You got the Dixie Mafia."

"How solid is your info? On the Dixie Mafia, I mean?"

She gave him a puzzled look.

"I mean," he explained, "is it just rumor, or do they actually exist around here?"

"Oh, they exist. They the ones doin' most of it. If it's

illegal, they're the first people think of, especially cookin' crystal."

"Are they the ones I've been hearing rumors about recently?" He questioned. "Or is that the Burners?"

"I'm not followin'."

"Word on the street is there's a gang on motorcycles causing trouble around here. Something about a bunch robbing people and assaulting them and burning up cars and buildings. I know there's an M.C. called the Barnburners in the area."

"I ain't heard 'bout that."

Mrs. Sadie's voiced changed when she answered him. It got weaker. Also, she averted her eyes.

If I could tell she was lying, I knew Dad had caught it. "Mrs. Sadie? I think you have."

"I know things ain't always what they seem in this county, Mr. Fitzwalter. You'd do best to remember that too."

"What do you mean?"

"Who's helping you down here? I hope you ain't by yourself."

He shook his head. "I've got the Alabama Bureau of Investigation coming down to talk Monday. I'm hoping I can meet with the locals after that."

Then it was her shaking her head. "You'd do best to be careful around them. The good guys don't always wear the white hats, if you know what I'm sayin'."

"I do."

"And I do know something about the people you talkin' about," she admitted. "The ones you say are new."

"Like what?"

"My advice? Leave them alone."

Dad looked surprised. "Why do you say that?"

"Let me ask you something. What else people tellin' you?"

"Nothing."

"Exactly," she said, pointing a gnarled finger at Dad. "So you don't know those people gettin' robbed or beat up or their houses and cars gettin' lit on fire, do you?"

"They're citizens."

She shook her head. "No, sir... they the criminals."

Dad looked puzzled. "What do you mean?"

"Your sources don't say the man robbed was a drug dealer," she explained. "Or that the house burned down was where they were cookin' meth. Or the car lit on fire was used in a stick-up, do they?"

"No, ma'am."

"Not all the bad guys wear the black hats either, Mr. Fitzwalter."

Dad didn't have an answer for that.

Mom decided to change the subject. "So, tell us about Max."

Mrs. Sadie seemed happy to go to another topic. "Max is a good boy. He scares some folks 'cause he's so big and so quiet, but he's good."

"Why doesn't he talk?" I asked.

She frowned. "I honestly can't remember the last time I heard him speak."

"Why not?"

"His mama is up in the looney bin for hurtin' him. He ain't made a sound since they arrested her. One of our friends thinks she hurt him because he was too loud." She shook her head in disgust. "Like you can just tell a young'un that small to be quiet. That woman did some bad things to him."

"That's terrible," Mom said with a frown. "Where's his father?"

"Doin' his best. He delivers bread, so he works long hours."

"Is he in some kind of special education program?"

She shook her head.

"Therapy?"

"Tried that. We took him to county mental health. They said it won't do him no good if he won't talk to the doctor."

Mom frowned. "How does he do in school?"

Mrs. Sadie smiled proudly. "He's real smart... makes good grades. Max might not talk, but there's nothing wrong with his head. He uses sign language some even though he can hear just fine, can write good and that figuring... the kind with the shapes and stuff..."

"Geometry?" I asked.

"That's it. Max can do all that. He got the prettiest handwriting and reads all the time. He's been on the Honor Roll in the paper ever since he started school."

"Interesting."

Mom was right. It was interesting. One would expect a kid that refused to talk to be committed somewhere, or at least receive medication or some kind of therapy. I had no idea how Max got along.

"Does he have trouble in school?" Dad asked. "I mean,

do people pick on him?"

Mrs. Sadie shook her head. "Oh no, he's got good friends."

That surprised me. "Friends?"

"Yes, child. Good ones. There's a group of them. They hang out together, ride motorcycles and help each other. They're basically family. My oldest grandchild hangs around with them a lot." She gave me a long look. "If you ever be needin' some help, Miss Marian, you do good to go to them. They might not dress pretty as you but they good people. Most people out for themselves, if you know what I mean."

My thoughts flashed to George, my ex, back in Dallas. "Yes, ma'am."

I STARTED ON WHAT was to be my room while Mom and Dad took Mrs. Sadie home.

I was thrilled with the small apartment. Not only would I have privacy, but it would give me a feeling of living on my own. The bathroom was big enough to have a double sink and a linen closet. The shower would've comfortably held two of me. I was also ecstatic to see it had its own hot water heater and wasn't connected to the one in the main house.

I had my own cable hook-ups. There was a kitchen area with a two-burner stove and a small oven, sink, and full-sized refrigerator. The bedroom had a walk-in closet.

I didn't have any furniture. Getting to redecorate was something of a bribe from Dad — an unnecessary one.

I heard someone's feet coming up the steps as I leaned my golf clubs in the corner by the window. The noise stopped at the top and I heard a knock.

I grinned. "Enter at your own risk."

Dad came inside. In one hand, he had a suitcase I recognized as mine. But slung over his right shoulder was a shotgun.

"Can we talk?"

"Of course."

He put the luggage down and unslung the weapon. "You remember how to use this, right?"

"Absolutely."

I'd been handling one since I was probably nine or ten. Everyone in my family shot — mostly skeet, but some bird hunting as well. I felt very capable with a shotgun.

"If you're going to be staying up here away from the main house, I want you to have this. Understand?"

"Yes, sir."

He held the weapon out to me and I made a show of taking it, checking the safety, pulling the pump down just enough to make sure it was loaded, but the chamber was empty, and bringing the muzzle back up towards the ceiling. While I'd never kept a firearm in my room, I wasn't surprised Dad thought of this. He was protective of me, but he was also practical. So was Mom, but in a different way.

"Where should I put it?"

He pondered. "Somewhere you can grab it quickly."

"Under the bed?"

"I was thinking closet."

"How about this?" I suggested as I turned, leaned it in the corner beside the closet, and opened the door so it was hidden.

"Good," he agreed.

"When do I get furniture?"

"You and your mom can work on that tomorrow," he replied. "She's got a week before she starts at the ER."

I nodded. It looked like I was sleeping on the floor.

"You see anything else you might need?" Dad asked. "Some ceiling fans look like they'd be helpful."

"Yes, sir. As soon as we get the furniture, I'll get everything squared away. Mrs. Sadie did a good job cleaning, but all this clutter bothers me."

"I asked her if she was free next week," Dad said, leaning against the doorjamb. "She's got church tomorrow."

"What about Monday?"

He shook his head. "She sits with some old guy out towards Saylis."

"She's nice. A little outspoken, but I kind of like that in old people."

"She has her opinions," Dad agreed with just enough edge in his voice. I picked up on it immediately.

"Something wrong?"

"I just think I'm going to run into a lot of people like her."

"Like her?"

"Yeah," he explained, "people that are okay with the law being broken if it doesn't hurt them. It has to be the same for everyone, every time."

I'd heard this from him before. "True."

"Anyway, we'll hunt for some furniture tomorrow. There might be somewhere in York, but we'll probably have to go to Mobile. We're going to have to get you a vehicle too, so I'd start deciding what you want."

"I can't take my bike?"

He shook his head. "The high school is just before you get to York. It would take you half a day to ride that far."

I sighed. "I'm not going to have to take the bus, am I?"

"Nah," he replied. "I'll get you to school till we get you mobile."

He stepped forward and hugged me tight. I returned his hug, breathing in the scent of the Gravity cologne he always wore. He pulled away first and looked at me seriously.

"One more piece of advice?"

I grinned. "Sure."

"You make up your own mind. I know Mrs. Sadie means well, but you trust your instincts. If or somebody doesn't seem right, you avoid them. You've got a good head on your shoulders, Kitten. Use it."

"Yes, sir."

It turned out we didn't have to wait or go to Mobile.

Clarence Furniture opened for us. Mrs. Sadie pulled some strings and got the owner to call Mom. I wasn't sure what she said to get him to open on a Sunday but

I suspected it was something like, "Hey, we need a lot of furniture. You open up and let us look and we'll buy from you." He had a really nice selection for a town the size of York and was even willing to deliver.

"What kind of car do you want?" Mom asked.

I shrugged from the passenger's seat and glanced at my outside mirror to make sure the delivery truck was still keeping up.

"I don't know. I mean, I didn't expect to need one 'til I was a sophomore in college."

"Be thinking about it. Not being able to go when and where you want to will get old quick."

When we approached the square, I saw it was more deserted today. I assumed it was because everyone was in church. Only the café looked like it had any business.

We slowed more as Mom came up behind a couple of motorcycles. They made an easy turn and Mom stayed behind them, keeping her distance. They approached the Sherriff's Department and I noticed a deputy coming out of the building and stopping to stare at the bikers.

I assumed the smaller one yelled something to his partner because he threw back his head and laughed. The smaller one then turned, extended his right arm, and flipped the deputy off.

"Well, that's rude," Mom remarked dryly.

The deputy yelled something back at the bikers and they both appeared to roar with laughter. Both bikes down-shifted, squealed tires, made the hard turn onto Highway 92, and sped off.

I just shook my head. "That wouldn't fly in Dallas."

"I'm not sure there's a law against giving a cop the finger, though I'll admit I've never asked — mainly because I've never really wanted to."

Mom pulled up in the driveway and I unbuckled. The delivery truck pulled past us before the driver put it in reverse and began backing it up.

"I need to pee," Mom said. "Will you show them what goes where?"

"I don't know where everything goes."

"Then show them where your stuff goes."

"Yes, ma'am."

Three guys emerged from the truck, opened the back doors, and stared at me expectantly.

"Okay," I instructed. "The desk and the queen bed go into the upstairs apartment. The breakfast table does too."

"Alright," the smallest of the three replied.

They started unloading and I leaned against the Range Rover to watch. They were quiet as they worked, moving pieces and putting them on the concrete.

I decided to see if they could explain what I'd witnessed. "Hey, y'all see the two guys on bikes in front of the Sheriff's office? They were right in front of us."

"Nah," the biggest one with the bald head and bushy beard answered. "They the ones I heard squalling tires?"

"Yep. One of them flipped the Deputy off as he went by."

The middle-sized one, wearing baggy pants and a white tank top, snickered. "That must've been Hood."

"Hood?"

He stopped working and pulled out a cigarette. "Yeah.

Crazy white boy on a motorcycle? That shit sounds like Hood."

"Who's Hood?"

"You don't know Hood?"

I shook my head as he exhaled smoke through his nose. "We just got here yesterday."

"He's a junior," he explained. "You'll see him and his crew around."

"Where your Daddy at?" The biggest one interrupted.

"He's inside. He's probably going over some files."

"What's he do?" Skinny asked.

"He's a consultant with the A.B.I."

That made all three of them glance at each other nervously. Good.

"You about through, Jermaine?" Big Guy asked. "We got shit to do."

He took one more drag and dropped the cigarette butt on the concrete before crushing it with the toe of his Nike. I let my gaze follow his motions, then looked him in the eye to let him know I disapproved. I might as well have been staring at the wall behind me.

Chapter 3

THE REST OF THE week was all work and no play, making Marian a dull girl.

I spent most of it in my apartment getting things situated. I painted all the walls, hung up my pictures, and arranged my furniture.

Dad had his meeting on Monday. I went to the hospital with Mom to help get her office set up so he could have some privacy. He said things went well but didn't elaborate.

With a week to go before school started, I had everything I needed. I'd ordered my school clothes online, went shopping with Mom for supplies, and got my computer and internet hooked up.

Monday night was Mom's first night at work. I was re-reading *The Grapes of Wrath* and listening to a local country station, which was about all I could pick up. Dad was out meeting with the Nottingham City Council.

Sighing, I looked at my picture board. The smiling faces

of my old acquaintances in Dallas looked back at me: Susan... Petra... George...

George.

I rolled my eyes and slammed my book shut, Hank Williams's voice singing, "Me oh, my oh," blocking out all other sounds. I hopped off the bed and glared back at George's photograph.

I was an idiot. I know that now. But I was smitten with the jerk until the beginning of the year. I wish I hadn't let flattery get him anywhere, but it did.

It got me into the backseat of his Challenger.

He was my main reason for not fighting Dad about his transfer. I could never be comfortable back in Dallas. People with big mouths ensured my secret wasn't so secret.

My hand shot out to do something... rip the picture into tiny pieces, I guess... when my eyes froze on the window overlooking the backyard.

The light beside the kitchen door was out.

That shouldn't have made the hair on the back of my neck stiffen, but it did. I shut the radio off and pulled the buds out of my ears. Stepping sideways so my profile wasn't visible in the window, I eased the curtain back and looked.

The back door to the kitchen was about halfway open.

Dad was a cop. We didn't leave doors open, accidentally or otherwise. And I knew no one had made it home. While I might not have heard them, I would've most likely seen headlights pass through the window or felt the vibrations of the garage door opening.

Someone was in our house.

Quickly, I stepped away from the window and let my hand drop onto my phone before I stopped to think about it. I couldn't call the police.

Well, I could... but what if no one was there? The last thing I wanted was for Dad to get a reputation for having a flaky daughter. For better or worse, my behavior reflected on him as a father... and as a cop.

I pulled my hand away from the phone and considered my options. Dad wouldn't hesitate to leave the meeting, but I didn't want to call him for nothing. I could lock my door and hide. I could take the risk and call 911. Or I could just go check.

I decided to have a look. If I was wrong, no harm, no foul. If I was right, I would put the intruder on the floor at gunpoint and then call 911. At least this way I didn't have to worry about potentially embarrassing Dad.

Decision made, I grabbed the phone and slipped it into my back pocket, then picked up the shotgun. Grumbling about the fact I was wearing a very non-tactical outfit — shorts, tank top, and tennis shoes — I put the stock to my shoulder and crossed the room before easing the door open and listening.

Not hearing anything, I crept down the stairs. Once both feet were on concrete, I peeked around the corner. Just as I suspected, there wasn't a vehicle visible through the back window of the garage or in the driveway. I took a deep breath and tiptoed to the kitchen door.

I paused at the door long enough to check the light bulb, getting more nervous when I gave it a twist and it came back on. I decided my best bet was to look for evidence that someone was still inside. If I saw nothing, I'd reevaluate. If there was something, I'd retreat and call for back-up.

Using the shotgun's barrel, I pushed on the door, relieved when it swung quietly, and took a step inside.

Before I could start looking for evidence of an intruder, I heard a bump in the living room. I raised the shotgun to confront the noise when someone wearing a hooded shirt came through the doorway.

The intruder's head was turned, so they were looking over their shoulder and not where they were going. They started turning back around when I made my presence known. Keeping the center island between us, I racked the shotgun. It broke the quiet with grim authority.

"Get your hands up!"

The intruder froze without completing his turn as I reached behind me and flipped on the light switch. He raised his glove-covered hands and I quickly got both of mine back on my weapon. I noted a sheathed knife on his right hip.

"Turn around," I ordered. "Slowly."

Instead, he kept looking back in the direction he came, like he was considering his odds.

"You won't make it," I warned. "Turn around."

He did as he was told and I started memorizing anything that might be important: height at a little over six feet, wearing jeans, a belt, boots, and leather gloves. It looked like he was wearing a t-shirt, but his head was covered by a hood — dark blue now that I had the light. A bandana like the biker's I saw Sunday covered the bottom part of his face.

"Let me see your face."

He sighed and lowered the hood to reveal reddish-brown hair. There was a moment's hesitation before he lowered the makeshift mask.

Despite having a short, neatly trimmed beard, he looked to be about my age. If he was older, it couldn't have been by much. His eyes were a bright blue. His expression didn't look angry or scared. He looked resigned.

"Don't shoot me."

His voice was a soft drawl that was more musical than the harshness I'd been hearing around here. His eyelids drooped, but he kept his hands where I could see them.

"Lie down on the floor," I instructed.

"Why?"

What did he mean, "why"?

"So I can keep you covered and call the cops."

"You don't have to do that."

Was he crazy?

"Seriously?"

There was no arrogance in his voice. "Look, Miss, I'm sorry I broke in here. But seriously, don't call the police. I'm begging you."

"You broke into my damn house!" I snapped. "Why the hell shouldn't I call the cops?"

"Because they'll try to take me to jail."

"That's normally the penalty for burglary."

"I'm sorry."

"You should've thought of that before you broke into my house and got caught."

"I don't want anyone to get hurt."

My eyes narrowed. "I like my odds."

He swallowed and seemed to measure his words carefully. "Look... Miss... I said I was sorry. Let me go and this will be the end of it. But I have to warn you, I'm not going to jail. There are people that depend on me."

He was threatening me?

"I'm going to tell you one more time," I warned. "Lie down on the floor. The next time I have to tell you, I'm putting a load of buckshot in your chest. You're in my house. Castle doctrine is in full effect."

His lips pursed as he weighed my words. I pushed the shotgun forward an inch for emphasis. Since I had the advantage, even if he got to the knife, I wanted to keep all the odds completely in my favor. I felt my trigger finger tighten reflexively.

"You don't want to do this."

"You didn't have to break in."

"Desperate times."

"Why?"

"Can I show you?"

"What do you mean?"

He started lowering his hands and reaching into his back pocket.

"Don't do it, asshole!" I snarled.

His hands shot back up. "I was going to show you why I was here."

"You... you took something?"

He nodded. "It belongs to another family, not yours."

"It's in my house."

"Which is why I snuck in here, to avoid this conversation."

"You could've just knocked on the door and asked."

He snorted indigently. "This is too important for me to put my trust in a cop. No, thank you."

"Well, that's rude!"

"It's an unfortunate truth in Barnsdale County. I had to. People are depending on me."

My arms were tiring. "Get down on the floor."

He shook his head again and slowly lowered his hands. I watched as he rested them on the counter where I could see them.

"Listen to me," he said calmly. "I'm not going to jail. I'm sorry I broke in, but I cannot, nor will I, go to jail. I'm going to walk around this counter and leave. You can let me go or you can shoot me. That's your choice. But I won't let them arrest me."

"If you have people depending on you," I challenged, "why are you so willing to get shot? If you go to jail, you live to fight another day."

"It doesn't work that way. If I get shot, I die knowing I did all I could to help them. I can't do that if I get arrested. I know you don't get that. But I can assure you, they know how it works around here and they'll understand completely."

This guy was either noble or crazy — or both.

I had to know for sure if he was lying or not. The conversation was so odd I'd gotten curious.

"Okay," I said. "I'll make you a deal."

"I'm listening."

"You put your knife on the counter. Once it's out, you

empty your pockets. If you're clean, I'll let you go. If you're lying, you're going to jail, and you will go to jail via the hospital because I'm going to blow your fucking kneecaps off. What do you say?"

"You see I didn't steal the silverware and I walk?"

"And you show me what you came for that's worth risking your life."

"I accept."

"Try anything stupid and you're getting a case of lead poisoning."

"Fair enough."

His hand dropped to the knife. He drew it without looking, his eyes steadily on me, and placed it on the counter before sliding it in my direction.

"We good?"

"So far."

He grabbed the end of his shirt and lifted it almost to his navel.

"What are you doing?"

"Showing you I'm not hiding a piece."

His stomach was flat and he had a trail of hair that disappeared into the waistband of blue plaid-colored boxers. His jeans rode just below that.

"I'm going to turn around now."

"Go ahead."

He did so and had nothing stuck there that I could see. He stopped when his back was to me, lowered his shirt, reached into his right hip pocket, and came out with a folded envelope.

"This is what I came for."

"Gotcha." It was probably wrong to think a criminal had a cute butt.

He put the paper between his teeth and his hands reached into both front pockets of his jeans. He then tugged them out to show me they were also empty.

"You don't carry a wallet?"

He shook his head and took the paper out of his mouth. "Not on B and E jobs."

"Good thing you don't have a gun."

"Not usually, though for the record I freaking hate being this close to the Sheriff's Department without one."

He definitely had his issues with local law enforcement. "Okay, so you're clean."

"Deal still on?"

"What are you holding?"

He brought his hands down, unfolded the envelope, and withdrew several pages. He then spread them out and held them for me to see.

"It looks like a land deed."

He nodded. "The lady y'all bought the house from has some acreage she needs to sell. The money is going to help out her daughter — the one she's moving in with. Her husband hid the deed. Like many people around here, he didn't trust banks, so he didn't put it in a safe deposit box. It was under a floorboard in the closet in a guest room — the last one on the left."

"You could've just asked us for it."

He shook his head. "If the wrong people got hold of this deed, they would've gotten control of the property, which means she can't sell it. And, like I've alluded to..."

"... You don't trust cops."

"Precisely."

"How do I know you're not full of it?"

"How else would I have known where it was hidden?" He explained patiently. "If you ask the right people, they'll vouch for me. Believe it or not, we've got one or two mutual acquaintances."

I couldn't find any holes in his story... yet. Considering what I'd heard about corruption in Barnsdale County, what he said about not wanting someone to get their hands on that deed made sense. And obviously it didn't belong to my family.

"Alright," I relented.

He breathed a sigh of relief and began folding the deed back up.

"What's your name?" I asked.

He smiled, and I had to catch myself before I smiled back. He had one of those devil-may-care grins that caused girls' panties to drop — and there was no way I was falling for that crap. I already felt exposed with bare legs and a shirt skimpy enough he could tell the color of my bra.

"Robert," he replied. "Robert Loxley."

"You the one I heard called Hood?" I asked.

"Among other things."

"Why?"

"Why what?"

"Why do they call you Hood? Because you wear that shirt a lot?"

"Who knows? None of my friends call me that."

I got the impression either he was lying or just didn't

care to discuss it. "What do they call you?"

"Robin."

To me, that was stranger than Hood. "Why?"

"That's a long story. My teachers and my grandpa are the only ones that call me Robert."

"Well, we're not exactly friends, considering I'm pointing a gun at you."

"True."

"Alright, Robert Loxley, you come back here again, I'm going to shoot first and ask questions later. Got it?"

"Got it."

I motioned with the shotgun. "Get out of here. If you're willing to die over it, it must be important. If I'd caught you sneaking out with the flat screen, I assure you I wouldn't be this nice."

He stuffed the paper back in his pocket while I watched him carefully. I noticed he was smart enough to nod at the knife for permission to pick it up. I nodded back since he couldn't reach me across the counter and I still had the gun.

"Do I get to know your name?" he asked as he sheathed the blade.

"You don't know already?"

"Fitzwalter. Everybody knows that. But I don't know your first name."

"Marian."

He smiled. "Marian. I like that name."

"You can wipe that smirk off your face."

He didn't. "Look, Marian, I owe you one. Seriously, I appreciate this. So you need something, come find me. You met Max, right?"

I nodded.

"If you can't find me," he went on, "you find Max. If you can't, ask around school for Alonzo Tuck, Mrs. Sadie's grandson. They'll help you and if they can't, they know how to find me. I mean it. You need anything, you just let it be known."

I remembered Mrs. Sadie's words about Max having "good friends." I wondered if she meant this guy. She used the phrase "good people," but then again, I had just caught him breaking and entering.

I couldn't see myself needing anything from a thief. "Forget it. Just get out of here before my parents get home."

He nodded and began moving counterclockwise around the bar. I moved with him, keeping it between us. He got to the door and looked over his shoulder.

"Thanks again. I'm sure we'll see each other around."

Before I could make a nasty comment, he was gone.

I counted out a full minute in my head, then walked out the door. All I could hear was crickets. I locked up the house and headed back to my quarters with the shotgun slung over my shoulder. As I reached the top step, a motorcycle started up in the distance.

Chapter 4

"THESE PEOPLE ARE NUTS..."

It was Tuesday morning. Mom had just gotten home and we were at the kitchen table having breakfast.

After Robert Loxley made his escape, I returned my shotgun to its hiding place. Sleep eluded me for a while.

I felt I'd made the right decision. I didn't believe anything good would've happened if I'd turned him in. Although he committed a crime, his story appeared credible. He had nothing else on him. My gut instinct told me it was the right thing to do. I was wary, but I couldn't see a downside to letting him go.

"What do you mean?" Mom asked.

He took a swallow of his coffee and continued. "The council meeting. Those people are out of their minds."

She gave him a puzzled look.

Dad was on a roll. "They asked the dumbest questions. One wanted to know where we were going to set up speed traps. Another wanted to know what we were going to do about littering. And this old lady with the gray perm?" He shook his head. "All I heard the entire meeting was about some kids knocking down her mailbox."

"They weren't up to speed?"

"That's what's so frustrating," he went on. "I honestly got the impression they were yanking my chain."

"Why would you think that?"

"Sheriff Wendensel got there before I did and addressed the council. He should've explained what I was doing here."

"What are you thinking, Bob?"

"I don't have anything concrete," Dad said, leaning back in his chair. "But considering all the rumors I've got of corruption, it wouldn't surprise me if Wendensel did this or at least muddied the waters just to bury me in B.S. complaints."

"Surely you don't think that," Mom said, sitting down and crossing her scrub-covered legs. "I mean, you've heard rumors of corrupt cops everywhere you've worked, and you've only caught a handful in your career, right?"

"And missed probably ten times as many because I couldn't prove it." He shook his head. "That's just Nottingham's. I've also got to worry about York's city council and the county commissioners — the actual power in this area."

I spoke up. "Just be careful, Dad."

He gave me a wink. "Always. We're still going car shopping today, right?"

"I guess," I grumbled.

"Still no idea what you want?"

"It really doesn't matter. I mean, it's not like I'm trying to impress anybody."

"So we want safe and dependable," Mom said.

"And good on gas if we can help it," Dad added.

"Agreed."

"You're quiet, Kitten."

We were headed west on 92 towards Derbyshire. We'd passed two car lots and had seen nothing that struck my fancy. Though I wasn't picky, their inventory appeared like junk from the road.

In Dallas, I had classmates driving BMWs, Audi's, and even one with a Porsche. I didn't need something fast or fancy. In fact, I wanted to avoid that if possible. I'd already considered how I needed to dress now. The last thing I wanted was to give off the impression I thought I was better than anyone else.

"Is that another one coming up?" Dad asked.

I squinted and strained to see. "I think so."

"I'll slow down."

I didn't think I'd fit in. So far, I didn't sound like these people, think like these people, or relate to these people. Regardless of others' thoughts, I didn't want my last two years of high school to be filled with isolation and struggle.

So far, the only people my age I knew were a mute, someone giving off a gangbanger vibe, and a burglar.

Something caught my eye. "Hey, Dad... check that out."

Sitting front and center of a shabby used car lot was a red Volkswagen Beetle — one of the vintage ones. At first glance, it looked like someone had restored it pretty well.

"Which one?"

"The red Bug."

He snickered. "Seriously?"

"Seriously."

He signaled and turned into the lot. "Okay then."

Up close, it looked even better. Someone had given it a fresh coat of paint. The mid-morning sun gleamed off the chrome bumpers. All the glass was intact. Someone had taken good care of it.

"Help you with something, folks?"

Dad and I turned around to find an older man with rotten teeth, whiskers, and a gray button-up shirt — with short sleeves and a lot of grease stains. The breeze had already messed up his comb-over.

Dad spoke up first. "Tell us about the Bug."

The man grinned. "It's a 1974 Volkswagen Super Beetle. The youngest Smith boy... you know the Smiths? Live in that trailer park before you get to York?"

Dad shook his head.

"Anyway, he restored it and sold it to me before he left."

"College?" I asked.

"Army."

Dad nodded. "What's wrong with it?"

"Nothing," the guy said proudly. "Body's solid, engine don't burn no oil, and you won't find one with interior this clean."

"Those wheels aren't original."

The guy shook his head. "Original had hub caps."

"Let's check it out," I said to Dad. "We'll start with the motor."

I went to the hood, grabbed the handle, and found it locked. Dad grinned and shook his head.

"Engine's in the back, little lady," the guy informed me.

"Oh."

My cheeks matched the car's color as I moved to the back. I grabbed the handle and pulled the trunk... hood... whatever... up.

"It looks clean," I announced, like I knew what I was talking about.

"Does it have a reverse gear?" Dad asked.

I looked up. "Huh?"

He turned his head in my direction. "Believe it or not, some of these don't."

"This one does," the guy confirmed. "It was the early models that didn't."

Dad opened the door and peered inside. "The stereo's worth more than the car. Does it run?"

The man snorted like he was insulted. "Like a sewing machine."

Dad looked at me. "You want to try it?"

I nodded. "Yes, sir."

"I'll get the key," the salesman announced before turning and leaving.

As soon as he was inside the little shanty I guessed was his office, Dad turned to me. "Okay. Be critical. Act like you're not all that interested. I don't want this guy taking us for a ride."

"Gotcha."

The salesman returned with a key in his hand. "I didn't get your name, stranger."

"Bob Fitzwalter," Dad replied, offering him a hand. "This is my daughter, Marian."

"Name's Bobby Joe," the man replied, shaking with Dad. "This for your little girl?"

"Yes, sir."

He held the key out to me. "Give it a whirl then, darlin'."

I took it and did my best not to grit my teeth. "Thank you."

I got behind the wheel and Dad moved around to the passenger's seat. It was a little tight for him, but he managed.

"You sure you don't want anything bigger?"

"You don't like it?"

"I don't care, Kitten. It's whatever you want. I'm not driving it. I guess we're going to have to teach you to drive a stick."

I glanced down. "Uh oh."

"We'll manage. Step on the clutch and start her up."

"Now," Dad asked. "How is it?"

"It's not bad," I admitted. Then I glanced at the speedometer. "Oops!"

I was already past sixty, heading for seventy.

"It's got a small engine, but it's so light that it'll accelerate in a hurry. Be careful with it."

"I will, Dad."

I got it to a perfect fifty-five and we continued to ride. Glancing out of the corner of my eye, I saw Dad concentrating as he listened to the car run.

"Okay?" I asked.

"Yep," he replied, sounding surprised. "This thing sounds pretty good, actually."

I beamed. "Excellent!"

"So you like it?"

"I think I do. It... fits me, I think."

Dad chortled. "Well, I'm going to have to try to deal with this old shyster. So try not to act too impressed when we get back."

I grinned. "Okay, Dad."

He draped his left arm over the back of my headrest. "You adjusting okay, Kitten?"

"This place isn't too bad. I'm getting a lot of reading done anyway."

Dad snickered. "Every father's dream. I'm not worried. You'll make friends pretty quick."

"Probably."

"You remember what I said about trusting your instincts?"

My mind immediately flashed to Robert Loxley in our kitchen. "Yes, sir?"

"I've got a hunch something is going on at your school."

He had my attention. "What do you mean?"

"Not at the school," Dad corrected. "If something were happening on school grounds, you wouldn't be going.

What I mean is, I think some people at the school might be responsible for some of the stuff happening."

"What makes you think that?"

He pointed to a side road. "Turn here and whip it around so I can drive. If you can keep from stopping before you turn, drop it into second. If you have to stop, put it in first gear."

I followed his instructions and was able to whip the miniature car around. I brought it to a stop and put it into first while he kept talking.

"It's just a hunch I have. Looking at the arrest reports, there are a lot of juveniles on them. Not only that, there are a lot of unsolved crimes that I think teenagers are doing."

"Why?"

"Timing mostly," he explained. "All of them happened on nights, weekends, or school holidays. The M.O.'s are on the sophisticated side — the only hole in that theory. But the timing fits. Reports I've read and people I've talked to say other than a few schoolyard fights and a couple possession busts, it's pretty quiet — about like your last school. What I'm saying, Kitten, is keep your eyes and ears open. Don't go out of your way to find stuff out, but if you hear something..."

"I'll let you know."

"Good girl. Now clutch, neutral, and pull the emergency brake so we can swap. Let me see if I can drive this matchbox."

"So what did you think, darlin'?"

It was difficult, but I didn't glare at him too hard. The weak woman routine was wearing thin.

"What's your bottom dollar price?" Dad asked.

"Four thousand."

Dad snorted. "No... seriously."

"Seriously... four thousand."

"I can pick one of these up every day of the week for less than two grand."

"Not in this good of shape or with that good a sound system."

"You can keep the sound system. She needs transportation, not entertainment."

"Thirty-five hundred."

"Two."

"Man, I got to make some money too!"

"What did you give for this thing? Eight hundred?"

"More than that!"

Dad leaned against the hood and folded his arms over his chest. Bobby Jo reached into his back pocket and brought out a pack of chewing tobacco. My nose wrinkled as he pulled out a wad of wet, black leaves and stuffed them into his mouth.

"Twenty-two hundred," Dad countered. "Cash."

Bobby Jo shifted the mess in his mouth to his left cheek. "It can sit here for that."

Dad shrugged.

"Thirty-two."

"Twenty-five."

It was fun watching Dad dicker with Bobby Jo. Dad

could've... and did offer to... buy me a new car. I honestly thought he was having fun wheeling and dealing.

"I got to make a profit," Bobby Jo said firmly. Then, he turned right and spat a long, black stream. "Thirty-two hundred is the lowest I'll go."

"There a warranty?" Dad asked.

"As is, Mister."

"Twenty-six."

"Man, you're crazy!"

"No, I'm not. I just know what I'm willing to pay and thirty-two hundred isn't it."

They continued to argue and I left them to it. Leaning into the unrolled window, I turned the key but didn't start it. I made a show of flipping the blinkers and walking around to make sure both sides work. Dad and Bobby Jo were getting heated.

"I ain't going past thirty-two," Bobby Jo said firmly.

"Twenty-seven."

"Not happening. You've got to work with me some."

"Three thousand," I butted in.

Both men looked at me.

"Three thousand cash. Otherwise we're going home."

Bobby Jo looked at Dad who gave him a shrug.

I reached into the car, took the key, walked forward, and held it out for Bobby Jo.

"Thirty-one," he countered.

I shook my head. "Dad, let's go."

"Alright," Bobby Jo relented, "three thousand. Let's go do the paperwork."

He spat again and turned with a huff before ambling

towards his office. Dad hoisted himself off the hood and put an arm around my shoulder.

"That's my girl," he said in a low voice, giving me a gentle squeeze.

"YOU SHOULD'VE SEEN HER, Ellie," Dad bragged. "She walked right up, held out the key, and told him he could take three grand or we were going home. He tried to argue some more and she said 'Dad, let's go' and that was it. Game, set, match."

Mom swallowed her food and smiled. "Well done, Marian."

"It was sort of fun," I admitted. "I was just afraid Dad was going to balk at me taking charge."

He wiped his mouth. "Nah, I would've given him thirty-two if you'd really wanted the car. But there's an art to making a deal. Your Mom's taught you well."

Mom smiled and reached under the table to pat Dad's knee.

"How's work been going?" I asked her.

She shrugged. "This place is crawling with meth."

"It's on the top of my list," Dad assured her.

"So you like the car, Mom?"

She smiled. "I drove one of the newer ones when I was in medical school. We had to get rid of it when I found out I was pregnant with Howard."

"It's got style," Dad spoke up. "It's not generic like what

you see everyone else driving. I think you made a good choice."

"Thank you."

"I did hear some interesting gossip at the hospital," Mom said.

"Do tell."

"One of the X-ray techs and the receptionist had to be separated. They got into a pretty heated argument."

Dad pondered. "Okay, I'll bite. Over what?"

"Cathy... she's the X-ray tech... is getting married soon. She was saying her dad was trying to get a piece of property to build them a house on. There was some problem about the deed being missing."

"Okay, go on..."

"That's the thing. I'm not sure how it works, but she said the deed had been lost years ago. Before her dad could find it or start the legal process to take possession of the property, someone produced it. She was convinced the lawyer that took it to the clerk's office had stolen it."

"So what started the squabble?" Dad asked.

Mom took a sip of her tea and continued. "Ernestine... the clerk... told her right quick the rightful owner of that land was the one that produced the deed and her daddy was nothing but a 'no-good thieving son-of-a-bitch.'"

Dad gawked. "Well, no wonder."

Mom nodded. "After they were separated and Cathy huffed off back to radiology, I asked a couple of the nurses what that was all about. They were... well, they kept looking around like they didn't want to be overheard, but they all agreed Ernestine was right and Cathy's daddy was trying to steal somebody's property right out from under them."

"That's... interesting."

If they only knew...

So Robert Loxley had been telling the truth. Despite his breaking in, I was relieved that letting him go was the right choice.

I took my dishes to the sink, said my good nights, and went up towards my room. Absently, I dug my key out and put it in the lock, freezing when it turned freely.

I really wished Cowboy was there. I was sure I locked up before we left to go car shopping.

I swung the door open but stayed outside. Reaching along the wall, I flipped on the light switch. The room got brighter and I blinked. Nothing looked out of place. I tried to listen closer, but all was quiet.

Leaving the door open so my parents could hear me scream if I was so inclined, I eased through the kitchen area. *The Grapes of Wrath* still sat on the table. The sink was still empty, and the floor didn't have any obviously fresh footprints like it would in a slasher movie.

I flipped on the bedroom light and went straight for my closet. To my relief, the shotgun was still in its place behind the door. I must have been unsettled by my visitor last night.

I locked my door before going to the bathroom to do my nightly routine. That complete, I wandered back into the kitchen area.

Figuring I was just tired, I grabbed my book, planning to try to finish it before I fell asleep. I'd read it before, but it was on the summer reading list, so...

I stopped cold in the doorway as my eyes fell on the bed. Lying on top of the pillow was a folded piece of yellow paper with my name scrawled across it.

“Who’s here?” I called out.

No one answered. After about ten seconds, I approached the folded paper like it was a live bomb. I picked it up, opened it, and looked at the handwriting.

Thank you again, Marian. I owe you one.

There wasn’t a name attached. Instead, below the message was a drawing of two crossed arrows surrounded by a circle.

Chapter 5

THE DAY I'D BEEN dreading had finally arrived. I was now a Junior at Barnsdale County High School.

"You got your lunch?" Dad asked.

"Yes, sir"

"And your bag?"

I swore he was more nervous than I was. "Yes, Dad."

"They have a rule against phones," he said, his coffee mug hovering at his chin. "But I don't care. Keep it on silent and in your purse. You call me if you need something."

"I'll be fine, Dad," I promised.

To be honest, I wasn't so sure.

I was wearing jeans and a green blouse along with sensible sneakers. My hair was down, and other than my watch and a couple of studs in my ears, I wasn't wearing any jewelry. I didn't want to stand out any more than I already would.

Mom wasn't home yet so Dad was seeing me off. When

he wasn't having meetings or holed up in his office, he'd helped me get used to the Volkswagen's manual transmission. I wasn't a pro yet, but I was confident I could drive to school without too much issue. Looking for a racetrack wasn't my intention.

"You remember what I said?" Dad asked.

I tossed my granola bar wrapper in the trash. "Keep my eyes and ears open and trust my gut."

He nodded. "I think you'll be fine. Heck, you'll probably be bored."

"I can handle it."

"You still got your O.C. in your purse?"

"At all times."

He stepped forward and hugged me. I buried my nose against his tie and squeezed him back gently. He let me go and smiled.

"Be good, Kitten."

"I will, Dad."

The trunk being in front of the car had its advantages. I could pop it open, toss my stuff in there, and never miss a beat. I finished my breakfast, started the car, and buckled up before backing out into the street.

The one thing it didn't have was air conditioning, which was going to suck. Luckily for me, it was August. It would be fall before I knew it. I cracked the window and turned down the radio, muting the morning personalities laughing at their own jokes.

My thoughts turned to school and what might await me. Dad's warning was fresh in my mind. I didn't know why. If word wasn't out already about who he was, it would be by the end of the week. No one would talk to me, at least not about anything criminal.

I slowed down as I approached a pickup truck. The truck was old, with the gas cap behind the driver's door and a fresh black paint job. The driver's hair was blowing in the breeze, a muscular arm absently flicked a cigarette butt into the oncoming lane. The passenger was still as a statue

I kept the textbook three seconds of space between our vehicles as I followed. Ahead I saw three motorcycles, and I wondered if Robert Loxley's was one of them. I glanced at my watch and saw I was going to be early.

Barnsdale High School looked like it was old when my parents were my age. It was a brown two-story building with a football practice field behind it, a couple of separate matching buildings and at least an acre of parking lot. Since everyone in front of me looked like they knew where they were going, I continued trailing the truck that was following the bikes.

They pulled into the last two parking spaces in the lot. Not wanting to appear like I was tailing them, I whipped the Beatle into a space about four down.

When I got out, I heard a gruff voice say something that was followed by good-natured laughter. I ignored it and collected my bags.

"Hey!" a voice called.

I turned around to see a guy approaching. He was wearing jeans, motorcycle boots, a t-shirt, and a black leather vest with his wallet was on a chain. He was thin with dark brown hair a bit on the long side. He had an easy grin.

"Seniors park in the next lot," he said, pointing.

"I'm a Junior," I replied.

"New here?"

"Yeah."

He held out his hand. "Dale Alan."

I shifted my bag over my shoulder and took his hand, giving back as much pressure as I got. I noticed the letters 'K' and 'C' tattooed on the knuckles of his index and middle fingers. Keeping the grip, I rolled our hands over to see the word 'ROCK.'

Dale grinned and made a fist with his left before holding it up. The word 'STAR' was tattooed there.

"Classy." I released his hand. "Marian Fitzwalter."

I thought I saw recognition cross his features. "Cool. Welcome."

"Thanks."

"You need anything, let me know. Just ask for Dale."

There was no chance of that. "Thanks, Dale."

"Catch you later, Marian."

Before I could say anything else, he turned and trotted back towards his group. I saw it was Max that was sitting in the passenger's seat of the truck I had been behind.

I also saw Robert Loxley in the mix.

He was wearing a black t-shirt under the same vest Dale was wearing. Getting a look at him in the daylight without the oversized hooded shirt, I could tell he was in shape.

Of course the local bad boy would be good looking.

He saw me and our eyes met. He finished what he was saying to someone next to him before he lowered his sunglasses and tossed me a wink where only I could see it.

My cheeks flooded and I grabbed my purse and lunch bag before I slammed the trunk shut. The group left ahead of me and I fell in a few steps behind. I dug my schedule out of my purse just to appear uninterested.

To Loxley's left was a giant. Robert Loxley I put at Dad's height, just over six feet. This guy had at least half a foot on them both. He had shoulder-length black hair that he had tied back. He was dressed just like the rest: jeans, boots, t-shirt, and vest. Like Dale, and Loxley too I noticed, he had a black wallet on a chain.

Loxley seemed ready for the NCAA championship, while this guy appeared prepared to face off against the Undertaker. I immediately guessed that a.) he was the one riding with Loxley when he flipped the Deputy off, and b.) he was the one driving the truck this morning.

Max was to the big guy's left, wearing overalls and a white t-shirt with the same heavy work boots. His hands were empty.

On Loxley's right was a girl. She had collar-length red hair and was whip thin. Her clothes fit right in with the boys', only she had a small black purse slung over her left shoulder instead of a chain tapping against her leg. Dale was on the other side of her.

So Robert Loxley had a girlfriend...

"What you got first period, John?" Loxley asked.

"Shop."

"Me too," Dale piped up. "Power tools first period. What a way to start the day!"

"You, Scarlet?"

"Fucking geometry..."

Max tapped his chest.

"You too?" Loxley asked.

He nodded.

Loxley smirked. "I'm Coach Frazier's T.A. All he'll want to do is drink coffee, dip Copenhagen, and talk football."

I wrinkled my nose.

"What's Tuck got?" Dale asked.

"Hell if I know," Scarlet replied.

Max shrugged his shoulders.

Dale, Loxley, and John veered off and I followed Scarlet and Max since they said they were heading towards Geometry. It was my initial class and homeroom as well.

I ALWAYS HATED SEATING arrangements that only made sense to the teacher. There were five vertical rows of desks. I ended up in the fourth seat of the fourth row. Max was in front of me and Scarlet was behind me.

I spent my time people-watching. I noticed two boys in the first and second seats by the door dressed sort of preppy. There was a girl on the front of my row and another at the front of the last one that gave off the same vibe. The rest of classmates-to-be were dressed in a range of styles, from sporty to white trash to gangster.

Mr. Gentry pointed out something on the board and I raised my head to look. It was then I noticed Max's head drooping. Waiting until the teacher turned back around, I craned my neck to check Max out.

He was asleep.

His eyes were closed, his arms were crossed over his chest, and he was breathing deeply. Out of the corner of my eye, I saw Mr. Gentry turning and I popped back and pretended like I'd been paying attention. He glanced at Max, shook his head, and went back to talking.

I didn't want Max to get into trouble. Gentry kept looking at him as he spoke. Each time he turned back from the board, his eyes fell on the sleeping giant in front of me. Figuring I needed to do something, I glanced at my pencil. I waited until Mr. Gentry turned back around and I hesitantly reached with it to tap Max on the shoulder.

Something bumped me in the back.

I snatched my hand away and glanced over my shoulder. Scarlet was scowling back at me.

"Leave him alone."

I turned back around without another word.

I could feel her glaring a hole in my back. My innocent gesture angered her for some reason.

The bell finally rang and Max woke with a start. He gathered up his book and stood like he was waiting for Scarlet.

"Go hang out with Mr. Ingram," she told him as a pregnant girl maneuvered past them. "He won't let anybody mess with you. I'll see you in History."

He rubbed sleep from his eyes, nodded, turned, and filed out of class with the rest of the students.

Scarlet then directed her attention towards me. "Let's walk."

She waited until I packed up. Only when I was ready did

she head towards the door. I followed her wordlessly as she lead us into the hall and made a left into the girl's restroom.

I stepped around the corner and she was immediately in my personal space. "I'll make this short and sweet, Rich Girl. You touch him and I'll cut your fucking throat!"

Not only was I shocked at her misinterpretation of what happened but also at her fierceness. She was probably two inches shorter than I was and fifteen pounds lighter, but she was a definite firecracker.

I tried to defuse first. "Mr. Gentry was staring at him. I was just going to wake him up so he didn't get in trouble."

"What do you care?"

I shrugged. "Mrs. Sadie said he was good people."

My answer seemed to surprise her. "Mrs. Sadie, huh?"

I nodded. "Yeah, he fixed our sink a couple weeks ago — the day we got into town. I was just trying to keep him out of the principal's office."

Scarlet rubbed her temples and sighed. "He won't go to the principal. They know what's what."

"And what's that?"

She eyed me suspiciously for a moment.

"Just asking," I said, putting my hands up like Loxley did facing my shotgun.

"He's lucky if he sleeps six hours a night," Scarlet explained. "He's probably been up since around three this morning helping his dad."

"He drives the bread truck, right?"

She nodded.

"I wasn't trying to get anyone in trouble," I assured her. "I just wanted to help."

"Why? Nobody around here does shit unless they can get something in return."

"I'm not from around here." The bell rang and I realized I was about to be tardy. "Hey, how do I get to Home Ec?"

"Follow me."

"So when Mrs. Sadie said Max had 'good friends,'" I asked, "she meant you?"

Scarlet shrugged. She was sitting in front of me and was turned around so we were facing each other. After passing out books, Mrs. Cotton had given us worksheets and told us we could partner up.

"Me," she explained, "Little John... Robin... Dale... Tuck."

"Little John?" I asked.

"Ironic, isn't it?"

"It is that."

"His dad is Big John," she went on, eyeing my paper and copying my answers. "All our families have been friends since we were in diapers. So we hang out with each other."

"You're the only girl?"

"Yep, only woman in this band of Merry Men."

"Why? I mean, are you seeing one of them?"

While I asked "one of them," I really meant "Loxley." I would keep that to myself.

If she noticed, she made no sign. "Nah, I've been one of the boys since the beginning. It's likely Robin and I are half-brother and sister."

"Really?"

"We think so. Rumor is my mom and his dad had a thing back in the day."

That was interesting. So she wasn't Loxley's girlfriend. At least that meant he wasn't flirting with me while dating someone else. Not that I cared, of course.

"What about you? What's your story?"

I shrugged and marked down another answer. "You mean you don't know already?"

She shook her head.

"I'm surprised it's not already making the rounds."

"Oh, I've heard them," she clarified. "Your dad is some sort of investigator who's here snooping. I'd rather get it from the source, so I figured I'd just ask you flat out."

"It's true," I admitted. "Dad's got background in organized crime and the governor's office hired him as a consultant."

"Interesting. Who's he after?"

I figured I'd said enough, so I gave a vague response. "Everybody. I hear y'all have a lot of bad guys around here."

"That we do. What do you have next class?"

I pulled out my schedule and glanced it over. "Anatomy. You?"

"American History. I don't have A&P until right before lunch."

I nodded and glanced over Scarlet's shoulder. It didn't look like anyone was paying us any attention. I looked back to see she was still copying answers. Figuring I needed to get finished, I picked my pen back up and went back to work.

So far, I'd seen preppies, jocks, nerds, cheerleaders — your typical high school mix. It was just like every other school I'd ever been in. I wasn't sure what to call the posse that surrounded Loxley.

That reminded me of something. "Hey, who coaches the dance team?"

"They don't have one anymore," she replied. "Budget cuts. Last year was the last one."

"Crap."

"You dance?"

"Some," I admitted. "And I'm guessing still no soccer?"

She shook her head. "Right now, your best bet is cheerleading. They had a girl break her ankle on a four-wheeler. They're going to hold an open try-out next Monday after school."

I didn't really care for cheerleading. But back in Dallas, cheerleaders came from higher-class families and were the popular ones. It was an easy way to make friends. I'd also taken gymnastics when I was a kid and obviously had dance team experience.

"I might do that," I said, mostly to myself.

Chapter 6

I SAID GOODBYE TO Scarlet and during the break found my locker, stowed my lunch and the books I'd been assigned, and got to my next class early.

There were only a couple of students in the room. I took the desk in the front row opposite the door. There wasn't a teacher in sight, so I unpacked a notebook and settled in to wait.

Dale grinned and threw me a nod when he and Little John came in. I gave him a plastic smile back. Little John ignored me. Both went into the back of the room, away from the teacher's prying eyes.

With nothing to do, I crossed my arms and leaned back.

"You're the new girl, right?"

I raised my head to see a clean-shaven, black-haired guy with dark eyes and an athletic build. He was wearing designer jeans and a white polo shirt. He looked well-dressed compared to what I'd been seeing.

"That's me," I replied.

He smiled, showing braces. Despite them, he was cute.

"Brent," he offered.

I smiled back. "Marian."

"Where you from, Marian?"

"Dallas."

"Cool. You just moved here?"

"A couple weeks ago," I answered. "Dad relocated."

"You're Bob Fitzwalter's daughter?"

I nodded.

He nodded back. "My dad is Prince Dean, one of the county commissioners."

"I haven't met him, but I think my dad has... or will soon."

Decent looking guy... easy conversation... I liked this.

"What class do you have next?"

"Spanish."

"Me too. If you wait for me after class, I'll show you where it is."

"That would be great!"

"And if you want, you can sit with me and my friends at lunch."

That solved that problem. "Sounds good."

"Cool, I'll see you after class."

"How do you like it here?"

I shrugged as we walked. "It's okay. It's a bit slower than I'm used to, but I'm adjusting."

He nodded along. "Yeah, it's boring sometimes."

"You been here all your life?"

"Sure have. You got any brothers or sisters?"

"Older brother. He's in law school at Tulane. You?"

"Two older brothers. One is a deputy and the other owns the truck stop at the Nottingham exit."

"Cool."

"Your mom's the new doctor, right?"

"She is."

"That's awesome."

This was the first conversation I'd had with someone my age since I got to town. Well, the first conversation that didn't involve brandishing firearms or subtly interrogating a wannabe gangster.

"Here's Mr. Culpeper's room," Brent said, opening the door for me.

"Thanks."

The first thing I noticed when I stepped through the doorway was Loxley sitting in the back of the room. Max was sitting on his right, a black guy with a shaved head and horn-rimmed glasses on his left. At the same moment, Loxley noticed me and a grin appeared on his face.

"I see two desks over here," Brent said, pointing.

"Alright."

I followed Brent, who went past the guy I didn't know, and sat opposite him. I squeezed into the corner.

"Morning, Marian," Loxley greeted.

"Morning, Loxley," I said back.

Before we could continue the exchange, a short, balding man wearing small, round glasses, suspenders, and a tie that looked like it was way too snug stepped into the room.

"Good morning, class," he said in perfect Spanish. "I am Mr. Culpeper. This class will not be in English. I repeat, there will be no English spoken in this class. I believe in the 'sink or swim' method of teaching. Questions?"

"Do what?" A voice from the opposite corner said.

"Excellent!"

I grinned to myself. Years of private school meant I could already speak the language fairly well. I was only here because I needed a foreign language credit to graduate. Spanish was the only choice.

"When I call your name," Mr. Culpeper called out in Spanish, "say 'here.'"

Most everyone got the gist of what he meant. He said their name, and they said 'here.' I smiled at Brent when his name was called.

"Marian Fitzwalter?"

"Over to your left," I called out in Spanish as I raised my hand.

He blinked in surprise. "You speak Spanish?"

"So-so," I lied. "I took it back in Dallas."

"Very good, Miss Fitzwalter."

Brent leaned over and whispered in my ear, "Not bad."

His warm, peppermint-scented breath on my ear gave me a shiver.

I was getting the impression I might be interested in this guy. It was still too early to tell. He seemed nice enough, but I needed to learn more about Brent Dean.

"Robert Loxley."

"Back here, sir."

I blinked rapidly in surprise. He'd replied in Spanish.

Mr. Culpeper was also astonished. "You speak Spanish too, Mr. Loxley?"

"Yes, sir."

"Where did you learn?"

"Here and there — mostly working with the migrants during picking season."

Mr. Culpeper grinned. "Thank you, Mr. Loxley."

He went on with roll call and I glanced behind Brent's head to look at Loxley. His arms were crossed over his chest and he was slumped back.

Like Dad, I did my best to read between the lines. Loxley broke into people's houses and just admitted he learned Spanish being a farm laborer. It wouldn't surprise me if this ended up being his strongest subject.

Mr. Culpeper began handing out books and I noticed Brent looking at me. I smiled and tucked my hair behind my ears. I got a nervous thrill when he smiled back.

It turned out I wasn't as special as I thought. Not only could Loxley speak Spanish, but so could the black guy I learned was Mrs. Sadie's grandson, Alonzo Tuck. Judging by his facial expression, it wouldn't have surprised me if Max could at least read and understand it.

Brent showed me to my American History class and was waiting for me at the door when the lunch bell rang.

"Okay," Brent introduced. "This is Jody, Will, Sonya,

Tina, Brian, Nick, and Hope. Guys, this is Marian."

"Hi," I said politely.

"Hi!" Hope responded. She was blonde, tanned, and sounded very chipper. "Have a seat!"

"You're the new cop's daughter?" Jody asked.

"Yeah," I replied, sitting down.

"We got Spanish together," Brent told him.

"I think I saw you in Geometry."

"I don't remember," I admitted.

"She probably couldn't see anything over the freak," Tina snorted.

"Huh?"

"She means Max Miller," Brent explained.

"Does he wear the same overalls every day?" she went on. "I mean, God, I know we live in damn Podunk, but he doesn't have to dress like it."

I kept my mouth shut.

"Who else have you met?" Sonya asked.

Before I could answer, Brent did it for me. "She knows Hood."

For some reason, everyone at the table turned and looked at me at the same time. Most of them were gawking.

"I don't know him," I explained. "I saw him in town when I first moved here."

"She called him 'Loxley'."

Was I detecting jealousy? "That's his name, isn't it?"

"I don't think I've ever heard anyone call him that," Sonya said, "except teachers."

I opened my salad and shrugged. "I don't know him well enough to use a nickname."

That seemed to satisfy them because they dropped the conversation.

"You heard about Joselyn?" Jody asked Hope.

Hope rolled her eyes. "I'm co-captain, remember?"

"When's tryouts?" Brent asked.

"Monday. Why? Do I need to add your name to the list?"

"No, but what about Marian?"

Hope looked me up and down. "You have any cheerleading experience?"

"No," I admitted, "but I was on the dance team back in Dallas."

"We don't do line dancing," Tina said mockingly.

I was speechless for a second but recovered quickly. "I also took gymnastics. I'm pretty sure I could give it a shot and not embarrass myself."

"Monday at four," Tina said, turning towards Jody.

And I was dismissed.

"Where is Hood anyway?" Will asked.

"Corner table, like last year," Brent replied.

"God, they're so... icky," Tina said.

"They are different," I admitted.

She rolled her eyes. "My dad says they take turns with that redhead girl."

"Scarlet?"

Tina gave me a condescending look. "You know her too?"

"I've got first and second period with her."

She actually rolled her eyes again. "White trash, honey. You'd better get used to seeing it around here."

That was about what I expected. Loxley, although smooth, was just a good old boy. In ten years, he'd be Bobby Jo with bad teeth and a crappy used car lot if he wasn't driving a tractor or cooking crank. Or in prison.

"Y'all hear what happened last weekend around I-10?" Nick asked.

"The truck that got hijacked?" Brent inquired.

He nodded. "What did they get?"

Brent shrugged. "It was a delivery truck, not a big rig. I think it was carrying, like, car parts or some shit. Someone needed some new rims pretty bad."

I quit listening as a tall, slender black guy flanked by two members of his crew began ambling towards Loxley's table. Alonzo Tuck intercepted them. Tina was squawking about a shop in the mall in Mobile being out of her favorite mascara, but I tuned her out.

Tuck nodded and joined the other three as they made their way towards the group. Little John saw them coming and stood up before crossing his arms over his chest and looking scary. Scarlet slid a little closer to Loxley. Dale came around Little John, a step behind. Max stood right behind Loxley.

Tuck said something to Loxley. I couldn't hear them over the chatter of the cheerleaders. He nodded back and the skinny guy stepped forward. I realized who he was — Jermaine from the furniture company. He said something else and Loxley held out his hands as if to say, "what?"

The quiet guy from the moving crew took a step forward, and Little John matched him. Loxley held up his hand like a traffic cop and they both stopped. He said something to the other ringleader. I assumed it was positive because Jermaine nodded in return.

Loxley turned and said something to Scarlet. She opened her purse, took out a small notebook and a pen, and began writing. Once finished, she tore the paper out with a flourish, folded it in half, and slid it across the table. Tuck took it and passed it to Jermaine who read it and nodded again before stuffing it in his pocket.

Loxley stood up and approached Jermaine. I noticed automatically that both sets of muscle stood back. Loxley and Jermaine shook hands and hugged, complete with a double back tap. The darker man cocked his head at his friends and they began sashaying off.

Dad taught me well because I looked in time to see Loxley's hand under the table. He was stuffing a folded wad of bills into his right front pocket. He was quick, but not that quick.

Whatever I had just seen looked dirty.

Tina's voice broke my concentration. "I wonder what 'Token' is up to."

I looked over at her. "Who?"

"She means Alonzo Tuck," Hope explained, "the guy with the glasses."

"Old Preacher Man," Jody added.

I looked at him, perplexed.

Hope answered, "His parents are missionaries in... Africa somewhere, but I can't remember where exactly. He's real active at his church."

He was still standing there talking to Loxley and crew. Tuck seemed at ease, despite being the darkest person at the table. It didn't escape my attention that he was one of the few people in this school wearing khakis. I noticed Little John wasn't puffed up at him like he had been at the guys that had just left.

"What's his story?"

"I heard his grandma takes care of Hood's grandpa," Sonya said.

"Takes care of?"

"He's blind."

"Huh," I said, because I didn't know what else to say.

"He's their houseboy," Tina added. "He's always stepping and fetching for Hood and crew. The other Blacks don't hang with him."

Tina was beginning to get on my nerves. Unlike the other girls, her gossip was pure venom. I made a mental note to be wary of her back-patting. She'd be looking for a soft place to stick the knife.

I went back to eating as the boys started talking about football and the girls about potential replacements for their injured cheerleader. From their talk, I could've very well been in the running. However, Tina made everyone sound bad.

"When is the next party?" Mallory asked.

"We could do it at your place," Jody suggested.

Tina wrinkled her nose. "All that chicken shit."

Brent turned to me. "Mallory's dad owns a huge chicken ranch just south of the prison. He's got a lot of land that's secluded. It's the perfect place to build a bonfire and have a party."

"Party?"

Tina snorted at me. “Watch it, guys. The narc’s daughter might tell Daddy.”

Now it was my turn to do the eye-rolling. “I’m not going to say a word. My dad’s not after anyone for having keg parties or smoking a little weed. It’s not what he does.”

“So you interested?” Brent asked.

“Sure.”

“Better search her ass first,” Tina taunted.

“I’ll volunteer,” Brent offered.

“Not on the first date,” I replied, half teasing...half not.

That got several catcalls from the others that made me blush. I dropped my head and let my hair fall in front of my face, which only made them whoop it up louder.

“Lay off, guys,” someone, Nick I thought, spoke up. “I think we embarrassed her.”

The bell rang, signaling the end of lunch. I polished off my water and started packing up.

“What class you got next?” Brent asked.

“English,” I replied.

He frowned. “Shit. I’ve got Computer Lab.”

“Sorry. What do you have last period?”

“P.E. All the football players do. We lift weights, then go straight to practice.”

That meant I wouldn’t see him after school. The others had left, leaving us alone at the table as I put my dishes back into my bag.

“Could... could I have your number?” Brent asked.

“Absolutely,” I said quickly. “It’s still a Dallas area code though.”

“I don’t care.”

I yanked out a pen as Brent tore off a piece of notebook paper. I scribbled it down quickly and passed it to him.

"Thanks." We stood at the same time. "I'll see you, Marian."

I smiled. "Bye."

Before I could turn, he said, "Hey."

I paused.

Brent glanced around before he stepped a little closer to me. "I'm not trying to tell you what to do, but... piece of advice? Stay away from Hood and his crew."

"Why?"

He licked his lips. "The word is they're into something. Something bad."

"Bad?"

"They're your typical rednecks, so it could be drugs, auto theft, anything. Tina wasn't kidding. If one out of every ten rumors are true, it would be a bad idea to get mixed up with them."

"You don't have to worry," I assured him. "I just know their names. We're not friends or anything."

That seemed to put him at ease. "Good. I'll try to call you tonight. I just don't know how long Coach is going to keep us."

"Okay. If not, I'll see you tomorrow."

He looked for a moment like he wanted to say something else, but he stopped himself.

"We're going to be late."

I slung my backpack over my shoulder. "Bye, Brent."

Chapter 7

"OKAY, EVERYONE," MISS CHEN announced. "We're going to hit the ground running and see how you all did with your summer reading assignments. Let's discuss *The Grapes of Wrath*."

Most of the class let out a collective groan. Not me. Literature was one of my favorite subjects. I loved to read. Mom and Dad had fed my addiction from a young age.

None of my lunch table was in sixth period English. However, Loxley and crew were there. Him, Scarlet, Little John, Dale, Max, and Tuck filled the back seats.

Miss Chen was young, barely out of college, I guessed, with black hair she had up in two braids. Of some Asian descent, she had a figure so nice that I noticed more than one boy checking her out. Her English was better than most of the people in this county I'd met.

First off," she began. "We're going to start at the end and work our way back. I want someone to tell me what character they believe did the most good in the entire story."

No one volunteered. She walked around to the front of her desk and looked us over. I noticed Max nodding off again.

"Anybody?"

You could've heard a pin drop.

Miss Chen sighed. "Alright then. Everyone take out a piece of paper. We're going to have a quiz."

"For a grade?" Scarlet asked.

"Yes, Miss Williams that's the normal point of a quiz."

The class groaned in unison again.

Unless someone wants to take a crack at the question," Miss Chen pressed.

I figured I could not only show off my smarts and score some brownie points with the teacher but bail the entire class out at the same time. I raised my hand.

"Yes, Miss Fitzwalter?"

"Tom Joad," I replied.

"And what did he do?"

"He decided he could help his family more by joining the labor movement."

"Good answer, Miss Fitzwalter."

Someone mumbled from the back of the room.

"Mr. Loxley," Miss Chen called out.

"Ma'am?"

"You have something to add?"

"No, ma'am."

"Something must be on your mind."

"No, ma'am," he repeated.

"Anyone else?"

The room went silent again.

"Then take out your paper."

"She answered the question," someone from the other side of the room called out.

"I seriously doubt everyone agrees with her opinion. I'd like to hear some that differ."

I heard that mumbling again.

"You don't, Mr. Loxley?"

I turned around and glared at him. What did he know? I doubted he could spell 'literature,' much less discuss it.

He sighed. "No, ma'am. I don't."

My eyes narrowed.

"Interesting," Miss Chen pressed. "You believe there was a character that did more good than Tom Joad?"

"I do."

He had to be kidding.

"Who then?"

"Rose of Sharon."

Did he just flip the book open and pick a name at random?

"What do you say, Miss Fitzwalter?"

I turned back to her. "Rose of Sharon at the beginning of the book was a flighty little girl with a lazy husband and a head full of dreams. At the end, her man left, her baby was stillborn, and she was still stuck in that labor camp with the rest of her family. Except Tom, of course."

That should shut him up, I thought.

"And you, Mr. Loxley?"

"I believe Miss Fitzwalter is confusing potential with actually getting something done," he countered. "Tom did leave to go help the movement, but we're left wondering if that actually did any good. Rose, on the other hand, took a negative — her child dying — and turned it into a positive by feeding that dying man."

I blinked rapidly in surprise.

Miss Chen came back to me. "Counter, Miss Fitzwalter?"

This time, I turned and addressed Loxley. "What good did that do? The man died. So your argument is invalid. If we're both going by potential, then I'd say Tom did more."

"But we're not going by potential," Loxley said before Miss Chen could interrupt. "The question was who did the most good, not who potentially did the most good. We're going by results. Did Tom do great things for the labor movement? Did he change things? Or did he get his head bashed in by a strike breaker? We'll never know."

I was getting irritated. We were going around in circles and I was right. He just didn't want to admit it.

"And again, the old man died."

"That's not the point," Loxley replied with surprising calm. "The point is what good was done. All we know is what Tom actually accomplished. He left. Rose of Sharon comforted a dying man. She took the loss of her child and used it to nurture another human being." His eyes met mine. "I'm going to take a guess you've never been hungry. If you had, you'd understand."

I had no response. The redneck had just schooled me, and schooled me good.

"That's very thought-provoking," Miss Chen said. "I'm surprised that no one mentioned Ma Joad."

I was still looking at Loxley when he shook his head.

"She was the rock of that family and really went above and beyond, but she didn't do the most good. Not in my opinion."

"Miss Fitzwalter?"

I swallowed. "I agree. Like Mr. Loxley said, she was a rock, but as far as doing the most good in the story? I can't see it. The family's situation wasn't really any better at the end of the book. It was equally bad as in the beginning, just in a different way."

I turned around to see Miss Chen smiling. "That was very good. Both of you. That's the thing about literature. Too many people read something and have a knee-jerk reaction. Literature's job isn't just to entertain. It's to make you both feel and think. It's to make you look deeper into the book and maybe deeper into yourselves."

She walked back to her desk. "Now you can take that paper out." She held her hand up before the complaints could start again. "Your assignment is to answer the question for yourselves. Who do you think accomplished the most and why? If you give me a solid reason for your choice, you get full credit. If you copy either Miss Fitzwalter's or Mr. Loxley's answers or don't support your answer with an explanation, you fail. I'll give you ten minutes."

"Well," Miss Chen said. "Some of your answers were interesting." She shuffled some of the papers. "Miss Williams?"

I looked over at Scarlet.

"Yes, ma'am?"

"You stuck to your guns believing Ma Joad was the most accomplished. You believe she was the one that got the family as far as they did. I don't agree with your answer, but I don't have to. You get an 'A.'"

"Thank you."

Wow. The rednecks were two-for-two.

"Mr. Tuck?"

My eyes jumped to him.

"Yes, ma'am?"

"While I disagree with your assessment on the Preacher, I did like your explanation. Your reasoning that he provided the family spiritual comfort was well done. You also get an 'A.'"

I wasn't feeling as smart as I thought I was.

"Mr. Alan?"

I tipped my head as I looked at him next.

"Yes, ma'am?"

Her mouth got screwed up. "Was you saying Grandma and Grandpa dying your attempt at a joke?

Several people laughed.

"They had to drug Grandpa to even get him to come in the first place," Dale replied. "He didn't want to leave. Plus, dying meant he didn't have to endure the suffering everyone else had to. That's an accomplishment, right?"

"You have a point, I guess... Mr. Miller?"

I turned just in time to see Scarlet give him a quick poke in the ribs with an elbow. He jolted awake and immediately focused on Miss Chen.

"You picked Uncle John. I like this answer. It's definitely outside the box. You put a lot of thought into your reasoning by portraying Uncle John as a flawed but generous man trying to redeem himself. You get an 'A.'"

Max nodded.

"Mr. Little?"

I wondered if I was about to be surprised again.

He grunted.

"Muley Graves... seriously?"

This was the first time I'd ever heard John Little speak more than one word. His voice was what I expected, a deep baritone. Despite sitting there looking like someone's pit bull on a chain, his answer came out rather eloquently.

"Muley Graves stayed put. Against the odds, he did the one thing the Joad family wanted to do but couldn't. He held on to his land a bit longer. We don't know how much longer, but unlike the rest of 'em, he didn't let the bank take what was his without a fight. To me, going down swinging is an accomplishment."

"I can't argue with that statement."

I was confused. Little John looked ready to fight at the drop of a hat. Scarlet threatened to cut my throat. Loxley broke into my house. Dale was a flirt with what looked like prison ink on his knuckles, and Max fell asleep in class. Yet, they each called Miss Chen "ma'am," they all provided 'A' answers, and they all received praise, not something not something typical of your bad crowd in a classroom.

The bell rang and everyone jumped up to leave. I saw Loxley was the last in line with his group and I stepped behind him.

I addressed his back. "Hey, can I ask you something?"

He stopped and turned around. He didn't speak, just nodded.

"How many time have you read that book?"

He shrugged. "A few."

"Why?"

"Why?"

"Yeah... why? I've read it three times, but not because I wanted to."

He shifted his weight, raised his head towards the ceiling, and blew out a long breath.

"What?"

His head came back down. "I need something to do at night."

"I don't follow."

"You have to have something to do indoors at night, especially when you don't own a TV."

"You... you don't have a TV?"

He shook his head.

I stepped forward. "Well, it was a good answer anyway." My voice dropped. "Now I need to give you some friendly advice."

"What's that?"

"My dad is driving to Dallas to pick up my dog. So I wouldn't be sneaking back into my room anymore."

"What do you mean?"

"Don't play dumb. Who puts notes on people's pillows? It's... creepy."

Loxley looked up again, blew out another breath, and said what might have been an f-bomb quietly to himself before looking back at me.

"I'm sorry." He actually sounded sincere. "I was going for charming. I wanted to make sure you knew I appreciated you not calling the cops. Seriously, I wasn't trying to be a creeper."

I huffed. "Thanks… but stay out of my room."

Again, he gave that half-grin. "Fair enough. But don't forget, I still owe you one."

"You can repay me by never setting foot on my property again."

His smile dropped. "If that's what you want, I won't come to your housc again unless I'm invited."

"Fat chance of that."

"Hey, Robin!" Dale called. "You're going to be late."

"Take care, Marian," he said before turning and walking out.

I watched him as he left, his stride reminding me of royalty. It was fluid, full of confidence, and the masses in the hallway parted for him like he was some kind of monarch.

"Miss Fitzwalter?" Miss Chen called.

I turned my head.

"I see you're to be my seventh period assistant?"

Mom had made my schedule when she registered me, so I wasn't sure. Quickly, I dug in my purse and found it. Sure enough, it listed "Chen" and "T.A." which I took to mean "teacher's assistant" during this period.

"Yes, ma'am."

She smiled. "Then let's get to it."

I was always weirded out being alone with a teacher

in a classroom, regardless of their gender. The only time students were speaking alone with teachers was when they were in trouble.

"What do I get to do?" I asked.

She pointed to a small table next to her desk. On it were several stacks of papers.

"Here," she said, handing me a red pen. "Read the answers. If they sound like they read the book, put 'A' on it. If they don't, put 'F'. And don't worry, I'll tell everyone I read them and not you."

"You don't have a class now?"

"Nope. This is my free period. Too bad I have bus duty or I'd go home."

I shrugged and sat down. I noticed that Loxley's paper was already graded with an 'A.'

"You seemed surprised that Robert came back at you with that answer."

I shrugged and kept reading.

"You ever lived in a small town before?"

"No, ma'am," I admitted. "I'm from Dallas."

"Really? I'm from Houston myself."

I scowled slightly. "Texans fan?"

"And I'm guessing you root for the Criminals... I mean Cowboys."

"Touché."

She turned her chair so she was facing me and crossed her legs. "How do you like this area?"

I shrugged again. "It's okay, I guess."

"Are you finding your way around alright?"

"What do you mean?"

Now it was her turn to shrug. "I mean, are you finding your feet? I know moving here can be a bit of a culture shock."

I looked up from the paper I was reading. "I think so. This place is confusing though."

"How so?"

"Take Loxley," I explained. "He looks like a typical dumb hick. But he speaks fluid Spanish and outdid me in my best subject. Or Little John. I didn't expect that answer to come from him. I didn't even know he could use a complete sentence."

"Nothing in this place is what it seems, Marian. When I first moved here, it seemed like I was constantly finding out my assumptions were off."

"Really?"

She nodded. "He should be graduating this year. Robert, I mean. John should've already graduated."

"Did Loxley fail a grade?"

"Ninth due to lack of attendance. But a stint in juvie will do that to you."

"What did he do?"

"Arson."

My eyes widened in shock. "Arson?"

"The rumor is he did it, but he did time on a lesser charge. He hasn't been in trouble since he got back, that I've noticed."

I kept my mouth shut about him breaking into my house.

"There is something wrong with this place."

"What do you mean?"

"I've been here three years and I've seen and heard so many things that are just... wrong. It's gotten to the point that I'm more likely to believe a wild rumor than what I see with my own eyes. People you think are dirty are clean and people you think are law-abiding are the criminals." She turned away from me. "This whole county is in trouble."

If what Dad told me was true, she wasn't far off. "There are a lot of bad people here... and I think Loxley is one of them."

"You might be surprised."

"You just said it yourself that he was an arsonist."

She shrugged. "Sometimes people do what they have to."

"Why did he have to do it?"

"I don't know. But my instincts tell me he's not the problem in this county."

"Then who is?"

"My guess? The people your father's after."

Of course she knew who I was. I swore all people in this county did was gossip.

"Dad will get them," I assured her. "He's very good at what he does."

She grimaced.

"What?"

"I don't think he will."

"You don't even know him."

"I can use the Internet. Your dad has a sterling reputation as a by the book investigator. The problem is, I don't think playing by the rules is going to solve this county's problems."

"Then what is?"

She pondered my question a moment before answering. "My guess is someone who's not afraid to break the law to uphold it."

"Then you have anarchy."

"We already have anarchy. We might be from Texas, but this is the real Wild West."

WHEN THE BELL RANG, I had completed grading and was relieved to have survived my first day.

No one bothered me as I trudged out into the parking lot. It was hot as Hades and not a bit of breeze was blowing. In the distance, I could hear a whistle and a coach screaming at the football team.

As I got closer to my car, I could see Loxley and his posse were already in the lot. All of them had their backs to me, except for their fearless leader, of course.

I couldn't see his eyes because of his sunglasses, but the slight tilt of his head told me he'd spotted me. I tried to ignore him and threw my bags into my trunk before fishing my keys out of my purse.

Despite my efforts, he was hard to ignore. He had a sort of gentleman rogue air to him. With Loxley, I was betting lots of girls made the same mistake I made with George — falling for a silver-tongued devil.

Huffing, I flopped down inside the Volkswagen and pulled my own shades out before starting it up.

Chapter 8

If there was one thing that filled me with dread, it was the phone ringing in the middle of the night.

I'd gotten home from school to find the house empty and a note from Dad saying he was going to be late. Mom was working. I did my homework, started my laundry, ate a sandwich, took a shower, and curled up in the living room with The Scarlet Letter to wait for him.

Brent didn't call. I tried not to let that disappoint me, but it did.

I vaguely remembered Dad coming home. I'd fallen asleep on the couch. He'd covered me with a blanket, kissed my forehead, and told me he'd set the alarm on my phone.

The ringing caused me to jump from a dead sleep and my blood turned ice cold. It was the house phone. I snapped my head around as Dad caught it on the second ring from upstairs.

Rubbing sleep from my eyes, I stumbled to the back

door and looked out. Mom's car wasn't in the driveway. I was beginning to panic, so I hurried upstairs to find out what was going on.

The door to their room was open. Dad was already in the pants he'd worn the day before and was securing his belt.

"What's wrong?"

"It's okay, Kitten," he replied. "There was some kind of accident. My contacts with the State Troopers thought I might need to see it."

"Is it Mom?"

He shook his head. "She's still at the hospital."

I exhaled with relief. "Do you need me to do anything? Make you some coffee?"

"I'm fine, Kitten. Just go back to sleep."

Instead, I stepped to him as he was putting his gun on his belt. My arms went around his waist and I hugged him tightly. He returned it in full.

"Be careful," I mumbled against his chest.

MY BUTT WAS DRAGGING when my alarm went off.

Mom wasn't home yet, so I left her what I didn't drink of the coffee. It looked like it was going to be hot and muggy again. Despite my sleepiness, I was still on time and for that I was grateful. I put Meat Loaf on and turned it up as loud as I could, hoping it would shake out some cobwebs.

During the drive, I saw the resident bikers sitting at a crossroads. There wasn't a truck today. Little John and Max were on their own bikes. They pulled in behind me, my music blaring.

Glancing in my rearview mirror, they were just... there. No laughing or yelling at each other, they were all staring straight ahead.

Out of habit, I lowered the volume as I turned into the parking lot. The space I took yesterday was unoccupied, so I took it again. Loxley and crew slid past me into their spots. I averted my eyes and sighed.

I knew I would go to bed early tonight.

"Hey, Hood!"

I turned around to see Jody and another guy I didn't know. Little John lit a cigarette and Loxley slid off his bike as they approached.

"You heard about Cory Boxer's dad?"

"Yeah."

Jody ran his fingers through his hair and blew out a long breath. "Any idea what happened yet?"

"Word is he blew a tire and rolled that log truck coming home late," Loxley said sadly.

"Oh well, one less low-life piece of shit—"

Loxley hit him.

I didn't see the punch. I only heard Jody cut off mid-sentence, saw his head snap back and his body go with it. He ended up flat on his back. A thin trickle of blood ran down his chin. Instead of advancing, Loxley snatched his cut off and held it out.

Both groups were already converging. Scarlet took the

vest from Loxley, turned, and draped it over her bike. Three more guys who looked like football players came running across the parking lot. Little John stepped forward and rose to full height.

"This doesn't concern you!" he growled at the incoming group.

"Get up!" Loxley snarled at Jody.

I shivered at the sound of his voice. It was low and dangerous, not the calm, good-natured tone I'd been hearing.

Jody slowly sat up and Loxley stood pat. Muscles rippled underneath the University of Alabama t-shirt he wore. He still had his gloves on, and I could hear the faint creak of leather when he balled his fists up again. I saw Max and Dale had joined the party.

"Whoa, whoa, whoa!" Brent came running in. "Hold up!"

Loxley didn't move.

"You okay?" he asked Jody.

"He busted my fucking lip."

"You open your trap again, it'll be your head!" Loxley warned.

Brent looked at him. "Come on, man. You don't want to do this here."

Loxley didn't answer.

"Get up, Jody."

Jody climbed to his feet and dusted himself off.

"Get to class," Brent told him. "I'll take care of this."

"This shit ain't over, Hood!"

"Name the time and place!"

"Let. It. Go." Brent's voice was ice, though nowhere

near as frightening as Loxley's.

Jody gave him a once over. Brent eyed him hard until he finally nodded, wiped his mouth with the back of his hand, and turned. All his boys went with him.

"What happened?" Brent asked Loxley.

"He was being a dick about Junior."

Brent sighed. "Idiot."

"Yeah…"

"I'll handle it, Hood."

"He runs his cake hole again you won't have to."

Brent held up his hand. "We don't need that, man. We keep the peace, right?"

Loxley said nothing.

Brent extended his hand and Loxley just stood there. An awkward pause followed. Brent never lost his easy smile and Loxley never relaxed his fists. This went on for about thirty seconds, but it felt like an hour.

"You don't want to not shake my hand," Brent warned.

Whatever that meant, Loxley finally relented. They shook, both of their biceps flexing like they were trying to make the other submit. Neither did and they finally broke apart. Brent looked at me and relaxed.

He walked up. "You ready?"

I nodded and slung my backpack over my shoulder.

"Let's go."

We walked side-by-side into the school, neither of us saying anything. It wasn't until we got through the door that he spoke.

"I'm sorry you had to see that."

"See what?" I asked. "You don't think boys fight in Dallas?"

"I told you he was dangerous."

"Jody was being a dick. Seriously, I can't believe he would talk that way about a dead person. What happened to this Junior guy anyway?"

Brent took a deep breath. "He rolled his log truck last night. It killed him instantly."

Cop's daughter instinct picked something up. Brent talked like a wreck happened, but Loxley said that was the word—like he wasn't so sure. Did Loxley think there was more to it?

"Anyway." Brent shifted his books to his left hand and his right arm went over my shoulders. "I'm sorry about not calling you last night."

I forced myself not to tense at the contact. "Don't worry about it."

"I'll see you in Spanish?"

"Count on it."

"It was pretty nasty," Dad said at the kitchen table.

"I figured by what the paramedics told me when they called to get a time of death," Mom replied.

When I got home, I threw on my helmet and went for a ride on my bike. Traffic was light so I'd gone towards the town square to get my bearings. Most of the shops were open, but it didn't look like anyone was doing much business.

The building with the most traffic was the tattoo parlor. What drew my attention was there were several bikes parked out front and I recognized them all.

I shouldn't have been surprised. Where else did I think bikers, even teenage bikers, would hang out?

Once I got home, I knocked out my homework. I was about done when I smelled steak grilling.

That was a bad sign.

Dad had a tradition that if he worked an awful scene, he came home with meat for the grill and a bottle of wine. Not to celebrate, but because a good meal followed by a hot shower "made him feel human again." He saved this tradition for the worst of the worst. The last one was eight months ago when he found five illegals in the back of a panel truck dead of heat exposure.

"What happened?"

"You know a kid named Cory Boxer?"

I swallowed my steak and shook my head. "No, sir, but I heard something about an accident last night that killed a truck driver with a kid named Cory. They had an announcement first thing this morning. The funeral is Thursday."

Dad nodded. "Yeah."

"So what's wrong, Bob?" Mom asked. "Was it just that ghastly?"

"No," he explained, "I mean... yeah, it was. But it didn't feel right."

"Didn't feel right how?"

He took a sip of his wine and continued. "I'm not an M.E., but he had some wounds that just didn't match.

Never mind the fact he was outside the truck, the door was closed with the windows rolled up, and all the glass was intact."

"You don't think the accident killed him?"

He looked at me. "This doesn't leave the dinner table."

"Yes, sir."

"I think someone beat him... severely. One of the worst I've ever seen."

"Do you have a suspect?" Mom asked.

He shrugged. "It could be anybody — Fox, Peckerwoods, Burners, Mexicans, Dixie Mafia. I honestly have no clue."

"Anything out of the ordinary?" I asked. "Something that made it unique?"

"Just the fact he looked like he'd been beaten up before the accident was set up."

Mom mulled it over. "What's the next step?"

"I've got to start asking questions. This would be the thirty-ninth murder in this county so far this year. They had forty-nine last year."

Mom and I gawked. "That's... insane!"

"Which is why I need to stop it."

"Is there any reason to think maybe it's one person or group?" Mom asked.

"Oh, no," he replied quickly. "For most of them I at least have a group of suspects — well, all but a few of them."

"That's not bad."

I took a sip of my wine. I was trying to make it last.

"Yeah, but the ones I can't figure out are the ones that bother me."

"Because you don't have any suspects?"

"Because the three look to be related. It makes me wonder if it's the unknown motorcycle gang in Barnsdale that no one seems to know about — or wants to talk about."

"How likely is that?" Mom asked. "I mean, there seem to be more than enough criminals running around."

"I told you," he stressed, "the M.O. is too similar."

"What M.O.?" I asked.

"Investigators recovered an arrow at all three scenes."

I blinked. "An arrow? Like a bow and arrow?"

He nodded.

"Someonc on the reservation?" Mom asked.

"I doubt it. It's an aluminum arrow. They sell them in every sporting goods or big box store in the nation. They're not uncommon."

"Still," I said, putting my fork down. "That's a start. Is there anything else?"

"All three victims had their own rap sheets and all had felonies, including murder."

"So you've got a criminal or group of criminals taking out other criminals?" Mom joked.

Dad was serious. "It honestly looks that way."

"Vigilantes?"

"That's my theory."

"Do you have anything else?" I asked. "Like… was anything taken?"

It looked like a lightbulb came on in Dad's head. "That's smart, Kitten!"

"What is?"

He polished off his wine. "I remember reading in the

case files a few instances where there was an attempted robbery, mostly hijacking, but the truck had no cargo. I thought to myself that it was dumb luck they got nothing. What if there is a group who are preying on the criminals and they've done more than we think? What if the Burners or Fox or the Dixie Mafia have had bigger losses and they aren't talking?" He reached over and mussed my hair like I was five. "I'm going to start cross-checking tomorrow."

I beamed at him.

"I'm glad you got your mother's brains."

Now it was Mom grinning at him. She leaned over and kissed his neck and I pushed my plate away.

"Okay. If you two are going to get mushy, I'm going to bed. I didn't sleep well last night."

"One more thing, Kitten. Do you want to go to the funeral on Thursday?"

I pondered. "I don't know the son. Pretty sure we're not even in the same grade."

"True, but he's a classmate. It would be good if you showed your support. Besides, you could help me."

"Help you?"

"Yeah, I plan on going just to offer condolences and let the family know I'm doing everything I can. Maybe if you went too, it would both send a message and give me a chance to get some intel."

"What do you mean?"

"If you go with me, it sends the message that I have a child about the same age as Cory. It'll show that I have a strong interest in making sure Junior's case is thoroughly investigated. I'm also hoping you might hear something I don't or someone that wouldn't talk to me might talk to you. With this curtain of silence around this county, I need every edge I can get."

It would give me a chance to miss school and help Dad. That sounded like a win/win to me.

"Okay, Dad. You drive?"

He snorted. "If it means we don't ride in that wind-up car of yours, deal."

I gave him a playful smack. "Don't dis my car, old man!"

"Knock it off, you two," Mom warned with mock sternness. "Let's clean up and get some sleep."

Her tone told me sleep wasn't on her mind and I needed to pour bleach in my brain.

Chapter 9

"You look nice, Kitten."

I smiled at Dad and smoothed out my skirt. I was going for basic with a one pieced dress that was snug enough to show I had curves but loose enough to not flaunt them. It was also short-sleeved and lightweight. Once again, it was hot as blazes.

"Thanks, Dad."

He reached over and adjusted the air conditioner. "You nervous?"

"No, sir. Well, maybe a little. I don't really know the family. I don't want it to look... morbid... that I'm here."

He smiled and turned off the highway onto a county road. "You're here as my daughter. You and I are showing our support for the family. Remember what Mom and I say about good manners?"

"That they don't go out of style."

"That's right. This is just showing good manners."

I nodded and turned back towards the window.

Holly Branch Baptist Church was off County Road 1. It was a brick church with white doors, windows, and a steeple, and it had a sanctuary with a smaller building beside it I assumed was where they held Sunday school classes and potluck suppers. The cemetery was to the left of the church.

Dad and I both slipped on sunglasses as we made our exit. I was wearing sensible shoes, but he still offered me his arm as we walked across the grass. An older gentleman wearing a navy-blue suit smiled, mouthed a 'good morning,' and opened the door for us.

The congregation around eighty percent white and twenty percent black. Dress ranged from work clothes to their Sunday best. Dad spotted an empty pew and led us in that direction.

As I sat down, I saw someone I recognized. I almost didn't.Scarlet.

She was wearing a skirt with a hem that landed just above her knee and a white blouse with black trim. Our eyes locked for a moment and she scowled before leaning down and whispering to an older gentleman in a black suit. All I could see of his features was the back of his head.

I settled in next to Dad and looked around. The carpet and the pew cushions were a dark green that contrasted with the deeply stained wood. A table in front of the pulpit had 'THIS DO IN REMEMBERANCE OF ME' carved into the side. In front of the table was a wheeled metal frame to hold the coffin.

A man with enough gel to stop a tornado from mussing his hair stepped forward. He raised his hands and the congregation rose. Those that weren't seated hurried to their places as the minister began leading us in singing the Doxology.

A young girl with blonde hair and a black dress with white flowers stepped up beside the man.

"His oldest granddaughter," Dad mumbled.

She sang "Precious Memories" and I thought I was going to need a tissue. When she finished, the preacher spoke a few words to thank us for coming before calling for us to sing "It Is Well With My Soul."

As we sang, a side door opened and, though his face was turned away, a person who couldn't be anyone but John Little began backing out. He got through the door and turned to take the side of the casket with his left hand.

Loxley was on the right. Behind them came Max and Alonzo Tuck. The end of the casket had Dale and an older man I didn't recognize.

All six men looked dignified as they walked, all with their chins up, shoulders back, showing no strain with their burden. They eased the silver casket onto the frame and filed into a line to sit on the front pew on our side.

Loxley was dead still while the preacher gave his eulogy. We stood to sing "Just As I Am" and sat down again as Mr. Boxer's oldest son spoke, telling stories of family fishing trips, Sunday fried chicken dinners, and how hard his daddy worked to provide. He got choked up at times, but he made it through.

The pallbearers rose and formed a semi-circle around the casket while the preacher stood up front. He signaled the congregation to stand before offering to let anyone that felt the need to come forward and make a dedication of their faith do so. We sang "Victory In Jesus," but no one took him up on his offer. Looking a little disappointed, he turned and nodded to the pallbearers.

The piano player began again as the pallbearers took their positions again around the casket. The preacher led the way and the boys filed out with the coffin. A crying older woman surrounded by the man who'd given the eulogy, a girl in her twenties, and a guy that I guessed was Cory came next. The usher then signaled for us to follow.

I put on my sunglasses as we went outside and saw a tent and platform arranged over a freshly dug grave. The family took seats as Loxley and company put the casket into place and stepped back. The rest of the guests, including me and Dad, stepped forward as the preacher talked again.

As we were asked to bow our heads one more time, I let my gaze wander to Loxley. Like me, he wore black sunglasses. His creases were sharply pressed and his tie was straight. Even without the sunglasses, I imagined the blue shirt looked good with his eyes. He kept his head bowed and his mouth in a tight line.

The preacher said 'amen' and Loxley's head came up. His expression never changed. I didn't know if he knew the Boxers very well or if there was something else on his mind.

The preacher stepped forward and offered his condolences. The pallbearers came next. Cory grabbed Loxley's shoulder as he bent down and whispered something fiercely in his ear but Loxley shook his head and mouthed 'not now.' Before Cory could object, he moved on to Mrs.

Boxer. Little John got to Cory next, and I heard him say in a low voice. "You worry about taking care of your ma."

Loxley walked away from the tent. The preacher and the guy from the funeral home followed. I tracked the three with my eyes, looking past Dad's head. They whispered for a minute and Loxley pulled a wad of money from the inside of his coat pocket. He peeled off a few bills and handed them to the preacher. He passed a few more to the other man. They nodded and mouthed their thanks before the money disappeared into their own pockets.

Little John came out to join his comrade, bringing out a pack of cigarettes. He opened it and extended it to Loxley. When he shook his head 'no,' Little John took one for himself and lit it. I saw Scarlet whisper something to the man she'd been sitting with before she patted his hand and moved to join them. Dale came next and said something to Little John. He must have asked for a smoke himself, because Little John handed him the cigarette he'd just lit and dug himself out another one.

I glanced around and saw Tuck talking with Dad. Max ambled toward his crew -- wearing a suit as well. He gave me a smile and a nod and I nodded in returned as he passed. He made it to his group and Dale and Scarlet slid apart so he could be in the middle. None of the others noticed me.

"Miss Fitzwalter?"

I turned as the usher that had met us at the door stepped forward.

"We're going to have fellowship now," he informed me. "The ladies of the church made an early lunch. We hope you and your daddy will join us."

I smiled. "Thank you."

"You're welcome."

He ambled off and I turned just in time to see Loxley walk back to the tent. Most of the well-wishers had made their escapes to the air-conditioned fellowship hall. Not him. He stopped at the old man that had been with Scarlet, leaned over, and whispered in his ear. The man nodded and stood. He had a cane with a curved end he kept in his right hand. He took Loxley's arm and they began walking carefully towards the group.

I made my way to Dad, whose head was whipping around like he was looking for me, and he smiled as I approached.

"Ready to go inside?"

"You go ahead," I replied. "I want to stay out here."

"Why?"

"You don't see cemeteries this old very often. I just want to check it out. Besides, I need a break from the crowd, and if I'm supposed to be keeping my eyes open, it defeats the purpose if we're both looking at the same thing at the same time."

He leaned over and kissed my forehead. "Don't be long. You'll need to get back to school."

"Yes, sir."

He walked off and I stood in the tent's shade. I crossed my arms and looked out over the graveyard.

I thought 'graveyard' fit this place better than 'cemetery.' To me, cemeteries were places that had monuments and everything looked new and orderly. Graveyards, on the other hand, had tombstones that were centuries old. Both might have ghosts, but the graveyards were the spookier of the two.

The closest tombstones had inscriptions so faded I couldn't even see with twenty-twenty vision. It wouldn't have surprised me if this church had been around years before the Civil War.

I leaned lightly against a tent pole and looked out over the grounds. The group had separated.

Scarlet was off to my left on the far side of the property, standing over a grave next to the fence. She had her back to me and her head was down. Max and Dale were with her just a couple of steps behind. Max matched Scarlet's pose while Dale was more animated, shifting from foot to foot like he couldn't be still.

Tuck was on the far right of the property with Little John. The smaller of the two meditated over a tombstone. Little John leaned against the whitewashed fence, smoking another cigarette.

Loxley and the old guy were standing nearly the dead center of the property. From where I was, I could see they were standing over a double grave. The man was leaning on his cane.

It seemed even outlaws had people they missed.

As I was slipping away towards the church, Dale, Max, and Scarlet caught my attention. Dale put a hand on her shoulder, which was shaking slightly. They held that pose for about a minute before her head finally came up. I guessed he asked her if she was okay because she swiped her right eye with her finger and gave him a nod. He released her and they began walking towards the middle of the cemetery.

Tuck was also moving that way. Little John was about three steps behind him, tossing his cigarette as he went. They all converged on Loxley and the old man.

They stood around the grave with their backs to me. I watched as they held their silent vigil. I didn't know the circumstances. Did they know the people buried there? Or were they just there for Loxley?

"Hail the Glorious Dead!" the old man proclaimed.

"Hail the Glorious Dead!" the other answered loudly.

I'd never seen anything like it.

It wasn't just their words. It was how they said them. The old man spoke strongly... proudly. And the others? It wasn't like Mass, where the priest would say something and the congregation would just mumble back at him. There was more to it. They were firm in their words. There was a significance to the moment that escaped me

Figuring I needed to disappear before they saw me, I eased around the corner and made my way to the fellowship hall. The smell of fried chicken made my stomach rumble. I saw Dad sitting with the family, a glass of iced tea in his hand. I moved through the sea of bodies to make my way to him.

"There you are, Marian," Dad said.

How Mrs. Boxer was keeping it together, I had no idea. Her eyes were red, but she wasn't shaking or crying. I didn't know where she was getting her strength. I made a note to pray before I went to bed that she would gain more. She was going to need it.

"This is my daughter Marian," Dad introduced. I extended my hand as he spoke. "This is Mrs. Boxer, her daughter Shea, and her son Cory."

"I'm sorry for your loss," I said sincerely. "It sounds like Mr. Boxer was a wonderful man."

"He was," she agreed with me in a shaky voice. "We were married for twenty-eight years."

"You're a Junior, right?" Cory asked me.

He had hair cut severely short, ears that were a bit oversized, and broad shoulders. His expression felt more angry than defeated.

"Yeah," I replied. "We just moved here."

"You see Hood?"

I didn't expect the question, but I recovered quickly. "He and the rest of the pallbearers were outside when I came in."

Dad looked puzzled.

Cory nodded and rose. "Excuse me."

As he walked away, Mrs. Boxer addressed Dad. "Do you know anything else, Mr. Fitzwalter?"

Dad shook his head. "I have my suspicions."

"You won't catch him."

He reached over and took her hand. "Ma'am, don't say that. It is my mission to see that justice is done."

Shea snorted.

Mrs. Boxer just nodded. "It will be done, but I doubt it will be from you."

"Why do you say that?"

"Because that's the way it's always been. You're going against a deep-rooted evil."

"I've dealt with evil all my life. It's my specialty."

"Not like this," she countered. "You're going against bad that's dug in like a tick. I fear it will take something with more teeth than your badge and your Texas-sized reputation."

Dad didn't look like he liked what she was saying. I bit my lip and kept my mouth shut.

"What would it take to get you to believe I won't rest until I find out the truth behind what happened to your husband?"

She shook her head. "I don't care about the truth. You and I both know it wasn't no wreck that killed him. What I care about is what is going to happen to the people that took him away from us."

Her son who gave the eulogy approached the table. "Excuse me, but have you seen Cory?"

"He went outside to talk to somebody," Shea answered.

"They're asking if we want to do or say anything else before they get on with burying Dad. I'd rather be out there to make sure they don't drop him or bury him without the casket." He snorted. "You know these undertakers are crooked as politicians."

"I'll go," I offered. "I'm pretty sure he's talking to the pallbearers."

"Thank you, Miss."

I stood up, smoothed out my dress, and made my exit. It seemed even hotter outside than it was when I'd come in fifteen minutes ago. I got to the corner of the building when I heard voices.

"What are you going to do?" Cory asked with anger evident in his tone.

"You know what I'm going to do," was the reply from Loxley.

"When?"

"When we know something."

"How long will that be?"

"We don't know," Scarlet answered. "Not only do we have to be careful, but we have to be sure."

"It can't wait long. This is killing Mama — and me."

Then it was Little John's turn to talk. "Look, man, I know you're hurting. I know you're pissed off. I would be too. But to do what you want, it has to be sure, it has to be cold, and it has to be final. Let us handle it."

"Please... don't take any longer than you need to."

"We won't," Loxley assured him. "We're already working on it. It will be taken care of." There was a pause. "We'll honor him the best way we know how."

I kicked a rock to announce my presence before I stepped around the corner. All heads snapped in my direction.

"Your mom and brother are looking for you," I said in a bored voice, jerking my thumb behind me. "They said it's time to say your final goodbyes."

Cory wiped his eyes and nodded. I kept my face impassive, though I had about a million questions. I glanced over Loxley's shoulder at the graveyard while I had the chance. I had to squint because of the distance to read the names.

Earl Loxley and Joan Loxley were engraved on the tombstones they had gathered around. I saw a couple of others with 'Loxley' on them, but I couldn't read their full names.

Who were Earl and Joan Loxley? What were they talking about? What was with this whole 'Hailing' thing? And what did Cory want?

Cory wandered past me, and I gave Loxley one more look before I fell in step with the grieving boy.

Chapter 10

"EVERYTHING OKAY, MARIAN?" BRENT asked.

"Yeah," I replied, sitting down beside him at the lunch table.

Dad dropped me off at the house to get my car before I went back to school. He said little on the way home, which led me to believe he was bothered by Mrs. Boxer's words I let him be.

"Hail The Glorious Dead" was still weighing on my mind.

"Where you been?" Tina asked.

I shrugged and opened my water bottle. "Dad wanted to go to Junior Boxer's funeral so I went with him."

"Good turn-out?" Brent asked.

"Yeah," I replied after taking a sip. "I didn't know that many people."

"So, did you leave before they broke out the moon-shine?"

I didn't know or care if Jody was making a joke. "I didn't

see any, no." I then turned to Brent. "I figured you'd be there."

"Why?" Tina asked for him. "We don't socialize with those people."

For some reason, the way she said "those people" stuck in my craw. I didn't know Cory or his family either, but that was beside the point. Junior Boxer drove a log truck. Did she think paper was made of unicorn farts? His job was as important as whatever it was her daddy did. Going to a school full of rich kids in Dallas that looked down on Dad's occupation made her words even more insulting to me.

"Because his dad's a county commissioner," I explained. "I figured he at least knew some of those that were there."

Brent gave a small shrug. "It's not his district. Plus, he's never done well with the blue-collar vote."

"Or the government check one," Tina added.

"Speaking of which," Jody said with a nod.

Alonzo Tuck was across the lunchroom. He'd stopped at the two pregnant girls. His hands were on the table and he was leaning over so he could whisper to the one from my Geometry class. I didn't know her name.

She nodded slowly and he nodded back. His hand went to his pocket and palmed something. He slid it to her. She covered it before anyone could notice what it was and mouthed, "Thank you, Alonzo."

He then turned to the other girl, and after a quick exchange she shook her head and smiled. Satisfied, he straightened up, gave them both a wave, and moved along.

"I think we just saw a dope deal go down," Jody remarked. “Ba-zing!”

I’d been around enough to know what I just saw wasn’t a deal. Tuck had only handed her money. I didn’t see her pass anything back to him.

Tina snorted. “We all know what the hell that was.”

“What?” I asked, since no one else did.

“Money from her baby daddy.”

“Tuck?” I asked. “He’s the baby’s...”

Tina snorted and gave me a look that said, “Don’t be stupid.”

“Tuck’s just the fucking houseboy,” Jody explained. “That cash came from someone else.”

“Who?”

“Word is it’s Hood’s.”

Brent stared at the table and said nothing.

“I haven’t seen them together since I got here.”

Jody just shrugged.

Was Loxley buying Grace off to make this all go away? Between my dad’s war stories, my mom’s tales from the E.R., and my own observations, I knew people could be cruel. To me, knocking someone up and abandoning the child, money or not, was unforgivable. Learning this about Loxley shouldn’t have surprised me, but it did.

The bell rang and we all stood up.

“Call me tonight?” I asked Brent.

“I’ll try,” he replied.

"Miss Chen, can I ask you something?" Class was over and it was just us two. "This is going to sound strange, but does the phrase 'Hail the Glorious Dead' mean anything to you?"

She peered at me quizzically.

"It's something I heard recently," I explained. "And I can't place it. Is it something someone wrote?"

She mouthed the words to herself very slowly. "The Lord of the Rings trilogy used the phrase 'victorious dead.' You sure it was 'glorious' and not 'victorious'?"

"I'm sure."

She pondered.

"I was just curious. Maybe I heard it in a song."

"Do you mind telling me where you heard it?"

I shifted my weight. "At Junior Boxer's funeral."

She looked at me, perplexed.

"Well, not exactly at his funeral," I added quickly. "It was after the funeral."

"Start at the beginning."

I took a deep breath. "I was outside and noticed a bunch of people gathered at a grave. It was... seven of them. Anyway, they were quiet for a minute. Then one of them called out 'Hail the Glorious Dead' and the rest repeated it."

"Hmmm."

She turned away and went towards her bookshelf. She had to come up on her toes to reach what she was looking for on the very top.

"Do you mind telling me who you saw?" she asked without turning around.

I did actually. It hadn't escaped my attention that she

was in the Robert Loxley Fan Club. I didn't know if what I had to say would bother her.

But I had to know. "It was Loxley and his crew."

She turned around. "That's what I thought."

I didn't like her look. It sort of reminded me of Tina, like she was weighing and measuring me. I jutted my chin and met her gaze out of pure stubbornness.

Instead of giving me an answer, she strolled to the door with a sense of purpose. She stuck her head out, looked left and right, and then closed it before turning to me.

Uh-oh...

"Can you keep your mouth shut, Miss Fitzwalter?"

"Yes, ma'am."

She approached me. "I mean it. I don't like to talk about the personal business of my students. So I need to trust you."

I swallowed. "You can trust me."

She put the book down and opened it. "Do you know what a cenotaph is?"

I shook my head.

"It's a Greek word," she explained. "It literally means 'empty tomb.'"

She found what she was looking for in the book and turned it around. I look down at the black-and-white picture of a war monument. The caption said it was in Whitehall.

"This is The Cenotaph in England," she explained. "They initially constructed it as a monument to those that died in World War One."

I didn't get it.

"Did you see which grave?"

"I could only pick out one — Earl and Joan Loxley."

She nodded. "I thought so."

She began flipping pages again as I asked, "What made you think that?"

She showed me the book again. "The south face of The Cenotaph."

It was another black-and-white photograph, a close-up to a carving of a wreath. Inscribed below were the words 'The Glorious Dead.'

"I don't get it," I admitted.

She sighed and tossed her left braid over her shoulder. "There are several Loxleys buried in that cemetery. Robert's aunt, uncle, and grandmother I know for sure... but that plot doesn't contain the body of either Earl or Joan Loxley. It's a cenotaph. They're not in there."

"They're not?"

Miss Chen shook her head. "No, they aren't. They've been missing for several years now and people have presumed them dead. From what I can gather, nobody ever found Earl or Joan's bodies."

"What happened to them?"

"Nobody knows. From what I've been able to gather, the report showed that their car was discovered in the swamp south of the Sherwood River, across the Florida line. Investigators found a lot of blood, but no bodies. They'd been missing for a week at that point. Earl and Joan were Robert's parents."

I was stunned. "How old was Loxley?"

"Eleven, I believe."

That was horrible. "So, I'm still confused. Why did they say that at their grave?"

Miss Chen took a deep, cleansing breath. "Marian, this is really where your secret-keeping ability comes into play."

"Alright."

"The Loxleys had enemies. Powerful ones. The family owns a lot of land that butts up to the Sherwood River. It's the perfect place to make moonshine or meth or use the river to smuggle drugs or stolen goods. It borders the national forest side of Florida and the river flows past the state line, then forks with one side going to Mobile and the other to Pensacola. The rumor is Earl refused to do business with the Dixie Mafia… to the point he even killed a man who threatened his family. And they murdered him and his wife."

"But not Loxley… I mean, Robert?"

"No," she admitted. "I haven't figured out why yet. I suspect he was staying with Mr. Thomas the night they disappeared, but I couldn't say for sure."

"So they were paying homage…"

"…To those gone, but not forgotten. The name 'Loxley' is English in origin. I have no clue where 'The Glorious Dead' came from, but if I had to guess, I'd say the Middle Ages. If Earl really killed to protect his family and died trying, he would be considered one of the Glorious Dead. I don't know how, but I'm guessing Junior Boxer did something to resist and died for it. I'd be willing to bet he received a similar homage when the family could be present."

I fell back into Miss Chen's desk chair, feeling gut shot.

Instead of answering any questions, it only gave me more. What horrors had Loxley seen? What was driving him? What was he doing about this? Was he even doing anything?

"It was an interesting display," I said, mainly to fill the silence.

She nodded sagely. "It doesn't surprise me though."

"Why not?"

Instead of answering me, she turned her head.

"Miss Chen? Why not?"

"I've said enough."

"Why not?"

She turned around and looked at me, stone-faced. "If you want those answers, you'll have to get them from somewhere else."

"So who do I ask?"

She shook her head. "I'm not going to tell you that either. If you want the answers, you'll find a way to get them. But it won't be from me."

"Are you afraid someone will... hurt you... if you talk?"

"No, I'm afraid someone else will get hurt if I say the wrong thing to the wrong person."

"Aren't you afraid someone will hurt me if I ask the wrong question?"

I must've had a point because her expression changed from blank to thoughtful.

"So I need to know," I pressed.

"No, you don't!" She snapped. "You need to keep your head down and mind your own business! This doesn't, nor will it ever, concern you!"

I recoiled like she'd slapped me.

Miss Chen didn't let up. "You've got two years and Barnsdale County will be a distant memory to you. You'll go to college, meet some rich guy, get married, have babies, and be a wealthy housewife. You'll join a country club in Dallas, drive an expensive SUV, be a soccer mom, and get Botox twice a year. This place won't even be a blip in your memory."

My teeth ground together and my fists clenched as my anger awakened.

If Miss Chen noticed, she didn't care. "Barnsdale County is an ugly place, Marian. You're not equipped to handle it. This place is nothing but sorrow. I know what I just said angered you, but believe me, it's for the best."

"The best?" I hissed.

"The best. The ugliness will wear on you. Sometimes I curse God for letting me choose to stay here."

Miss Chen had given me the impression she was out of the loop about the other side of Barnsdale County. I realized then she knew a lot more than she'd let on.

"Why do you like him so much?" I asked.

"Robert Loxley? Why wouldn't I?"

"Because he's a criminal!" I snapped. "He committed arson. You said so yourself. He punched a guy dead in the mouth yesterday in the parking lot over an insult and would've stomped a mud hole in him had someone not intervened. I heard he's got a girl pregnant and isn't even in her life. Why do you think he's so great?"

I didn't know why I left off breaking and entering.

"Who told you he had a child?"

I shrugged. "Word gets around."

"I seriously doubt he's done that."

"I don't."

"Why?"

I threw my hands up in the air. "Because he's a thug! You don't get the nickname 'Hood' by being a gentleman."

"And you don't earn the admiration of so many people in this depressing place by being one of the criminals."

Who admired him besides that merry band of delinquents he hung out with?

She hopped up on her desk and let her feet swing. While she was sitting taller than I was, it didn't give off that impression. Instead, she looked like she was trying to put us on the same level — acquaintances instead of teacher and student.

"You want to know why I don't think Robert is the evil you think he is?"

I nodded.

She took a deep breath and began. "I told you I had him in my class in ninth grade, right?"

"Monday. Yes."

"That was my first year of teaching here. He was just 'Robin' to most people, not Hood."

I kept my trap shut and let her continue.

"The other teachers had warned me to keep my students at arm's length," she went on. "Some of their lives outside school are horrifying, Marian. I hope you don't find out for yourself."

I gave her one nod to signal her to continue.

She did. "The year I got hired... Robert's freshman

year... I was chaperoning the football game. It was November, the season was almost over, and it was nasty cold. I stayed to talk to Mrs. Jones... she retired at the end of last year... and we were parked on opposite sides, so I was alone going to my car."

I leaned back in my chair and listened.

"I had my keys in my hand, had already hit the unlock button, and was ten feet from the door when they grabbed me."

"They?"

"Five men," she explained. "Boys really. None are here anymore. They've either graduated, dropped out, or been arrested. All black, all young, and all on me." She took a deep breath. "They took my purse... The biggest one had his hand over my mouth. I couldn't scream. I was kicking and thrashing, but there were too many of them and I was all alone."

I swallowed the lump in my throat. "They... hurt you?"

She shook her head. "Someone came out of the wood line swinging an axe handle. He dropped the man holding my mouth. His blood actually hit me in the face."

I leaned forward, her story drawing me in.

"The man was enormous... like really huge... and he had that stick, but it was still four on one. They backed off, regrouping to take him down, and I saw his face — well, sort of."

"Sort of?"

She nodded again. "He was wearing a hooded sweatshirt and a hockey mask."

"Like... that guy in those cheesy horror movies?"

"That's the one. But I assure you when someone built like the Terminator and holding an axe handle is standing there, 'cheesy' isn't the right word. Before the other four could attack, someone jumped one of them from behind. When the others turned on him, the big one waded in with that stick. I don't think the fight lasted more than a minute."

I started to see where this was going

"He approached me and offered me his hand when it was over," she said, her head dropping so she was looking at her shoes. "I was so frightened that I took it. I asked him who they were, but neither one answered me. He just escorted me to my car while his partner was systematically kicking each attacker in the ribs."

"Then what happened?"

She licked her lips. "Like his partner, he was wearing a hooded sweatshirt. But he had a bandana around the lower part of his face. He bent over, picked up my keys, and handed them to me."

Sounded familiar. "Did you get a name?"

"No," she replied. "I asked. He just opened my car door for me like a gentleman, closed it for me, and then pointed for me to leave."

"Was it Loxley?"

"I didn't know Robert really well then," she admitted. "I didn't put two and two together that it was him and John Little until I saw them in class the following Monday. Of course I questioned them about it, but they denied it. "Robert even laughed and told me even though he was an orphan he was definitely too poor to be Batman."

“But it was?”

“It was. Their height, build, and eye color were right. There aren’t many people John’s size. And I’ve seen Robert on his motorcycle since then. He wears the same bandana.”

“Lots of people do.”

“But with it on, he looks just like the guy.” Her eyes came up to look at me. “I don’t believe anyone like that can be what he’s made out to be. They waded into a five on two fight just to protect someone they didn’t even know. That says more to me than any high school rumor.”

This kept getting even morc confusing. I had one side saying he was white trash. I had another calling him noble. I saw him with my own eyes steal and assault someone. I’d also seen him tenderly escort a blind man to his son- and daughter-in-law’s headstone and leave a note on my pillow. Each new thing I learned contradicted the previous one.

Chapter 11

"HELLO?"

"Hey, Marian… it's Brent."

"Oh!" I perked up. "You called."

"I said I would."

"You said you'd try," I corrected.

"So, did you want something?"

I didn't want to be forward here and ask him out. I was still old-fashioned like that. I took a shot that he would ask me. Worst-case scenario, I showed I was interested and maybe led him that direction — if I didn't make a fool of myself.

"Not really," I admitted. I flopped back on the bed. "I just wanted to talk to you outside of school, you know?"

"I gotcha."

Score for me! "You home yet?"

"Yeah, I just walked in the door. You ready for Monday?"

"Cheerleading tryouts? Yeah, I am. I don't think I'll

screw up too bad."

"You'll do fine," he assured me.

"I hope so."

It was quiet for a moment. I was drowning here and I didn't have a lifeline.

"Well... if there's nothing else..."

I went with the only thing I could think of. "What was that about the other day?"

"What do you mean?"

"You and Loxley," I clarified. "You two met in the middle of that group like a couple of Mafia dons brokering a deal."

He got quiet.

"I asked the wrong question, huh?"

"No," he replied. "I guess you probably need to know if you're going to live here."

That sounded ominous. "Know what?"

"Well," he began, "the truth is we sort of were brokering a deal."

"You were? I was just... running my mouth."

He chuckled dryly. "This whole place is corrupt."

"I know. It's why my dad's here, remember?"

"True. But it extends all the way down to the school."

"I don't follow."

"Sometimes people are in charge because of who their family is. Sometimes it's because a lot of people will follow them. And sometimes? People are in charge because they're willing to do whatever it takes to get to the top."

"And Loxley will do whatever it takes?"

"Yeah. I told you he was bad news."

"People are sort of vague about that."

"That's because it's best not to mention it. You don't want to incur his wrath, I can assure you."

"You are."

"Loxley's crew won't touch me because of my dad. They do, and they have to deal with every law enforcement agency in the tri-county area. It's too much heat."

"That makes sense. So what does that make you?"

"The Peacemaker," he said with a touch of annoyance in his voice. "I can't stop most of the shit that goes on. I can only really protect my friends and anyone not really involved."

"Like the other morning?"

"Precisely."

"I understand."

And I did. Had I been in Brent's shoes, I would've probably used the 'my dad is a cop' move if it would've kept some thug from beating up my friend. Unless that friend was Jody. He kind of deserved to get blasted in the mouth.

"So you get it?"

"Of course," I assured him. "I was just curious. I feel like I've kind of stepped off into a foreign country."

"You do, huh?"

"Yeah, I mean, I still don't have that many friends. Heck, half the people I know are criminals. Know, mind you, not hang out with. I still feel like I'm treading water."

"Oh yeah?"

"For real."

"You want to do something?"

Was this going to be it? "What do you have in mind?"

"Nothing major. We usually do the hang-out thing in the school parking lot on Saturday night unless something else is going on. You want to hang out with me?"

It didn't escape my attention he said "me" and not "us." "I'd love to."

"Cool. We usually get there after dark. You want me to pick you up or meet you there?"

I thought it over really quick. I trusted Brent, but on a first date, I preferred to be on my toes.

"I don't mind," he added. "You live in Nottingham, right?"

"Yeah."

"It wouldn't be any trouble."

"Okay," I agreed. "What time?"

"Six?"

"My curfew is usually eleven. That okay?"

"Yeah, that's fine. I can have you back, no problem."

"Awesome! I'll be ready."

"Cool. I'll see you at school tomorrow."

"Okay... bye!"

"You ready?" Brent asked.

"Yeah," I replied. "Nice car!"

He had a small convertible. It was very new, very shiny, and very fast-looking.

Brent opened the door for me and I settled into the leather. He then hopped over the other door and landed in the driver's seat. He gave me a sly smile that I couldn't help but return.

"Ready?"

"Oh, yeah!"

He started the car as I buckled up.

"So what else do you do besides play football?" I asked.

He shrugged. "Play basketball. Rodeo some. Hunt when it gets cooler. The regular stuff. How's your dad's work going?"

"Slow," I admitted. "I know it's only been a week, but he's still trying to get his feet under him. It's like no one wants him to though."

"People are like that. Anyone he arrests is related to someone. They're going to protect their people. So he doesn't have any suspects or anything?"

I tilted my head in his direction. "Not that I know of. Why? You know something?"

"Why would I know something?" He sounded defensive.

"I don't know. But after the other night when you were talking about Loxley, I figured you knew who the bad guys were."

"You're the only person our age, besides his friends, that doesn't call him Hood."

I shrugged. "I told you. I don't know him well enough to call him by his nickname. But if it makes you feel any better, I don't like him enough to call him 'Robert' or 'Robin.'"

"Good point."

We came up on a dually truck hauling a horse trailer.

Brent dropped the hammer and swerved. The car rocketed around and I pulled my clip out of my hair so it could be free.

As we came out to the crossroads, I was surprised to see Loxley and Little John sitting there on their bikes. Brent didn't even look at them as he zoomed past. I only gave them a glance, but I noticed both their heads whip around when they saw me in the car.

Brent pulled into a space right in the middle as if someone had saved it for him.

The parking lot looked like the lunchroom, split into different groups of kids segregated by race and economics. I saw the two pregnant girls sitting on the tailgate of a small pickup, sipping from bottles of water and talking. Jermaine was hanging out with a mostly male group and all black. Five boys that looked young enough to be freshman were riding skateboards around a small corner of the parking lot and attempting to do kick flips.

"Ba-zing!" Jody exclaimed, coming up to Brent's door. "My man!"

"Sup?"

They slapped hands and Jody leaned on the window frame. "Sup, Marian?"

"Hi, Jody."

I shifted as I caught his eyes falling to my chest. Brent didn't seem to notice.

"You got any?" Jody asked him.

"In the trunk."

Brent popped the latch and Jody disappeared. He returned with three beers.

"Here," he said, passing Brent two.

Both were looking at me, so I took one. No sense in being unsociable.

"What's the word?" Brent asked.

Jody, who was in the process of digging a snuff can out of his back pocket, shrugged. "Be damned if I know."

I heard motorcycles and I made myself not look in their direction.

Jody noticed the sound though. "Looks like the fucking trash is out."

Brent just shrugged.

"Hey, I'm going to see what J-man's holding. You still want to get wet on Labor Day? It'll probably be our last chance."

"Yeah," Brent replied. "Dad hasn't had the boat winterized yet. Pass the word. We'll take that bitch out Monday."

"Crawford Landing?"

"That works."

Jody pumped his fist.

Brent turned to me. "You like the water?"

"I do," I admitted.

"So you want to go out on my dad's boat?"

"Monday?"

He nodded. "You got plans?"

"Mom's working and I think Dad is going to Dallas to get the rest of our stuff. I'll be free."

"They'll be gone all weekend?"

"Mom will be on nights, so it'll pretty much be me."

"Want some company Sunday?"

"Thanks, but they're weird about me having people

over when they're not at home."

"Aw," Jody mocked. "No party at Marian's house?"

"Afraid not."

"Weren't you going to talk to Jermaine?"

Jody threw up his hands and muttered, *"I'm going"* as he walked away.

"So what's the plan?" I asked to make conversation. "We going fishing... skiing... swimming?"

"Probably going to the rope swing," he replied. I noticed he had a dimple in his chin that only made him look cuter. "Can you drive? I'm going to be pulling the boat on a trailer."

"I don't mind."

Looking past Brent's head, I noticed Jody and Jermaine shook hands. Jody stuffed something in his pocket before he handed Jermaine some money, then said something else and Jermaine looked past him in our direction. He cocked his head as if to say, "all right," and they separated.

"Jody just bought weed."

"You going to rat him out?"

I shook my head. "It's not my business, but I thought..."

"Thought what?"

"That was Loxley's department and you kept the peace."

"It's a little more complicated than that."

"It is?"

"As long as they don't hurt anybody, it's best if I stay out of that shit."

"Dealing pot here isn't hurting anybody?"

"No," he corrected. "If Jermaine and some other spook

were beefing, that would hurt someone."

I was a little taken aback at the word 'spook.' "But just dealing?"

He shrugged. "There's a market. If I got Jermaine's ass arrested, someone else would be dealing Monday. Actually, several would and they'd brawl over who controlled it. It would create a power vacuum. That's when fucking trouble starts. It's like the government's war on drugs. The worst part of it isn't the addicts. It's the brawling over turf."

"Very libertarian of you."

He shrugged. "One thing I've learned from my dad is around here you have to live with the scum and learn to stay clean. Otherwise you'll end up dirty too."

Something caught his attention, and he nodded his head past me. "Looks like Hood needed a fix too."

I looked that direction to see Loxley, Little John, Dale, and Jermaine were talking. I watched along with Brent.

He took a long swallow of beer.

"See? Everybody is dirty somehow."

"I didn't see a deal," I admitted. I then took a small sip to be polite. "It looks like they're just talking."

"You sure like to give him the fucking benefit of the doubt."

His words had a harshness to them that caught me by surprise. I glanced in his way. He was looking at Loxley like a fighter would stare at his opponent from across the ring.

"I don't even think about him," I lied.

"Every time we talk, it seems you bring his ass up."

"Once," I admitted. "When you two had words last

week. The other times someone else had brought him up."

He took another swallow and fumed.

"You really don't like him, do you?"

"I fucking hate him."

Wow. I didn't think it ran that deep. "Why?"

He exhaled and his face relaxed. "His family and mine don't exactly get along."

"And when you say don't get along..."

"Think Muslims and Jews. Hatfields and McCoys are probably more accurate."

"That bad, huh?"

He polished the beer off and dropped the bottle in the back seat. "Yeah."

"Why?"

"Shit's been going on for generations. Seems the Deans and the Loxleys have squared off over all sorts of things."

"What started it? Two guys feuding over a woman?"

He snorted. "Nothing that fucking romantic. It's been a culmination of things: property disputes, arguments over business deals. Shit like that."

"So you two are just continuing it?"

"No," he corrected. "I just sort of... fell into it."

"What about him?"

Brent blew out a long breath. "I think he's got a grudge. You ever hear about his parents?"

"I've heard something about that."

"He blames my family."

"Why?"

"My brother is a deputy, remember? I'm sure Old Man Loxley has been filling Hood's head with lies for years."

"They think it was a corrupt cop?"

"Word is the old man does. At least last I heard."

The plot thickened.

"So what has he done about it?"

"Been crazy. You hear he's done time?"

"I think so... arson, right?"

"Yeah. He blew up a house with a fucking meth lab in it."

"Why'd he do that?"

"Because he thought my dad had something to do with it."

I blinked in surprise. "Obviously not."

He nodded in agreement. "It was on our land, but Dad didn't know the shit was there. He didn't even know that old house, trailer really, existed. We only used the land to grow timber. He hadn't been out there in a fucking decade at least."

The one thing I wanted right then was to hear Loxley's side of the story. That thought really made me disappointed in myself. Here I was with Brent and I wanted to talk to Loxley.

I forgot all about it as Brent turned and rested a hand on my leg just above my left knee. My body flooded with warmth and I smiled nervously. Thankful I shaved my legs before he picked me up, I rested my hand on top of his-mainly to keep him from thinking he was going much further.

It had gotten dark while we were talking and the dim light made him look more mysterious. He tilted his head more towards the back seat and gazed at me. I bit my bottom lip. His hand gave my leg a gentle squeeze, which made me feel even more nervous.

Slowly, he leaned in. My body was tingling, and I was extremely uneasy. He was going to kiss me and I wasn't sure how I felt about that yet.

"Ba-ZING!"

It was like being dunked in cold water.

"Hey, man. I'm getting another beer. You want one?"

Brent groaned. "Sure." He opened the car door as he spoke. "I'll get it. You need another one, Marian?"

"I'm good. Thanks."

Across the way, I saw Loxley, Little John, and Jermaine had been joined by a bunch of kids, both black and white. Several people held money and were waving it.

Brent returned with a fresh beer and his gaze followed mine. "Looks like we've got some entertainment."

"What's going on?"

"With people waving money, I'm guessing an arm-wrestling match. They do that shit sometimes."

"Hell yeah!" Jody yelled from Brent's side of the car. "Let's go check it out!"

"Okay."

I didn't really care to, but if Brent was going I figured I'd tag along.

We exited and met in front of the car. With his beer in his left hand, Brent threw his right arm over my shoulder and we went to join the crowd.

We got there as a black guy that looked like he weighed closed to three hundred pounds lumbered through the crowd. He was shorter than Little John but wider — much wider.

Jody sounded excited. "Pookie's about to kick his ass! I'm getting me some of that action!"

The crowd parted as Brent led us to the front. Little John removed his cut and unbuttoned his shirt before he shucked it off. He was wearing a wife beater underneath that showed off his mountain of muscle.

His right upper arm had a very interesting tattoo: a World War Two biplane. It black and gray with splotches of red, like someone splattered paint on a pencil drawing. The plane's nose pointed down towards his wrist like the aircraft was setting up to dive bomb a target.

"Hood," Brent said politely.

Loxley's eyes settled on me for a split second before he turned his attention back to my date. "Brent."

"What are the odds?"

"Two-to-one on Pookie."

Brent gave a nod like that was okay with him. Loxley gave me one more look and headed over to where Little John was getting set. I noticed Scarlet had joined them.

I stood by impassively as Little John beat the larger man. Brent looked bored. Jody lost a hundred bucks.

While I did my best to watch the match, my eyes kept glancing at Loxley. I noticed his would occasionally dart to me before returning to business. People collected wagers and gathered around to congratulate the winner. I stayed back with Brent.

Those weren't my people.

Chapter 12

"HEY, KITTEN. HAVE A good time?"

"It was okay," I replied, setting down my purse. "I'm getting a glass of tea. You want any?"

"Sure."

I went to the refrigerator and grabbed the pitcher before heading towards the cabinet for a couple of glasses.

Brent had been less than affectionate after the arm-wrestling match. He wasn't mean or anything, but he didn't try to kiss me again. I was confused, but relieved. I figured it was probably for the best. The last thing I needed to do was kiss on the first date and make him think I was easy.

I poured our drinks and moved to the table. Dad had a bunch of folders spread out. There were two boxes at his feet. He was glancing at files and put them into a bunch of different stacks.

"Confidential?" I asked as I put his drink in front of him.

"Nah," he replied. "Have a seat. I actually wanted to show you something."

Curious, I sat down beside him.

"Remember the other day when we were talking about the killing where an arrow had been left behind?"

"Yes, sir?"

He took a long swallow before continuing. "You remember telling me I should look for arrows or evidence of them at non-homicides?"

I nodded and took a sip of my tea before wincing. Mom didn't use enough sugar.

"You were right."

"Really?"

He pulled out a file folder and opened it. "This one is an attempted hijacking. Supposedly, the truck was empty." He slipped a photograph out and slid it in front of me. "You see anything?"

I studied the picture carefully. It was a side profile of an unmarked panel truck. The right front tire had been blown out. Other than that, I saw nothing that set off alarm bells.

"No, sir."

He took his pen and tapped the road. The spot he was showing had something there. It was too straight to be a random stick, but I couldn't tell what it was exactly.

"What does that look like to you?"

"No clue."

"Me either... but you know what it could be?"

I shook my head.

"An arrow shaft. It's the right diameter, I think."

"It could be. Any witnesses?"

Dad took another drink and shook his head. "Driver was knocked out. He didn't remember anything."

"Why did they hit an empty panel truck? They thought something was there?"

Dad grinned. "They said it was empty. But the driver was a man named Morgan Hayes, a known Dixie Mafia associate."

"You think there was something illegal in there and they lied about it?"

Dad nodded. "That's why it's in the maybe pile."

"Why use an arrow to blow out a tire? Why not a gun?"

"Maybe they didn't want the noise. Here's a better example."

He pulled another file and opened it. Inside was another photo, this time of a burned-down building.

"Shotgun shack north of York, almost to the county line," he explained. "Now, there was no question about it--this was a meth lab. But the fire marshal found something interesting."

He pulled out a sheet of paper and slid it to me. I studied it, but it had all sorts of chemical names I'd never hope to pronounce. Out of a list of about thirty, I noticed a handful that he'd highlighted.

"I don't take chemistry till next year, Dad, so you're going to have to translate."

"This is a printout of what the fire marshal had tested. He hit right at the source of the fire." He took a deep breath. "Let me back up. He believes it was a fire, then an explosion. Not the other way around. Don't ask me to explain how… fire investigation isn't my specialty… but he's willing to testify to that fact if necessary."

"Okay?"

"That's the thing. Since there are all sorts of volatile chemicals, normally meth labs explode, then burn. Not vice versa. That's why he started doing tests. You see those things I highlighted?"

"Yes, sir?"

"They're not supposed to be there."

"Okay, but what are they?"

"In English? Aluminum, four-forty steel, and two different plastics."

He had me at 'aluminum.'

"It was an arrow."

"Precisely. I got a confirmation email from the fire marshal today. He said that although he couldn't testify that it was an arrow because it was too burned, he could confirm that it was consistent with the materials used to make an arrow."

I thought about the three killings, and how they'd all been killers in their own right. "And since we know this was a crime scene…"

"I think it's a match."

"Good job, Dad!"

"I don't think it's going to help," he grumbled. "The truth is, even if it's three crimes or thirty, these perps got away clean each time. Whoever they are, they're not only good. They're lucky too."

"No one is lucky forever, Dad. How old are these?"

He pondered. "Um… these with the arrows are no more

than a year or two old. Why?"

"Honestly? I'm curious about some classmates."

"Give me some names?"

"Can you do that?"

He snorted. "I'm the police with privileges authorized by the governor herself. I can check on anyone I want."

He pulled a pen out of his shirt pocket and reached into his jacket hanging on his chair, coming out with a small notebook.

"Robert Loxley— a.k.a. Hood."

Dad's lips twitched. "I've heard that name before."

"He was at Mr. Boxer's funeral. Cory asked me if I'd seen him, remember?"

"That's not the only time I've heard it. So you think he's into something?"

"You know how rumors fly around school, Dad. I'd like to get some truth from an unbiased source."

"You didn't answer my question."

"I don't honestly know."

"Ok. Anybody else? Known associates?"

"The first one is John Little... a.k.a. 'Little John'."

Dad wrote the name down.

"The second is a girl. Scarlet Williams."

"Common spelling?"

"Yes sir."

"Who else?"

"Dale Alan. Alan with one 'L'."

He wrote it down. "Go on."

"The next is Max Miller."

"The same kid that fixed our sink?"

"Yes, sir."

"You think he's into something?"

"Not necessarily," I explained, "but he hangs around Loxley and the others."

Dad nodded and wrote the name down. "Okay, who's next?"

"Alonzo Tuck?"

That caused him to look up. "Mrs. Sadie's grandson?"

I held up a hand. "Just like Max. I think he's associated."

"That's a pretty good list, Kitten. What do you have on them?"

I bit my bottom lip. "Honestly? Just a hunch."

"So why check them out?"

I sighed. "School is full of gossip. I've just heard more of it about them, especially Loxley, than I have anyone else. And let's be honest. His street name is 'Hood.'"

"Is the school dangerous, Kitten? We'll home school you for a year if we need to."

"School's fine," I assured him. "I don't think it's any more dangerous than Dallas. I guess I'm just... paranoid... since that's why you're here."

He leaned back and started tapping the notebook with his pen. I polished off my tea and rattled the ice cubes in my glass.

"I'm leaving Sunday and going to Dallas," he said finally. "I'll be bringing Cowboy back with me."

"Awesome!"

He grinned. "Yeah, I kind of miss the big lug too."

I had seen no signs of Loxley in my house since the note. Now I sort of hoped he'd try it. I'd loved to see Cowboy take a chunk out of him.

"You want to ride with me?"

"Actually, I wanted to talk to you about that. I got invited to go to the river for Labor Day. If it wasn't the last trip before the end of summer, I wouldn't push it but..."

"Who's going? Anyone on this list?"

"Not hardly. It's mostly the upper crust of this county. Brent Dean invited me."

"Invited, huh?"

Dad didn't sound either positive or negative about it. If a voice could be blank, that's how he sounded.

"Is it okay?"

"I don't see why not."

His tone didn't convince me. "Spill it, Dad."

"I'm investigating his dad too, you know."

I didn't, but I wasn't surprised. "I haven't seen or heard anything about them. On the surface, Brent seems as American as apple pie. He dresses nice, he's good to me... so far... and I haven't seen him get into a bit of trouble."

"The apple rarely falls far from the tree, Kitten."

I just shrugged. What I'd told Dad was the truth. While I'd heard plenty of rumors concerning lots of people, especially Loxley, Brent's name didn't come up at all.

"And don't forget, you don't have to settle."

"What do you mean?"

He looked at me with serious eyes. "I'm your father. You know what that means, right?"

"No one will ever be good enough for me?"

"Exactly. So it will be up to you to decide who is. My point is you don't have to be in a hurry to decide."

"I'm not," I assured him. "But after George, I just... I don't want to say I want to get back in the swing of it. But when my time with George was good, it was good. I want to see if maybe it can be good again with someone else."

"But you're taking your time?"

"I am. Besides, aren't I supposed to find my husband in college? It's a major, right?"

Dad frowned. I couldn't help but burst out laughing.

THE WEEK COULDN'T HAVE ended soon enough.

I made the cheerleading squad. There was only one other girl that was even close to me in ability. I went first and nailed my routine. It made me proud. My closest competition went second and she nailed hers too. I thought we'd have to do some sort of tie-breaker.

Hindsight being twenty-twenty, I shouldn't have been surprised. I later realized it had been a formality. The other girls barely paid attention to anyone else's routine.

The rest of the contestants were less than cordial. They didn't cause a scene, but they didn't bother to thank the other girls for the opportunity or congratulate me. They simply gathered up their stuff and left. I think I was the only one that noticed.

I got fitted for my uniform and they put a rush on it. So now I had practice after seventh period. The schoolwork wasn't hard by any stretch. I got through my classes with little issue. After our conversation about the Glorious

Dead, Miss Chen had little to say. I graded papers or did as much of my homework as I could, so I had less to do at night.

Scarlet stopped talking to me. Well, she never really started after that first day. She shot me dirty looks, but I could ignore those. I neither knew nor cared what her problem was. I just chalked it up to her personality.

Max would at least smile at me in the hallway — if no one was looking. Otherwise, like if I was with Brent or one of the others, he was as stone-faced as ever.

Dale didn't care. He would wave if he saw me looking. To avoid questioning from my clique, I ignored him.

As far as Little John went, there was nothing. We'd never spoken, so that didn't change. I was just another face in the crowd to him.

Alonzo Tuck was polite to me, but he was polite to everyone. We hadn't had an actual conversation. He was another mystery to me: the only one of color in that group of peckerwoods.

Then there was Loxley.

He was beginning to irritate me. Well, that wasn't exactly fair. What was getting on my nerves was that I thought about him. I chalked it up to either the mystery surrounding him, his ability to be charming at times, or that maybe I was cliché and chicks are supposed to like bad boys.

I was losing my mind. It must've been the heat.

Not talking to Brent every night didn't help. I knew he was busy and got home from practice late and that he was tired. He was easy on the PDA. I got my hand held or his arm around me whenever we were on break or at lunch, but nothing a teacher could call us out on.

I didn't have any sort of urge for anything else, concerning Brent or anybody else. When I got 'The Talk' from Mom, she had warned me she was a late bloomer so it was possible I'd be the same way. I wasn't opposed to a kiss or holding hands or anything, but I did it because that's what people dating were supposed to do.

"You packed?" I asked Dad.

It was Saturday night. Brent hadn't asked me out, but that was okay. It meant I didn't have to say no to him to be with Dad tonight. Besides, I knew I'd see him Monday bright and early.

"I'm ready. Got an agent driving me to Mobile. I'll catch a flight there to Houston and then a connector to Dallas."

"And you'll be home Monday?"

"Cowboy and I will see you Monday night."

"Good. I can't wait to see him."

"Oh, I checked on those kids you asked me about."

"That was fast."

"It was easier than you'd think. Miller and Tuck were clean. They had nothing criminal at least. I'm still checking other sources, especially about Max, since we know about the history of abuse, but they've never worn cuffs as far as I can tell."

"That's good."

"Dale Alan is pretty clean too. He's got a couple of

speeding tickets, a 'possession of drug paraphernalia,' which could mean anything from a pipe or even a lighter if he pissed the cop off, and one truancy complaint, but that's it."

That surprised me. I figured he'd been in trouble more than that.

"The other three are interesting though."

"Oh?"

"Scarlet Williams pled down an assault charge and did a couple of months at a juvenile facility. Report said she slashed her father's girlfriend with a knife."

I winced. "Ouch."

"I'm checking DHR. There's got to be more to that story. I didn't realize she was the youngest of the three."

"Me either. What about the other two?"

"John Little Junior, a.k.a. 'Little John', was caught with his dad, 'Big John', in a stolen car. The elder Little is doing six years for it in Staton. Little John did eighteen months. He should've graduated last year. Police report leans towards he was just with his dad."

"Then why prosecute?"

"That bothers me. That and the fact he did his time in county jail instead of juvie. He was going into the Army, but the conviction squashed that, for now at least. I'm still checking."

Now for the cherry on top. "And Loxley?"

"Robert Loxley did nearly a year. Juvie. He was charged with arson. He walked on that charge but got some lesser ones. Contempt of court was one of them."

"He walked? Or he didn't do it?"

Dad's lips twisted into a grimace. "I honestly don't know. He tried to plead guilty, but they wouldn't accept it because his guardian wouldn't sign off." He shook his head. "That entire case was weird. It's like he was trying to go to jail on purpose, the powers that be were trying to convict him, his guardian was trying to keep him out of jail, and the judge was on the guardian's side. It was a total cluster. Oh, and get this: the judge was voted out in the next election after being on the bench for almost two decades."

"It does sound weird. Do you think he did it?"

"He said he did."

"The system disagrees with you. I've heard that rumor a few times and no one has said they thought he didn't do it. It was some of Brent's dad's property he was accused of setting fire to."

"You know why?"

"According to Brent, the Loxleys and the Deans have this whole family feud thing going on and have for several generations."

The wheels were turning in Dad's head.

"What?"

"I'm curious, that's all. It comes with being a cop. Something else weird. 'Robin' is listed as an alias but 'Hood' isn't. I had to double and triple check to make sure I had the right guy."

"That is kind of weird."

Chapter 13

The Sherwood River was beautiful.

Following Brent's directions, I left the house a little before eight. He had assured me we weren't meeting until 8:30, but I wanted to give myself plenty of time to get there. I found Crawford Landing with no issue, even though the directions included 'turn on to the dirt road just past the house with the two rusted tractors in the yard'.

Crawford Landing was a well-kept public boat ramp a few miles off the main highway on the far eastern side of the county. It had a concrete ramp that looked big enough to put a yacht in, with a wide wooden pier to its left and a couple of picnic tables by the water. The trees were mature and provided plenty of shade.

With nothing to occupy my thoughts my mind went back to my conversation with Dad, which had me once again going over everything I knew about Loxley. Every time I convinced myself he was trouble, I'd remember something he'd done that moved him into the 'good' category. But every time I'd start leaning towards good, I'd remember something that pushed him back towards 'trouble'.

I huffed and tied my hair back before getting out and unloading my car. All I had were the basics: a couple of towels, some sunscreen, my binoculars, and my wallet. I'd also brought a small cooler with some bottled water, in case all they had was beer.

I walked to the dock and sat down. The sun-warmed wood toasted my butt and the clear water cooled my feet. Absently, I tucked a loose strand of hair behind my ear and made sure I'd taken out my earrings. I was wearing jean shorts that were short enough to be flattering but long enough to cover what I wanted covered, and a blue Cowboys t-shirt over my blue two-piece.

Dad said I didn't have to settle when it came to guys. And while that was true, I didn't want to be alone. I wanted someone I cared about and who cared in return. That could've been Brent. He was nice-looking and came from a good family. I couldn't tell what the future held obviously, but what if was him?

I felt blessed. Mom and Dad had been together for a long time. They had a son who was nearly out of college and me almost done with high school, they had satisfying careers, and they didn't hurt for money. They had each other and it had been that way since they were young. In a world where love didn't last forever, theirs had weathered all storms.

I wanted that.

The roar of a diesel engine caused me to look up. I saw a white dually come around the bend towing a very large and very new pontoon boat. An arm waved at me from the driver's seat. I smiled, recognizing Brent, and waved back.

Jody's Toyota with the custom paint and oversized spoiler came in next. He parked across from me while Brent made the loop and maneuvered to back the boat into the water. I couldn't help but gawk. It was huge.

"The party barge is here!" Jody announced. "Ba-ZING!"

Tina, Will, and some girl with black hair that stopped at her collar got out. I didn't recognize her.

A Dodge pickup pulled up behind Jody and two more guys I recognized from our lunch table got out, followed by Hope and Sonya. It looked like we were going to have a full crew.

"Hey, Marian," Brent said from behind me.

He was wearing a pair of orange and white board shorts and a blue Auburn t-shirt with the sleeves cut off. He had good arms.

"Hey."

He looked over my shoulder. "Let's get this thing off the trailer and load up."

"Got it," one guy called back.

They were lugging a cooler that it would've taken six of me to carry. Like me, the girls had a bag each. I grabbed my stuff and followed them to the dock.

Hope made the introductions. "Marian, this is Selena. She's a sophomore. She just moved here from Monroeville. Selena, this is Marian. She's in my class and the newest member of the squad."

"Nice to meet you," Selena replied.

She had an easy smile and a friendly voice. But I was wary. I'd learned nothing in Barnsdale County was what it seemed.

"You too."

Brent backed the boat into the water, and one guy worked the winch to get it freed. Jody and Will worked the tie-downs.

"All aboard!" Jody called out.

We filed on while Brent moved the trailer and locked up his truck. I put my stuff next to the driver's seat, figuring Brent was going to be behind the wheel. The coolers went up front and I noticed Jody was already cracking open a beer.

I checked my watch and my stomach immediately rolled. It was way too early.

Brent hopped aboard and untied us before he slipped around seats and bodies to flop down. He grinned at me from behind expensive sunglasses. I grinned back.

"Ready?"

"Oh, yeah."

He turned the key and the boat roared to life. Looking like he knew what he was doing, he backed the boat into the channel, put it in forward, and we were cruising. We were heading in the direction I came from.

And that set Tina off. "Why are we going this way?"

"I thought we were going to the rope swing," Brent said back as he eased off the throttle. "That's right before you get to Nottingham Bridge, right?"

Her face looked like she smelled something dead. "We have to go past Loxley Farm."

He shrugged. "So?"

"You know I don't like those people."

"It's a goddamn public waterway," Jody told her, though he seemed unhappy at the mention of the name 'Loxley.'

"It's not a problem," Brent assured her.

She crossed her arms over her chest and huffed.

The river was beautiful. The water looked inviting, and while most of the forest I'd seen in this area was pine, the woods lining the water looked to be mostly hardwood. I stretched my legs out beside Brent and took it all in. Since it was already getting muggy, he kept us going fast enough that the breeze kept us cool, but slow enough we could talk over the engine.

"So you made the cheerleading team?"

It was Selena asking the question.

"Yeah," I replied.

"Cool. You ever been on the Sherwood?"

I shook my head.

"I've been once or twice. Further upriver, of course. It's a fun place."

"It looks nice."

Most of the time the banks were close enough that I felt confident I could swim across, but there were a few spots I wouldn't have wanted to try it.

Hope pointed out a cliff coming into view on our left. "That's Crypt Point."

"Crypt?" I asked.

"Mm-hmm. If there wasn't so much tree cover, you could see. There's a bunch of old mining shafts up there."

I reached into my bag and dug out my binoculars. I got them into focus and could make out some squares through the leaves that looked like they were very old and made of a dirt and wood mixture.

"I get why it's called Crypt Point now," I remarked as I lowered my specs. "Those do look kind of like 'em."

"The stories say that bootleggers used them to dispose of bodies."

"Hey, Brent?" Nick called from the front.

"Yo?"

"Can you turn the radio on?"

"Sure."

He flipped a switch and country music played from several speakers. I leaned back in my seat and admired the boat. Briefly I wondered if we were far enough south I might see an alligator. Will stood and shucked off his t-shirt, showing a pale but decently built torso. Past him, I saw Tina spreading out her towel and kicking off her sandals.

"What's that?" Selena asked.

I brought my binoculars back to my face and looked.

"That" turned out to be a large johnboat, olive green with a tin top. There was man sitting at the console in the back, a puff of smoke appearing over his head. Another man was standing at the front and had what looked like a bow and arrow. He was staring at the water.

"Looks like Hood and Little John," Brent answered, "bow fishing."

Loxley let the arrow go smoothly and lowered the bow before he began winding a reel below the grip. Little John stayed sitting as his partner worked. Loxley knelt and reached in the water before coming up with a fish that looked big even from this distance.

"Good-looking stripe," Nick remarked.

Loxley nimbly walked to the middle of the boat. He pulled the skewered fish off the arrow, kicked a lid open with his foot, and dropped the fish in before closing it back. Then he began rewinding the spool.

As we got closer, I could make him out better. He was wearing cut-off shorts. Not denim shorts like mine. Shorts with fraying around the legs that looked like they started as jeans. The knife I'd seen the first time we met was on his side. He was wearing sandals and sunglasses, but no shirt.

"Wow," Selena said under her breath.

'Wow' was right. Brent had what I thought of as 'pretty muscles.' He got them from a gym. He had muscles like an athlete. Loxley had more 'useful' muscles. He got them from hard work. Brent was the guy on the beach doing curls for the girls. Loxley was the cowboy digging holes for fence posts. I watched as he drew the arrow again.

Loxley had a nice profile, like a statue you'd see in an art museum. He fired and started reeling again. And again he knelt and came up with a nice-sized fish.

"Wow," Selena said again softly again. "Who's the hottie?"

"Stop drooling, Selena."

I lowered my binoculars at that and noticed that while Brent said Selena's name, he was looking at me.

"Speed up," Jody called to Brent. "Throw some wake at that piece of shit."

"Nah."

Instead, Brent slowed even more and turned their way. Selena was openly checking Loxley out. Little John saw us coming and hopped up. I noticed he was also shirtless and looked even more imposing than usual.

Brent killed the engine and we drifted up beside their boat. Loxley turned and lowered his bow. Little John said something I couldn't hear and Loxley nodded.

"Killing anything?" Brent asked.

"They seem to be moving," Loxley replied with a shrug.

"How long you been at it?"

"A couple of hours or so."

"How long you going to be at it?"

Loxley smirked. "Well, since someone drove up and scared off my school with their wake, we're probably going to have to move."

Brent didn't apologize or even react to that.

"Where y'all headed?" Loxley asked.

"Rope swing."

"Ah."

It was then that Loxley noticed I was sitting there. As he tended to do, his eyes lingered on me for about a second before he turned back to Brent. But that second was long enough to make me feel flushed.

"Y'all need anything?" Loxley asked.

Jody snorted.

"Nah, we're good," Brent replied.

That earned him a nod from Loxley.

I cut my eyes to look at the rest of the group. The two Seniors, Nick and Brian, looked indifferent. Hood and

Little John were just two guys they'd heard of but probably didn't know.

Sonya and Hope looked bored. They didn't appear uncomfortable or hostile or anything, just... indifferent like the two boys.

Brent's decision to halt irritated Tina. She was making a point of sitting with her back to the other boat. She'd taken an emery board out and was rubbing it against her nails.

Brent had his usual reaction to Loxley. He adopted a business-like manner and seemed to keep any emotion in check.

"We're going to try closer to the farm," Loxley told him. "Y'all need anything, blow your air horn three times."

I saw Little John grimace and shake his head behind Loxley.

"We won't need it," Brent assured him.

Loxley just shrugged. "You never know. I've been stranded on this river before. It sucks. You need help, we'll be around."

"Thanks," Brent replied, obviously not meaning it.

He sat back down and fired the engine up again. Loxley's head turned towards me and he nodded in my direction. Before I could react, Brent started the boat and pulled away.

"Damn, he's hot," Selena gushed.

Brent didn't say a word.

Tina did though. "You'd need rabies shots, a tetanus shot, and about ten pounds of penicillin if you let that touch you."

"Did you see that body?"

I kept my mouth shut, but it went without saying that I had.

"He's fucking trash, Selena," Jody said. He tossed his beer bottle over the side and reached into the cooler for another one. "You'd be tainted for life if you let that up in you."

The people in the front of the boat picked up a conversation and the ones in the back let the radio do the talking. Figuring I needed to let Brent know I wasn't as affected as Selena, I squatted down beside him and rested my forearm on his thigh.

"So, when are you going to let me drive?"

That got me a smile. A small one. "You know how to operate a boat?"

I shook my head. "But you could teach me, right?"

"I could teach you lots of things."

Part of me liked the sound of that, but a tiny corner of my brain flashed 'danger.' Was that part of the attraction?

Before I could ask 'like what,' we rounded another bend.

"Why don't we stop here?" Selena asked. "This is pretty."

And it was. We came to a sandy beach on our right. Behind it was a small grassy spot with a gentle slope above. The grass was a lush green and appeared to have been recently mowed. A little further down was a small but well-maintained dock next to a ramp.

"That dock is on Loxley Farm," Brent informed her.

About the time he said that, I saw a truck parked under a nearby tree — Little John's.

"We should stop," Jody piped up from the front. "One of us could hop out and knock that fucking pickup out of gear. I bet with a little push it would end up in the drink."

My eyes narrowed behind my sunglasses.

I saw Nick roll his. Brian shook his head, obviously annoyed. Brent ignored him and picked up speed as we passed. We went past a patch of woods, then another slope. I could see corn on top. Rows and rows of corn.

"Can you see the house from the river?" Hope asked.

Brent shook his head. "They own a couple hundred acres. I don't know where the house is exactly."

"You mean 'hovel,'" Tina piped up from the front.

"I've never seen it."

"I bet it's a shitty-ass shack with no electricity and a fucking outhouse in the back," Jody taunted.

Tina snickered.

Chapter 14

SHERWOOD BRIDGE WAS OLD, and it looked it. It was a two-lane structure on Highway 19 with steel trusses that were rusty and tired. It looked like it needed to be in a black-and-white photograph, and I wondered why the state hadn't replaced it. I doubted I could drive over it without holding my breath.

"How deep is it here?" I asked.

Brent looked at his depth finder. "Twenty feet or so."

We rode for several more miles and, to my surprise, saw another bridge spanning the river. This one was newer and looked much sturdier.

"Which one is that?" I asked, pointing.

"Nottingham Bridge," Brent explained. "When they widened the highway, this became the main route into Florida instead of 19." He adjusted his sunglasses. "They were supposed to close Sherwood Bridge for repairs once this one was built, but they never did."

"Who the hell cares?!" Jody yelled from the front. "Ain't

nothing in that area but Saylis white trash!"

Roughly two hundred yards down from the bridge was another sand bar to our right. It was almost as nice as the one we saw on Loxley's land. Brent didn't stop there though. He went to our left, towards the opposite bank.

"You see the ladder on the Florida side?" Brent asked.

I raised my binoculars and studied where he was pointing. It took me a moment to see what he was talking about.

The bank was steep on that side and heavily wooded. At the foot of a large oak growing near the edge, there was a metal ladder secured to the trunk with what looked like red bungee cords.

"I got it."

Brent cut the engine, and we drifted towards the bank. "Someone tie us off."

Jody, polishing off his third or fourth beer, called back, "I got it."

It was then I saw the rope hanging from a branch of the oak. I calculated it would probably be about a six-foot drop into the water.

I grinned. It looked like fun.

Jody tied us off to the side, and I stood up before removing my sunglasses and holding them out to Brent. He grinned and took them. I then grabbed the hem of my t-shirt and pulled it over my head.

I tossed the shirt into my bag and started unbuttoning my shorts, hoping that at least Brent liked what he saw. It was the most modest two-piece I could find, but it was still two pieces. It covered the important parts. Cutting my eyes, I saw from Brent's expression that, yes, he did like what he saw.

Nimbly, I took my sunglasses from him and slipped them back on. A shudder ran up my spine as I looked up. Brent wasn't the only one that noticed I'd stripped. I sat down quickly to get away from Jody, who was now leering at me.

Brent stood and removed his shirt, which made me feel better. Just as I suspected, he had pretty muscles.

"You mind putting some sunscreen on my back?"

Lord have mercy... "Sure."

He handed me the tube and turned around. I squirted some into my hand and went to work.

"Like what you see?"

I swallowed quickly and nodded. "I think I do."

"Good," he replied. "Me too."

IT WAS THE MOST fun I'd had since I moved there.

I went off the rope swing so many times that my arms would barely hold me on my last trip. We swam and we dove off the boat. I'd forgotten to pack a lunch but Selena shared her snacks with me.

"I'm going to hate going back to school tomorrow," I admitted.

My back was leaned against Brent's chest as we stretched out on one of the front seats. One of his fingers was making slow circles around my upper arm. I'd almost been able to relax. Almost.

"When do we need to head back?" Selena asked.

Brent glanced at his watch. "Soon. Dad wants his boat home before dark. Otherwise, he might send someone to find me, and that wouldn't be good."

I glanced towards the west and estimated we only had a couple of hours of daylight left. "Then let's pack it up. I don't want you getting into trouble."

I turned around as I spoke and once again, our heads were less than a foot apart. I bit my bottom lip and stopped breathing.

"I'm not ready," he whispered.

For a second, I thought he meant to kiss me. Then I realized he meant something else.

"Me either, but I don't want you getting in trouble on my account."

He groaned and eased me forward so he could get up. "Okay, everybody. Let's load up."

There was some grumbling, but everyone started exiting the water. I grabbed my towel and dried off quickly, though I was mostly dry from sitting in the sun with Brent. It was still hot as the dickens, so I pulled my shorts up over my bottoms but stayed in my swim top.

We got packed and got everything stowed. Everyone climbed back into their seats. Jody was wobbling. I was glad I hadn't had any beer. Sitting in the sun drinking would've equaled throwing up for me, and that wouldn't have been very ladylike.

Brent turned the key. The motor turned over... and over... and over... but didn't start. He swore to himself, turned the key off, turned it back on, and tried again.

Again, nothing happened. He sighed, sounding defeated, and hit the key one more time. Again the motor turned, but it didn't fire.

"What's wrong?" Jody asked.

"It won't fucking start."

"Why the hell not?"

"Hell if I know."

Tina reached into her bag and pulled out her cell phone. "I've got no service."

I dug out my own and checked. "Me either."

"Anybody?" Brent asked, looking at his.

No one did.

"Guess we're padding," Nick joked.

"You can't paddle a boat this big," Brent replied. He sighed and slammed his hand on the steering wheel.

I put a hand on his shoulder. "Hey. Chill out. We'll figure it out."

"What the hell are we going to do, Marian? We're stuck out here."

I started thinking, but I couldn't come up with anything. I knew nothing about boat engines or the area.

"We could start a fire," Jody slurred. "If we made that sonofabitch big enough, someone would see it."

"It's all national forest on both sides," Brent replied. "Not even our dads could get us out of that."

"What's downstream?" Nick asked.

Brent thought it over. "Fucking swamp, swamp, and more swamp. There's nothing 'til you get past the fork. But that's... twenty or thirty miles at least and that's just to there."

"Maybe someone's house?"

"That may be what we have to do. I mean, we can't paddle this bitch at all, much less upstream."

Dad was going to be upset. He'd get over me missing curfew. But he would've assumed the worst. He'd be putting out an APB if I wasn't home at a reasonable time.

"That's the only thing I got unless someone's got a better idea," Brent said. "Maybe we'll come up on someone else and they can tow us."

I sighed, and my head dropped, causing my eyes to fall on the boat's console. Underneath the steering wheel was the air horn.

"Loxley," I said aloud.

"Huh?" Brent asked.

I pointed to the air horn. "Hit it. Maybe Loxley and Little John are still around."

Jody snorted. "I'd rather sit my ass here."

"Me too," Tina agreed.

"My parents are going to have a duck," Hope said.

"Mine too," Selena piped up.

"And Brent will get in trouble if he's late," I added.

"Man, just do it," Nick called from the bow. "If you don't, we'll be out here all fucking night."

Brent glared at the air horn like it had personally offended him.

"Here," I said, reaching down. "I'll do it."

My hand got to the can when Brent's flew out and grabbed me by the wrist. I squeaked in surprise as he clamped down.

Our eyes locked and he looked... crazy for a moment.

I cowered, then his eyes turned back to normal and he slowly let me go.

"Go ahead."

I rubbed my wrist and gazed at the finger-shaped red marks for a moment, trying to decide if he meant it.

He slumped back in his seat.

I pulled the horn from its holder and held it up in the air before giving it three quick blasts.

"They probably quit fishing hours ago," Tina grumbled.

I stood there like an idiot. Panic was setting in. Mom and Dad would be worried and I was going to spend hours in the dark on a river I didn't know.

I blew the horn again, making my three blasts just a touch longer.

"You hear that?" Selena asked.

"No fucking way," Jody slurred.

Sure enough, it was the sound of another boat coming from the east. I walked behind Brent to look over the stern. Truthfully, I was hoping someone... anyone... would hear it. I didn't honestly expect for it to be Loxley.

But it was. I breathed a sigh of a relief.

Little John eased off the throttle and they pulled up beside us.

"Hey," I said before anyone else could speak. "The boat won't start."

Loxley didn't even look at Brent. "Is it getting fire?"

He was speaking 'engine' and I wasn't fluent. "Huh?"

"Does it do anything when you turn the key? Does it turn over? Or is it just dead?"

"It'll turn like it's trying to start. It just won't."

"Show me?"

I glanced at Brent. He nodded. I turned back to Loxley. "Go ahead."

Loxley grabbed the rail to our boat and nimbly hopped aboard. He glanced at the very back of the boat and grabbed the padded area I thought was a shelf before pulling it back to expose the engine.

He bent over and studied it, giving me a good view of his muscular back. "This isn't the original engine, is it?"

I glanced at Brent.

"No," he said finally. "Mother fucker blew up last year. Dad got a rebuilt one and had it installed over the winter."

"Plug wires?" Little John asked.

"Nah," Loxley replied. "Don't suppose you've got a screwdriver, do you?"

Brent shook his head, but since Loxley wasn't looking, he couldn't see.

"Nope," I answered.

Loxley squatted down and pulled his sunglasses up to rest them on top of his head. He drew his knife and went into the engine.

"Okay, give me a minute."

I looked over his shoulder to see if I could figure out what he was doing. He was using his knife as a makeshift screwdriver to remove some sort of plastic cap.

"Anybody got a nail file?"

Tina, of course, had turned her back when Loxley and Little John approached and was filing her nails again.

"We need that, Tina," I called.

She huffed.

"Damn, Tina!" Nick snapped. "I don't want to be out here all night!"

He reached over and snatched it out of her hands. She glared as he passed it to Hope, who passed it to Selena, who passed it to me.

"Here," I offered.

Loxley took it and brought the plastic cap all the way, then looked at a piece and began rubbing it with the file.

"It doesn't have an electronic ignition," Loxley explained. I didn't know if he was talking to me or Brent. "It's got a points system. That's how I knew it was an older motor. An electronic ignition isn't expensive and takes about five minutes to put on. It'll keep this from happening again."

Brent stared off to his right and didn't answer.

Loxley continued to scrape as I watched. The entire front of the boat had gone quiet. Tina, who had slipped up while I wasn't looking, rolled her eyes and turned the key, so the radio came on.

"Shit!" Loxley snapped as he popped back. "You crazy?"

"What?"

"Turn that damn thing off."

"I want to listen to the radio."

"And I don't want to get electrocuted while you do it." He then looked at me. "There's an electric current that runs through there. Turning the key completes the circuit. Get my meaning?"

I turned the key off, asking no one's permission. Nick muttered something at Tina that I was pretty sure wasn't complimentary. Brian shook his head in disgust.

Loxley went back to scraping and I went back to watching. He seemed to know what he was doing. I glanced over at Little John, who had a foot propped on the edge of the bow of their boat and was leaning on his leg. He could've been watching what Loxley was doing or watching his back. I didn't know.

Loxley put the cap back in place and started screwing it down. The entire process took less than ten minutes.

"Try it now."

Without taking his eyes off whatever he was staring at, Brent turned the key. The motor kicked over twice and started.

Loxley grinned.

"Thanks," I said.

He shrugged. "You're welcome. Y'all headed home?"

I nodded.

"Crawford Landing?"

"Yeah."

"We'll follow you and make sure you get there."

"We're good now," Brent piped up.

"That was a temporary fix, man. If they get fouled again, they won't fire. They stop firing, you're not going anywhere. You might need us to tow you back."

Brent glowered.

"Thanks," I said, mainly to expedite the process.

He shot me a wink that I liked more than I should have and then rejoined Little John. Brent put the boat in drive, turned us around, and started heading home without even glancing back.

“It was nice meeting you,” Selena said.

I smiled. “You too.”

We were all loaded up. Nick was driving for Jody, for which I was grateful. Everyone except me had beer, but I lost count at how many he drank. He might have been a dick, but the last thing I wanted was for him to wrap that car around a tree.

I glanced at my wrist and saw obvious bruises in the shapes of fingers. Brent’s fingers. I didn’t know how I was going to handle that just yet.

Loxley and Little John followed us until Brent made it to the dock before turning their own boat around. No one waved or said anything. The party was definitely over.

Sometimes grudges just didn’t make sense. Was whatever that was between those two worth us getting eaten by mosquitos and stranded on a river in the middle of nowhere? I didn’t think so. But then again, it wasn’t my grudge.

Brent was checking to make sure the boat wouldn’t slide on the trailer when I decided to approach him.

“I’m sorry,” he said before I could open my mouth.

“For?”

He nodded towards my arm. “That was wrong. I shouldn’t have grabbed you. But... you know I don’t like bastard.”

“That’s not an excuse.”

"I know."

My gut was telling me he wasn't sorry. In fact, it told me he was just trying to smooth this over, like he did that day with Loxley. I tried to check my anger, but I wasn't getting anywhere.

A man putting hands on me was where I drew the line. I didn't know if it was because George had been so... rough... or if I was just raised with an overabundance of self-respect, but I wasn't putting up with that crap. Not anymore.

"That was your free one," I warned Brent. "Next time it won't be pretty."

He looked at me smugly which only made my temper shorter.

"I mean it."

"Okay, Marian."

I huffed and turned to storm off.

"Hey."

My head snapped back around.

"You opposed to some free advice?"

"I'll listen to it."

He pushed himself off from leaning against the boat. "You need to stop being so nice to Hood."

"I didn't realize I was nice to him."

"You need to just flat out ignore his ass."

"Why?"

"Because you're going to get a fucking reputation."

"So?"

"Marian, you know what I'm talking about. People like us don't associate with people like him. It's asking for trouble."

"Because he's poor?"

"Because he's fucking Alabama white trash," Brent snapped. "His family is trash, his friends are trash, and the people he associates with are trash. And if you keep letting him in, not only are you going to be lumped into that group, but you're going to get hurt."

"Hurt?"

"He doesn't care who the fuck he runs over as long as he gets what he wants."

"We're not friends. I barely know him. Today was just... it served a purpose. No one is going to get in trouble. We're safe. It's over with. I wish you'd just let it go."

"I wish you'd just let him go."

"Are you jealous?"

He snorted. "You're the one that brought him up."

"No," I corrected, "you did. Just like any other time. I've brought him up twice: once when I asked you about the meeting after he hit Jody, and today, which saved our asses. It's everyone else in your little group that talks about the world-famous Hood."

He didn't answer.

"Forget him. If I wanted to be with him, which I can assure you I don't, I'd be on that boat with him. It's you I wondered all day was going to kiss me, not him."

That wasn't what I wanted to say. But it sounded good. It also looked like I was right. Brent stepped forward and yanked me to him. He kissed me full force and I submitted.

It wasn't what I expected. I don't know what I expected, but that wasn't it.

The kiss was hard and left no room for doubt. It just didn't send the sparks I thought it would. I took it. My body locked up at the fierceness. Needless to say, it didn't light my world on fire.

Brent finally pulled away. "Like that?"

"Yeah, but next time, how about kissing me because you want to, not because you're trying to prove a point?"

Chapter 15

"BE... AGGRESSIVE... B-E AGGRESSIVE..."

The next few weeks moved with little issue.

Dad was still beating the bushes and scouring crime scene reports to lock on who was doing the dirty deeds in Barnsdale County. Mom kept working the ER and coming home tired. And I had school. For the most part we settled into a comfortable routine.

Dad had closed two cases so far. Both were armed robberies. He believed both were the Dixie Mafia, though he couldn't prove it. Those arrested were bailed out shortly after the A.B.I. served their warrants and Dad was afraid they were going to run. It frustrated the hell out of him.

But he was excited. He had it on good authority on good authority that someone knew something about Junior Boxer's death. Dad said the tip sounded credible, and he was meeting the person tonight. They were meeting somewhere tonight.

School was still strange. Everyone stayed separate and I

stayed with my group. I kept my eyes open, but nothing really looked out of place lately. I was doing my best to ignore that part.

Brent and I were doing pretty well. We'd had a few dates — dinner in York, hanging out in the school parking lot, and a movie in Mobile. I got a kiss when he picked me up, a hand on my thigh as he drove, an arm around my shoulders at the theatre, and another kiss goodnight on my doorstep.

It wasn't doing it for me, and I couldn't figure out why. He was handsome and well-off, and when the conversation wasn't about Loxley, he was sort of fun to be with. But the more I thought about it, the more it seemed like there was something I was missing.

I'd never been an expert on how love was supposed to work, but Brent seemed to treat me like an appointment. When I dated George, we saw each other on the regular. Until the end anyway. With Brent, we usually went on dates on Saturday nights. Nothing after the game on Friday and nothing on Sunday. I could understand Friday, sort of, since we had the football game. But it would've made sense if we at least got to hang out a little before I had to be home. And what about Sunday? He could come over so we could order takeout and watch the Cowboys.

But that didn't happen. He still touched me. I got kissed. But it didn't feel real, and I couldn't understand why.

I guess he could've been distracted by the team. The Rebels were 0-2, and it looked like we were going to lose another one.

Cheerleading was harder than I expected. It wasn't the

routines or the responsibilities — making signs, practicing, pep rallies, or anything like that. It was being... cheerful. When I was on the dance team, I didn't feel like I needed to keep a crowd 'in the game.' My job was to do my routine that just happened to be at halftime. To be the entertainment. The rest of the time, we rooted for our team and joked around with the band. Of course, my old school in Dallas won a lot more games.

But now I had to be upbeat regardless of the score. It sucked.

I'd gotten so good at the routines that I could do them automatically. It gave me a chance to observe the crowd. Some little girls that always sat front and center, mimicking our cheers. Some of them even wore their Pee Wee uniforms. The student section spent more time socializing than watching the game. The same old people sit in the same seats every game and they probably had since the stadium was first built.

And then there was Loxley.

This was one of the few times I saw him alone. He always sat near the top of the bleachers, away from the crowd. He would stretch out his legs and prop them on the seat below. When September moved into October and the nights started getting cooler, he wore a hoodie under his vest and a leather motorcycle jacket over both. Nothing about it was odd. What had to be odd was that he never got there until after halftime.

"L-E-T-S G-O... let's go, let's go... L-E-T-S G-O... let's go!"

I glanced at the scoreboard and saw that we had about

a minute left in the game. The score was 35-6. We'd lost again. Sighing, I started taking down signs and cleaning up our area.

"Well, that sucked," Tina remarked.

I nodded in agreement.

"Has Brent talked to you about the party next weekend?"

"No."

"We're having a big blow-out Saturday night after next," Tina explained. She wasn't doing anything to get us ready to leave. "Kegs. Music. All that good stuff. You going to come?"

"Probably."

I wasn't sure if I would or not. If Brent wasn't going, I knew I'd miss it. I could only stand so much snark.

"Cool," she said, sounding like she was trying to be sociable. "I guess I'll see you Monday."

She left before I could say anything else and I went back to rolling up signs.

"Hey, Baby."

I turned around to see Brent standing there, looking all sweaty and GQ in his uniform. Despite that, I still had to bite my tongue to avoid informing him my name wasn't 'baby.' It shouldn't have bothered me, but it did.

"Hey," I replied instead.

"Hope you had a better time than I did."

I shrugged. "It was okay. Where you headed?"

"My parents want me home."

Why did he look away when he said that? Surely he wasn't lying.

"Okay."

"We still on for tomorrow night?"

"Sure."

"Cool. You okay with just hanging out?"

"That's fine," I replied, even though it wasn't. He didn't notice.

"Great. You want me to pick you up?"

"I'll drive. There's no sense in you having to drive past your house to take me home."

"Works for me."

He leaned over and gave me a quick kiss that left me both wanting more and wishing he hadn't bothered. He gave me one last smile and trotted off.

About the time he rejoined his team, I got the feeling I was being watched. Quickly, I turned around and scanned the bleachers, but I didn't see anyone openly undressing me with their eyes. I checked the section where Loxley had been sitting, but he wasn't there.

The Bug was in the parking lot on the far end of the stadium and I waved to the rest of the girls before lugging off my duffel bag and the signs. I got a few smiles from adults and I made a point of smiling back. I put on my jacket before I got through the far gate, found the dumpster, and tossed the signs before I walked towards my car, digging my keys out as I went.

My trunk sounded loud as I opened it and threw my bag inside. I rubbed my temples to ward off the headache I felt coming and moved to open my door.

"Hey! Hey, Baby! Hold up!"

I turned around to see six boys heading my direction. Two I recognized from school. One of them was the mean-looking one from the furniture place. The rest looked older, including the big guy with the beard that was part of the same crew.

They got to within six feet and he grinned. "Where you headed, beautiful?"

"Home," I replied. "I've got curfew. What's up?"

"The night's still young," he said with a leering grin.

I shifted as he openly checked out my legs. "Not for my parents."

"Aw," he pressed. "Come on, Baby. I got some of Jamaica's finest and we was going to go fire one up. You scared to break out of that shell?"

"Sounds fun, but I've got to go."

"What you need to do is join the party," he pressured. "Pretty thing like you... I bet we could have us a damn good time."

His words sounded like a suggestion, but his tone made me think he and his boys were willing to press the issue. I could feel the anticipation in the air from his crew. It didn't help I was still wearing my cheerleading outfit, and he wasn't the only one looking at me like he wanted to eat me up.

"Maybe some other time," I said, trying to smile.

"No time like the present."

The group spread out to surround me and I started calculating my odds. There was no way I could get into my car before they grabbed me if that was their intention. And my instincts told me there was a high probability that was on their minds.

My mouth had gone completely dry and my heart was racing. They inched closer. Fear flooded my system.

"So what do you say?" he asked, his grin showing ultra-white teeth.

"How's it going, Antonio?" a voice said from behind them.

He turned, and through the crowd I saw Robert Loxley standing there with his hands in his pockets. His posture was completely at ease.

"Sup, Hood?"

Loxley glanced past them and his eyes fell on me. My head dropped as I fought to calm down. He then turned back to the ringleader.

"What's going on?"

Antonio grinned. "We was just asking this fair maiden if she wanted to grace us with the pleasure of her company."

To my surprise, Loxley started walking my direction. Like Daniel in the lion's den, the boys parted for him. He walked right up to me before turning around and standing at my right shoulder.

My entire body relaxed and I could breathe easier.

"You don't want to do that," Loxley warned.

Antonio's smile dropped. "Say what?"

"You know who she is?"

"Yeah. She's a cheerleader. Them hoes always ready to get down."

Loxley shook his head. "That's not what I mean."

"Oh." His grin returned. "You talking about Dean? He won't mind if we handle his business for him... since he ain't here to do it hisself."

"That's not what I mean either."

"I don't follow you."

He tilted his head at me but kept his eyes on the ringleader. "You ain't heard? Her Dad's with the A.B.I."

Antonio's entire demeanor changed. He went from trying to be smooth to cold-blooded in the blink of an eye.

"So you probably don't want to party with this one."

My tension ratcheted up a notch. Loxley calmly put his hands back in his jacket pockets. I could feel the leather brush against my elbow.

"Well," Antonio said. "See, we got a problem."

"You do?"

"We do," he corrected. "The way I see it, I just implicated myself in some shit. I can't just let that go."

Loxley chuckled dryly. "She ain't going to say anything."

"How you figure?"

"She knows what's up. Besides, her daddy is after the big fish. He ain't worrying about the small stuff."

Antonio's eyes cut to me, back to Loxley, and finally back to me.

"He's right," I admitted. "Dad's here looking into the top shot callers and the Dixie Mafia is his number one target. He doesn't care about people smoking a little weed." I gave a shrug. "And honestly? Neither do I. As long as you aren't raping and killing, it's none of my business."

The fact I just sounded like Brent didn't escape my attention.

"She's good," Loxley assured him.

"You think?"

"I'll vouch for her."

I blinked rapidly in surprise.

"You do, huh?"

"I do."

Antonio looked to his left and right before turning back to Loxley. "All right, but just so we understand. She opens her fucking mouth and it won't go so good for her. Or for you. You said you'd vouch."

"You really think it's a good idea to threaten *me*?"

Loxley's question caused two of the boys I didn't know to back up a step. The shortest one glared. Antonio seemed to deflate.

"She won't talk," Loxley said again.

Antonio gave my bare legs one more look before our eyes met. I flinched slightly at his gaze. It wasn't friendly. He cocked his head and moseyed off, his posse turning to follow him silently.

As soon as they were out of sight, I turned to Loxley. "You like being Johnny-on-the-spot, don't you?"

He grinned and I felt a touch warmer inside. "It's sort of my thing."

"Well," I said, tucking my hair behind my ear, "thanks."

He gave a shrug. "Not a problem."

Standing close enough to touch, I wasn't afraid of Loxley. Despite seeing him punch someone, never mind the rumors I'd heard and what I knew of his criminal record, my body registered absolutely no fear. It was strange.

"But you're still not allowed in my room," I warned.

"We have an agreement. I would never break my word without a good reason."

"By whose definition?"

"It's my word, therefore it gets to be my definition."

"My dog would kill you."

He just shrugged again. The gesture looked as if he meant 'if you say so.'

"What are you doing here anyway?" I asked.

"I like football."

"You do?" I was a little surprised.

"Yeah," he replied. "I always have."

"How much do you watch with no TV?"

"Not as much as I want to. I try to catch the game on Friday night if they're not too far away. On Saturdays, we all go to this restaurant-slash-dive bar near the farm and watch Alabama."

"If you like football so much, why don't you play?"

"I used to, back in grade school. But let's just say my circumstances have changed. I'm just too busy now."

"You're so busy you've got time to hang out on the river?" I challenged.

"I was fishing. I caught my limit and Little John's. Needed to put some meat in the freezer for the winter."

I ignored that. "And if you like it so much, why don't you get here earlier?"

"They stop taking money at the start of the third quarter."

He seemed embarrassed to admit that.

My mouth started running before my brain could stop it. "You've got money."

"I do?"

"I saw that deal go down with Jermaine the first week of school."

He smirked. "You see a lot. That money isn't for football tickets."

"It's for paying off baby mamas?"

That wiped the smile off his face. "What are you talking about?"

"I saw Tuck pass some money to that pregnant girl the day of Mr. Boxer's funeral. So it makes me wonder, Loxley, are you not only a criminal but a deadbeat too?

"A what?"

"A deadbeat."

For the first time since he'd approached, I saw his face cloud in anger. "You think Grace's baby is... mine?"

"Isn't it?"

"Not hardly."

"Tuck's?"

He snorted.

"Little John's?"

"Wrong again."

"Dale's?"

"No!" he snapped. "And before you ask, no, it's not Max's and obviously it's not Scarlet's. Why do you assume the worst in us, Marian?"

"Because you're a criminal," I snapped back.

"Some crimes need to be committed."

"No, they don't." Now I was getting angry. "The law must be upheld. Otherwise you've got anarchy."

"I guess it's escaped your attention that we already have anarchy."

I had no answer for that.

"That's the way it's always been in Barnsdale County,"

he pressed. "People that can take what they want to, do. Everyone else is expected to bend over and take it. But guess what? My family chose a different option. I can't stop them. I would if I could. But I can't look at myself in the mirror if I don't at least try to help a few people."

"I don't follow."

He sighed. "And you won't, Marian. You're in a different league than I am. In your world, Mom and Dad are still alive and you have a car and rich friends and a cute boyfriend that you think is all that and a bag of chips." He took a deep breath. "But every apple has brown spots underneath. You just don't see them."

"Because no one bothers to show me."

"Why should I?" There was a bitterness in his voice that surprised me. "You're better off sitting in your pretty house and not getting dirty. Trust me, Marian. It's for the best."

"I can make up my own mind," I growled at him.

"Yeah, seems pretty made up to me."

"About you? Yeah. You're a criminal. You commit crimes. I've seen your rap sheet, you know."

"If that's what you think, okay." He pulled his hood up over his head. "You be careful going home, Marian."

Before I could say anything else, he turned and walked away. I watched him until he disappeared into the darkness.

Chapter 16

"Hey, Kitten," Dad called from the kitchen.

Cowboy was lying beside him. He thumped his tail happily at seeing me before hauling his massive bulk to his feet. I rubbed his ear and steadied myself so he didn't knock me over.

I had nothing but Loxley on my mind as I'd driven home. Once again, I was being pulled in two different directions. The more I listened to what people said and the more I saw with my own eyes, the more confused I became.

What was it about Robert Loxley?

"Hey, Dad. Anything new?"

"We've got a suspect," Dad announced proudly. He kept talking before I could ask the obvious question. "Tyler Williams. Forty-two years old. And get this, not Dixie Mafia."

"No?"

He shook his head. "My source gave me some solid intel, namely two people who claimed Tyler confessed. I've also got a motive. Tyler's a local screw-up that was trying to make his bones."

"Did he do it?" I asked. "Get in, I mean?"

"My source didn't know. They didn't even know why Junior was killed."

"He didn't know?"

Dad leaned back. "So he said. Anyway, the Sheriff's department is running point on this one. I'm crossing my fingers I wake up to an interrogation. With any luck, he might be willing to make a deal."

"Here's hoping," I grumbled.

He changed the subject. "How was the game?"

"We got stomped."

"Sorry. How'd Brent do?"

"Didn't catch a pass. But in his defense, the quarterback never had time. Their defense was straight beast mode."

He chuckled.

"How's Mom? She wasn't home when I left."

"She had a tough night. They had some girl from out-of-state die of a drug overdose. It kind of shook her up."

"Meth?"

"Prescription pills. The name on her driver's license and the one on the bottle didn't match."

"Think it could be a clue?"

"It could be. The Sheriff's department is handing it."

"So the Sheriff is trying to play nice?"

"That or he's trying to head me off at the pass. I'll see when they get some information."

"You don't trust them, do you?"

He shook his head.

I continued to rub Cowboy's ears as he rested his head on my lap.

"Dad, can I ask you something?"

"Sure, Kitten."

"Is it ever alright to commit a crime?"

"Why? You planning a bank robbery?"

I grinned. "No, just a philosophical debate I'm having with myself."

He pondered my question. "Well… I hate to say that it's complicated, but…"

"It's complicated," I finished for him.

He nodded. "What brought this on?"

"You remember us talking about those kids I asked you to check out? Specifically, Robert Loxley?"

He nodded.

"Yes, arson is a crime. But it was a meth lab, which is a crime too. So did one cancel out the other?"

Dad pondered the question.

"I guess it doesn't matter. I mean, the law is the law, right?" I wondered aloud.

"I've broken it."

"You have?"

He grinned. "I broke the speed limit taking your mom to the hospital when she was delivering you and your brother."

"That's a little different."

"The law is the law, right?"

"Speeding versus arson?"

Dad's face lit up. "That gives me an idea. You know how

any time you're helping me look through files and I say we have to figure out the 'why' to figure out the 'who'?"

"Yes, sir?"

"The way the law works is, to prove a crime was committed, you have to prove intent. Otherwise it's an accident and at the most you get some kind of criminal negligence charge."

"So if they intended to kill someone..." I lead.

"... it's a crime. I'd say it depends, but I guess I could go along with that. All actions have consequences whether they're noble or not."

I nodded along.

"But personally? If someone hurt you or your mom and I didn't get justice legally, I can't say I wouldn't press the issue myself."

"So would you have arrested Loxley?"

"I would've had to. He still committed a crime. Actions have consequences, remember?"

"And if you were the one that committed the crime, you would expect to be arrested?"

"You're smart."

"Seriously?"

"I mean," he explained, "yes, I would expect to be arrested. If they hurt you or your mom, I probably wouldn't care if I got caught. They'd probably find me at the crime scene, still standing over the deceased. But that explains Hood."

"I don't follow."

"Remember me telling you how weird the plea deal went? How he tried to confess and how the county tried to lock him up and throw away the key, but his grandfather wouldn't let him plead guilty and how the judge sided with him?"

"Yes, sir."

"Hood didn't care about being caught, did he?"

"He didn't try to escape or anything?"

"Exactly. We were wondering if he for sure did it. That makes me think he did."

And there was another piece of the puzzle that was Robert Loxley. Unfortunately, it didn't answer any questions.

"So, are you friends with this guy?"

I shook my head quickly. "I see him around, but it's a small school. I've only spoken to him a couple of times and each time he's been really polite. Not what you'd expect from a thug. I've got some classes with him and if his grades are as good as they are in Miss Chen's class, I'd have to say he's not the dumb white trash redneck people say he is. I guess what I've seen is just different from what everyone tells me."

"I don't know the kid. I only know what's in the file. But that's enough to thank God you're not dating him."

"Fat chance of that."

"How are things with Brent?"

"Is this Bob or Dad asking?"

He reached over and mussed my hair. "Both."

"They're good." I hesitated, unsure how much to say. "He's doing and saying all the right things."

"You say that like it's a bad thing."

I shrugged. "I think Barnsdale County has made me paranoid."

"What do you mean, Kitten?"

I stared at the table. "Nobody is what they seem. I keep expecting to find out something about Brent that I don't like."

Dad had asked about the bruises on my wrist. I lied and told him it was from someone grabbing and pulling me out of the water into the boat. I'd handled it and I didn't want Dad to get involved.

"You taking my advice?"

"You mean remembering that I don't have to settle?" I asked and answered. "Yes, sir. He's the best of the lot and even with that, I'm just… enjoying his company. I doubt we'll get serious. It could happen, but I don't see it right now."

"George has you jaded, huh?"

I'd never told Mom or Dad what happened exactly. They knew we'd broken up, but I'd never said why and they didn't push too hard. I assumed they chalked it up to my first heartbreak.

"Yeah, he turned out to be a real prize."

Dad reached over and grasped my hand. "Kitten, not all men are like that. Trust me. That being said, there are plenty who are. That's why I asked you if you were taking my advice. And I didn't mean about Brent."

"What did you mean?"

"Trusting your instinct. If something feels wrong, it probably is."

"I am," I assured him. "But right now, they're as confused as the rest of me."

"Keep listening to them. They'll figure things out before

the rest of you."

SINCE I DIDN'T FEEL like driving to York, Saturday morning found me at the Piggly Wiggly. I'd been eating healthy for weeks and it was time to splurge. I was craving lasagna. Mom would be off tomorrow and I figured I could treat the family.

The store was old, with enough of the fluorescent lights either out or flickering to make it dim. I pushed the squeaking shopping cart — for some reason, people around here called it a 'buggy' — through the produce section to get the fixings for the salad.

Ahead of me was the pregnant girl Tuck had given that money. Grace. She was studying the bread section at the end of the aisle. I grabbed a couple of tomatoes, bagged them, and figured I'd get a French loaf to make garlic bread.

"Hi, Grace," I said politely.

Her response was downright cold. "Marian..."

She threw a loaf of white bread into her buggy and pushed off without another word.

Chalking it up to pregnancy hormones, I turned down the back aisle and headed to get some meat.

Grace was studying the chicken. I picked up a pound of ground beef and placed it in my cart as I watched her.

She was cute with large brown eyes, a button nose, and freckles. Her right shoe was untied. I could swear I felt tension from her as I walked by.

I grabbed a jar of sauce since I wasn't in the mood to look up a recipe and added it to my bounty. Like most grocery stores, this one was designed for the customer to start at one end and move to the other while shopping. That meant Grace and I were never far apart.

She passed me as I was getting my sauce. I did my best to ignore the awkwardness as she moved towards the juice. She maneuvered around a floor display, stepped on her shoelace, and tripped.

Reacting, I turned and caught her under the arms. My knees buckled slightly, but I was able to keep her from hitting the floor.

"You okay?" I asked as I hoisted her back to her feet.

"I'm fine!" she snapped.

"Your shoe's untied."

"Don't worry about it."

I figured she couldn't tie it in her condition. "Here... let me."

I knelt, and she stepped back. Looking up, I saw her eyes spark with anger.

"I said I was fine!"

Slowly, I stood back up. "I was just trying to help."

"Why?"

Why?

"Because."

She sniffed. "Leave me alone... bitch."

The girl who could audition for Teen Mom was calling me a names?

"What's your problem?" I snapped.

She squared her shoulders at me. "You. Stay the hell out of my business."

"I didn't know I was even in your business."

"I heard you and your friends talking about me."

My blood ran cold.

"Why don't you ask your boyfriend whose baby this is instead of gossiping with those other bitches?"

"I was just curious. Why would Brent know?"

Her mouth opened, but before she could say anything, she slammed it shut.

"Seriously though," I said, trying to calm her... and myself. "Are you okay?"

"I said I was."

"I'm sorry I asked the wrong question. Unless it's escaped your attention, I'm new here. I saw Tuck give you some money and I was trying to figure it out. You'll have to forgive me. My dad's a cop and stuff like that catches my eye. I didn't mean to make you uncomfortable."

She looked uncomfortable now. "Just stay out of my business."

"Why did you tell me to ask Brent?"

"Isn't he the one that told you this was Hood's baby?"

She said she heard us talking about her. That should've meant she knew it was the girls and Jody who told me, not Brent. Thinking back, I didn't remember him saying a word. But then again, he tended to get quiet when Loxley was the topic.

"No... he didn't."

She shrugged and looked away. "Then don't ask him. I don't give a shit."

Now I understood why her baby's father was such a big secret. Grace was pretty defensive about it.

"Look, Grace, I'm sorry if I hurt your feelings. It wasn't me talking about you. I'll admit I was curious, but I'm not in your business. I promise."

She turned around. Her right hand rested on the top of her stomach. She glanced down at it and mumbled, "You lie down with dogs, you get fleas. At least that's what they tell me."

I didn't know if she meant the people I hung out with or her pregnancy.

"At least let me tie your shoe?"

She huffed and leaned against her shopping cart before extending her foot.

Once again, I knelt. Balancing her foot on my thigh, I pulled the laces tight and tied the shoe quickly and snugly. Finished, I eased her foot back to the floor and stood up.

"Thanks," she mumbled.

"I'm not your enemy, Grace."

"You're not my friend either, Marian."

I shrugged. "True, but I could be."

"Why would you want to?"

"Why wouldn't I?"

Now it was her turn to shrug. "No one else is."

"Loxley and his crew are."

"That's reason enough why you shouldn't be. Ask your friends."

"Look, I'll admit I don't know what's going on around here. But I trust my gut. And my gut says you're an okay person who's in a not-so-ok situation. Now I don't know how bad or anything, but I can assume it's at least not great. So if you want to be friends, that's great. If not, I understand."

"What are your other friends going to say?"

"I need a few friends who aren't 'skanky bitches.'"

"Okay... I guess."

"Cool. Now, if we're good, I've got to get home."

"Yeah... thanks for the assist."

I grinned. "My pleasure."

I slid my 'buggy' past her. As I was heading to the check-out, I realized someone had been watching our exchange.

Make that two someones. The first one I recognized. Alonzo Tuck. He was propped up against a canned drink display. He smiled at me but didn't speak.

The other was a man at the meat counter. He was standing with an employee in a white coat and a red apron, but he wasn't looking at him. Tall with white hair parted to the left, his eyes were brown, hard, and staring at me like I was bird crap on his freshly washed car.

I got in line and did my best to ignore him.

While I was waiting, it gave me some time to think and remember Cowboy needed dog food. Feeding a Great Dane was like feeding a horse. Hurrying so I didn't lose my place in line, I raced over and grabbed a bag, wincing as I struggled to pick it up.

"I got it," I heard.

I turned in time to see a dark hand relieve me of my burden. Tuck tossed the bag over his shoulder with minimum effort. He was just a bit taller than I was, but obviously stronger.

"Thanks."

"No problem," he replied. "Lead the way."

We got back to my cart and he put the bag on the conveyer belt. I still had one more customer in front of me, so Tuck stood by as I started unloading the cart.

Figuring I could be polite, I asked, "How's Mrs. Sadie?"

"She's good. She sent me to get her some milk. How's your mama and daddy?"

"They're fine. Mom's off tomorrow, so I figured I'd make her some lasagna."

It got to be my turn and I watched as the cashier rang me up. Tuck moved around and put the bags in my cart without being asked. I let it slide, but I kept my guard up. His own friend, Scarlet, had warned me no one was nice unless they wanted something.

Tuck pushed the buggy and I led him out into the parking lot towards my Beatle.

"Thanks," I told him, not sure if I should be concerned or not.

He shrugged. "It was a pleasure, m'lady. The truth is, I wanted to talk to you a minute."

"Oh?"

He nodded and looked around quickly before he leaned in. "You're asking a lot of questions."

"You here to warn me to stop?"

"No, ma'am," he corrected. "I'm here to offer advice."

Everybody seemed to have that.

"What's that?"

"You want answers? You come see me. I'll give it to you

straight."

"How would I know that?"

Tuck shrugged. "I don't have any reason to lie."

I didn't know if he did or not. "And what answers do you have?"

"Whatever answers you want."

"What made you decide to talk to me?"

"Grandma says you and your family are okay people. I also saw you talking to Grace."

"So you know who the father is?"

He snorted. "Sure, but I ain't telling you that. People talk to me because I keep their secrets — like one of those priests. But even if I can't or won't tell you, that doesn't mean I wouldn't point you to someone who might."

This was interesting. If he was half as honest as Mrs. Sadie seemed to be, I might actually get some answers.

"That the only advice you've got?"

"No, but you've probably heard the rest."

"Tell me anyway."

"Nobody in this county is what they seem. Not Robin, not Brent, not anybody. You keep that in the back of your mind, okay?"

"I will. Thanks, Alonzo. I might take you up on your offer down the road."

Chapter 17

As soon as I'd gotten the groceries inside, cramps hit. I huffed, counted the days in my head, and realized the cause.

I devoured a sandwich, took something for the pain, and tried to take a nap. Cowboy stretched out on the floor beside me. Sleep wasn't coming. I started to cancel on Brent.

After a couple of hours, I got up and took a hot shower, which helped some. I kept my wardrobe casual: jeans, a black and red Barnsdale t-shirt, and my cheerleading jacket. Out of habit, I grabbed a couple of water bottles. After leaving Dad a note and letting Cowboy use the bathroom, I drove to the school.

As I was pulling up, I noticed no one was in their usual spots. All the cars were in the freshman lot. Everybody was at the football practice field, past the basketball goals up on the hill.

I got out, stuck the bottles in my jacket pockets, and

made my way over. It looked like a game had just finished up. Brent and Jody were on the field with Brian, Nick, and the other guy from the boat, Will. All four were shirtless despite the chill in the air.

The only person I saw on the sidelines that I knew was Selena. She noticed me about the same time and waved. I returned the gesture and made my way over.

"What's up?" I asked.

"Brent and Jody met some guys to play a couple of hours ago. Word got out there was a game and people started showing up. Brent and Jody's team just smoked some underclassmen. I don't know how much money was involved."

Brent saw me. That caused him to smile, and he began heading my direction.

"Hey, Baby."

Ugh. "Hey yourself. Good game?"

He shrugged. "Yeah, it was okay. I think we're about done now. It wasn't even close."

I glanced past him to see Jody collecting money before quickly focusing back on Brent.

"Glad you had fun."

It could've been PMS, but I was a bit irritated that he'd spent the afternoon playing a pick-up football game. He could've at least called me, even if it was to see if I wanted to come watch and cheer him on.

I chalked it up to hormones. "So, you did good?"

"Basketball's more my game," he replied.

I nodded along.

"If I keep my grades up, I'm hoping someone will notice.

Maybe I can go to college somewhere and get out of this town."

"Maybe."

This was another issue I'd noticed. When we weren't arguing about Loxley or talking about Dad, the conversation revolved around him. Brent didn't know about Cowboy. He didn't know my birthday. He didn't know that I preferred sweet pickles over dills, or that I'd always wanted to learn to ride a dirt bike.

Before I could say anything else, Jody came up. "Dude, guess who showed up to fucking play?"

Brent turned as Loxley, Little John, and Dale walked out. It looked strange to see them on the field in jeans and boots. Loxley shook hands with someone I didn't know and strolled up to where we were.

"Hood," Brent greeted.

Loxley squinted with the sun in his face. "I heard there was a game."

"Not for free," Jody snorted.

"You charging admission now?"

"I mean, it's a C-Note per man," Jody growled. "We play five-on-five and the winner takes all."

"Don't suppose you're down for three-on-three?"

Brent snorted. "Winner calls the game."

"I'll be right back."

Brent rolled his eyes and Jody snickered as Loxley strolled off. Brent said something about getting Will, Nick, and Brian together while I watched. To my surprise, the first person Loxley spoke to was Jermaine. They talked for roughly a minute before Jermaine nodded.

As Loxley was returning, Brent met him before he got back. “You got a game?”

“I got four.”

Brent gave a ‘tsk’ and shook his head. “Five-on-five is the rules.”

“You afraid to take on us four?”

“Not a chance, but I’m calling the shots, not you.”

Loxley turned around and looked over the crowd for a moment before he called, “Yo, Cory!”

Cory Boxer pointed at himself.

“Yeah, man, come here.”

Cory came jogging up. “Sup?”

“We need a fifth. You down?”

Brent snorted. “He ain’t got any money.”

“But I do.”

Cory gulped.

Loxley reached into his pocket and produced a roll. Brent looked at Jody, who eyed that money like Cowboy eyeing a T-bone.

“Ten count rush and the QB can’t cross the line of scrimmage until he’s got heat,” Brent said. “TD is seven. Four downs to make ten yards and we’ll mark the spot each time it’s converted. Full tackle. First to thirty-five wins.”

“Works for me.”

Loxley turned and walked towards his team. From across the field, I noticed Scarlet, Max, and Tuck had made it.

“We’re going to smoke this fucker,” Jody said through clenched teeth. “Those sod busters can’t play ball.”

“We got this,” Brent agreed.

Nick looked across the field. "We're playing them?"

"Yeah," Jody sneered. "No problem."

To my surprise, Nick and Brian shared a worried look.

Loxley came back as Little John was stripping off his t-shirt. "Who's holding the cash?"

"Who you want?"

Loxley's eyes fell on me. "Marian, you mind?"

To my surprise, Brent just smirked. "Go ahead. It's going in my pocket, anyway."

Loxley held out the bills. I shrugged and took them.

All ten guys met in the middle of the field to discuss something. Whatever they had to talk about, it only took a moment. Loxley stripped off his hoodie, which left him in just a t-shirt. He tossed it toward his crew and joined his team at roughly the twenty-yard line. It looked like Brent was playing QB and Loxley's team was on defense.

The first drive looked like it was going to be a massacre. Brent threw easy ten-to-fifteen-yard passes to Nick, who was so much taller than Dale he caught almost everything. He would get tackled immediately, but they moved the ball. Nine plays and my boyfriend and his team were on the board.

Loxley's team came out. They huddled up and Loxley began talking. Whatever he said must've been good because all of his team agreed and they went to their positions.

Being a Cowboys fan all my life, I knew a decent amount about football. I was surprised to see Dale and Jermaine line up on the far side of the field as receivers. Little John was either at tight end or in the slot on the right. Cory lined up in the backfield.

My eyebrows shot up as Jermaine came into motion and I realized they were running... a jet?

Loxley, holding the ball out, simulated a snap, turned, and pitched it to Jermaine as he came across. He was probably the fastest on the field, had a solid head start, and when he turned the corner he was running like an antelope. They scored on the first play.

Jody swore at Brent, who responded with "shut the fuck up."

Brent and company got the ball, and it was simply a repeat of the last drive, a pass to Nick. The only difference was when they got into the red zone, Brent pump-faked and tossed their second TD to Jody.

The other team lined up in the exact same formation and again Jermaine went into motion. Loxley faked the pitch and handed it to Cory straight up the middle. Jody, playing the linebacker, thought he had an easy tackle, but Cory cut right. When Jody turned, he ran smack into Little John. Cory wasn't the fastest person on the field, but Dale caught up with him and was able to throw a block on Brian so Cory could score.

Two plays. Two touchdowns.

Most of the kids, surprisingly, seemed to cheer for Loxley's team. Only the ones in our small circle were on Brent and Jody's side. The numbers on opposing sidelines made it clear who the majority were pulling for.

On Brent and Jody's third possession, Dale and Jermaine double-teamed Nick. Brent had to dump it off to Jody and Brian to move the ball. Loxley's team got them to fourth down inside the ten, but Brent was able to hit Will in the back of the end zone over Cory to take the lead.

Loxley took the ball and glanced my direction. He grinned before his team took their same formation. That smile worried me. Jermaine went into motion and Loxley snapped as he got close. Once again, Loxley faked the pitch to Jermaine, only this time he also faked the handoff to Cory. By the time he went through all that, it gave him a seven-step drop. Loxley cocked his arm, planted his foot, and on Brent's count of eight threw the ball deep.

Selena and I hopped up at the same time as the ball flew. Will, distracted by all the motion in the backfield, lost Dale, the guy he was supposed to be covering. Dale had to run wide open but was able to get under the ball and trotted into the end zone with no one even close.

"That's...," I gawked, "over fifty yards in the air! Close to sixty!"

"Damn!" Selena exclaimed.

Looking over, I saw Brent chewing out Will, who was shaking his head. I frowned.

"You get the impression Hood is toying with them?" Selena asked.

"I hope not," I muttered.

Loxley and company followed the same game plan as they had on the previous drive: double-teaming Nick. Loxley, playing the middle of the field, didn't bother to rush Brent, making their coverage five-on-four. Three different times, Brent had to dump the ball off to get a first down. The defense held them to fourth down again inside the ten, but Brent broke and scored to make it 28-21.

All they had to do was score again.

Loxley's team swapped their formation on the next series. Little John remained in his hybrid slot/tight end position. Cory Boxer mirrored him on the other side. Dale lined up as a fullback, with Jermaine as a running back.

From there it was short gains. A lot of them. Jermaine and Dale took turns toting the mail. Little John made several tough catches over the middle. Loxley threw short, quick passes to move the sticks and converted a fourth and long by bootlegging away from Jody's rush. A pass on the out route to Little John put the ball in the end zone to tie the game. I lost count of how many plays they ran.

If Brent's team scored, they won. When everyone lined up, I realized Loxley's team had changed their defense.

Jermaine was playing back, like a free safety. Loxley stayed roughly at the middle linebacker spot. Dale lined up on Nick one-on-one. Cory and Little John positioned themselves as inside corners, like in a nickel package.

The first play was almost a disaster for Brent.

Seeing Nick was one-on-one again, he took the snap and loaded up to throw. Nick had his hand raised to signal he was open over the shorter Dale, and Brent let it go. As Nick stretched out to make it, Jermaine, who had come across to cover over the top, leaped and caught the ball but landed out of bounds.

The crowd groaned at the near miss.

On second down, they tried the same thing. This time Loxley was counting and by the time Nick threw his hand up, it looked too far to throw it. Brent tried to run and got roughly four yards before Loxley corralled him.

I almost cheered despite myself. It was a nice tackle.

They lined up on third down and Brent abandoned trying to throw to Nick. Needing only six yards to get a fresh set of downs, Jody released inside Little John. Brent hit him on a slant that Jody had to make a fingertip catch to secure. Loxley was waiting and put him down two yards short of the marker.

Fourth down.

Brent and Jody came together and began whispering fiercely. They exchanged a high five and lined up. Jody was alone on the far side of the field, covered by Dale.

"Stay at home!" Loxley yelled.

"Stay at home!" Little John echoed.

Jody went into motion and Dale went with him. The ball was snapped and Brent pitched to Jody, coming around the corner. Jody moved five steps, turned, and threw the ball right before Little John creamed him back to a wide-open Brent.

Dale had followed Jody too far inside, and the fake worked. Brent took off down the field with nothing but green grass in front of him. Our side was cheering as he sailed clearly down our sideline.

Brent passed me and almost three steps later, Loxley came by like a blur. They made it to the twenty and Loxley was on him. We were screaming, but it didn't look like Brent could hear us. He got to the fifteen and Loxley was close enough to touch. He got to the ten and Loxley's arm came over the top of his shoulder. As they were approaching the five, somehow Loxley's arm was able to dislodge the ball, so it came out between Brent's arm and torso and popped upwards. Loxley grabbed the ball right off Brent's upper back before they got to the five, secured it, turned, and began running the other way.

I stood there in open-mouthed shock.

Loxley sprinted down the sideline with the rest of the guys coming at an angle. Jody got to him first, but Loxley made a hard stop, causing his would-be tackler to go flying past. Nick grabbed him by the shoulder and Loxley wrapped both arms around the ball and kept chugging. Brian came in next and was able to connect shoulder-to-shoulder. That, combined with Nick's weight, brought Loxley down. As he stood up, Brent came charging in, snapped his elbow and caught him flush on the nose.

Loxley ended up on his butt with a grunt. That emptied the side of the bench that I was on, which caused Loxley's side to rush the field.

Selena and I might have been the only people from Brent and Jody's side of the field to not jump up. I was too stunned. Watching Brent, who I thought was one of the good guys, sucker punch Loxley, left me dumbfounded.

Loxley popped up. Blood was leaking down his nose, staining his white t-shirt. Without wiping it off, he walked up and tugged at Little John to get him back.

"We're letting it go, John. Let it go. We got this..."

"I'm sure it was an accident," Tuck said, trying to keep

the peace.

Loxley shrugged. "I don't give a shit if it was or not. This game's about to be over with!"

His words caused his side to back up. Little John gave Brent one last menacing glare before he turned and stormed off. There were a few more taunts from non-participants as the field cleared.

"Dude!" Nick bitched at Brent. "Seriously?"

It was first and ten from around the thirty-five-yard line. I couldn't say for sure, but it looked like Loxley glanced at me from the corner of his eye as he walked a few steps away from his teammates, spit a mouthful of bloody phlegm, and returned to his position. There was a quick conference, some pointing, and they came to the line.

The formation was different again. This time, Dale was at the end of the line and Jermaine was on the other. Little John was lined up as the blocking back and Cory was behind him. Loxley came to the line of scrimmage, looked at the defense, and snapped the ball. He pump-faked to Jermaine, turned, and hit Dale on an out pattern that got them a first down.

From the twenty-five, they lined up again and Loxley snapped. He faked a handoff to Little John up the middle, another pump fake to Jermaine, and then hit Cory on a little screen. He rumbled inside the ten-yard line.

As they were going to the line, Loxley looked over at me, then back over the defense. Then back to me. He gave me an arrogant smirk before he turned back to the game.

"Check! Check!" He turned to the opposite side. "Check!"

All his teammates turned their heads towards him.

"Clemson! Clemson!"

I saw Dale and Jermaine both grin. Little John looked over his shoulder and whispered something to Cory, who nodded.

Loxley snapped the ball again and pitched it to Dale, who was coming around behind the line with Cory lead-blocking. He got about four steps and flipped it to Jermaine, who was going the opposite direction. Jermaine abruptly stopped before he got to full speed and threw an easy pass. It went right back to Loxley, who caught it two yards deep in the end zone all alone.

Brent ran, trying to cover, but was definitely too late. The crowd on their side erupted. Loxley spiked the ball right in front of him, bowed up, bumped foreheads with Brent and said something I couldn't make out.

When Brent turned around, his face was a storm cloud of anger. Jody had his hands on his hips, an ugly scowl on his face. They'd just gotten punked in front of the entire student body, and they knew it.

Loxley strolled through the crowd of well-wishers with a purpose. He stopped right in front of me.

"M'lady, I believe that's ours."

I glanced down and remembered I was still holding a freaking grand in cash. I held the folded stack out to him.

Loxley grasped my entire hand. His palm was rough and calloused — and warm. But his touch was gentle, as though he were holding a baby bird he didn't wish to either drop or harm. He kept my daintier hand a heartbeat longer than proper, but not long enough to be called out before releasing it, and took the money.

"Thank you, Marian."

Before I could say anything, he turned and went to rejoin his crew. Seeing Brent heading my way, I took out one of my water bottles. I figured he could use the drink and his ego could use the soothing.

When he snatched the bottle, his hand struck mine, causing it to fly back. I cried out as pain shot down my hand into my wrist — the same wrist he'd bruised at the river.

My eyes narrowed as we locked gazes. His face was twisted and ugly.

"Let's go."

"Yeah," I snapped. "Let's."

I stormed off. I didn't know where he was parked, nor did I care. That was twice he'd been physical with me and I didn't like it. I just knew I wasn't in any mood to deal with it.

No one stopped me as I got into my car. I slammed the door angrily, wincing again as it jarred my wrist.

My eyes started misting as I drove. My boyfriend treated me like a possession and the town outlaw treated me like a princess. Brent put bruises on my wrist and Loxley left notes on my pillow.

I fucking hated Barnsdale County.

Chapter 18

"HEY! HEY, MARIAN!"

I kept walking.

"Hey, wait up!"

Brent came running up as I headed to Spanish. I kept my head down and my feet moving.

"I tried to call you yesterday."

"Yeah, well, I was busy."

"You're mad."

"Ya think?"

"I'm sorry."

Once again, his tone sounded like he was trying to pacify me instead of actually apologizing.. My teeth clenched and I kept walking.

"Seriously," he went on. "I'm sorry, okay?"

"Bite me."

"That an offer?"

"Not in the mood, Dean."

"So I'm 'Dean' now? Like Hood is 'Loxley'?"

That got me to stop. "When you mistreat me, you're damn right!"

"I said I was sorry."

"I said you had one freebie and you blew it."

"I didn't hit you."

"It was rough enough."

"Don't you think you're overreacting just a bit?"

That pissed me off even more. "Get away from me, Dean. I'm warning you."

He smirked. "Or what?"

'Or what' was right. It's not like I could pull a Loxley and deck him.

So I ignored him. I went to my seat in Spanish and opened my book without looking up. Brent sat in his seat beside me and let me stew. I couldn't decide what I was angrier at — his smug attitude or his insincerity.

My eyes cut towards Loxley, and I again was struck by how odd my situation was. I was arguing with the 'safe' guy about his temper and the bad boy held my hand like he thought I was made of glass.

The bell rang for lunch and I grabbed my stuff, trying to hurry out. Brent was waiting for me at the door.

"I said I was sorry," he said again.

"You did."

"Really," he went on. "I am."

He then stopped talking as the source of most of his agitation strolled past. Instead of walking towards the cafeteria, Loxley was headed to the office and the principal was waiting for him at the door. Both were frowning. Loxley didn't even seem to notice us.

"It's just... I can't stand that guy," Brent said as soon as he was out of earshot, "and he uses it. It's like he does stuff just to yank my chain."

"He can't if you don't let him."

Brent gave me a curious look.

"If you just ignored him, he wouldn't hold any power over you. He's living rent free in your head. Just stop letting him get to you. You'd be a lot happier. Not only that, he'd probably be the one getting mad because you treated him like he was beneath you."

"And what about keeping the peace?"

I shrugged. "I didn't mean ignore him completely. But if you only deal with him when you have to, instead of making it a point to speak to him and interacting with him, it will drive him crazy."

Brent grinned. "You're pretty smart."

"So my parents say."

His grin widened and he leaned in, giving me a peck on the corner of my mouth. I stood still and let him.

"So am I forgiven?"

Was he? I didn't really want to. But I could get where he was coming from. I tended to see red about George. We all had character flaws. His rivalry with Loxley was one of his, just like my tendency to see the good in people was one of mine.

"Let's go to lunch."

While we walked, he threw his arm around me again. We took our usual table and he acted like things were completely back to normal. Tina was as catty as usual, so I ate my leftover lasagna and did my best to ignore her.

"Hey," Jody said. "Check this out."

I raised my head to see three men wearing brown uniforms and police duty belts through the large windows. They entered the front door and turned into the principal's office.

"What's going on?" Hope asked.

"I bet they're going to do a locker inspection," Tina said.

"They going to search students?" Nick asked.

Tina shrugged. "Only if they think you've got a reason to be holding."

My fork froze inches from my mouth. What worried me was my can of Mace. This wasn't the pepper spray normally sold to the public. It was the stuff issued to police officers.

Dad would cover me, of course. He'd admit that he gave it to me and told me to carry it. But that wouldn't matter. If I got caught, I'd be expelled. I'd have no option but to be homeschooled. That wouldn't look good on my permanent record.

My fork went back into my Tupperware, my appetite gone. No one seemed to notice. Brent was bragging about the four-wheeler he was getting for Christmas, and Jody was talking about preparations for hunting season.

Our table wasn't the only one that noticed the deputies enter the building. The cafeteria became abuzz with whispering. Glancing around, I saw both Jermaine and Loxley, who I hadn't seen come in, giving their troops instructions. I tried to figure out what I could do about the Mace, but I only came up with one answer — I had to ditch it.

The problem was, how?

It was police-issued. If someone found it, I would be on a very short list of suspects. That's also assuming the person who found it was honest and turned it in. The thought of someone using it to harm someone else made my already fragile stomach even queasier. And to top it all off, there was the risk of being caught disposing of it.

The bell rang and I decided the only thing I could do was to just keep my mouth shut.

"You heard about the party this weekend?" Brent asked.

I was too nervous to speak, so I nodded.

"You want to go with me?"

"I guess. You know where?"

"Yeah, it's on Mallory's dad's property. Want me to pick you up or meet you there?"

After the past weekend, I felt better having my own car. "I'll drive."

He shrugged. "Okay."

We rounded the corner and saw the deputies were hard at work.

To my surprise, they were actually frisking students, lining up teenagers, mostly male, against the wall with their hands pressed and their legs spread. Deputies wearing black gloves were patting them down.

I saw Little John standing three down from Miss Chen's room.

"Come on," Brent said confidently. "They're not going to bother us."

I followed him stupidly as he took my hand and walked me towards my class.

"This you?" Jody mumbled to him.

Brent smirked.

"Ba-ZING!"

"No way I was letting that shit go..."

My heart bottomed out in my stomach as I realized what they were talking about. Brent somehow set this up. I dropped my head and stared at the floor as we walked past. I could feel glares from the people against the wall.

"Get your hands off me!"

The voice was Scarlet's. She had a finger pointed at an overweight, bald deputy.

"The handbook says that you're subject to search at the principal's discretion," the deputy barked at her. "Now turn and face the wall or you'll be subject to arrest."

"You're not touching me!"

Brent was grinning like the cat that ate the canary.

Miss Chen appeared. "What is the meaning of this?"

Scarlet spoke up first. "He's not searching me!"

Miss Chen glared at the deputy.

"Rules are rules, ma'am."

"The rules state that someone of the opposite sex isn't allowed to either physically search a student or administer corporal punishment," Miss Chen angrily explained. "So unless you'd like Miss Williams's family to call their lawyer, I suggest you abide by her wishes."

"She's getting searched and Deputy White ain't here."

"Scarlet, would you consent if I searched you?"

Scarlet swallowed nervously, but she gave a slow nod.

Miss Chen looked at the deputy. "The handbook allows teachers and administrative staff to do the searches. Are you opposed to me doing it?"

The deputy pondered for a moment before he shook his head.

"Scarlet, please turn around and put your hands on the wall."

"But I will be supervising," the deputy added.

Scarlet was shivering, but she did as Miss Chen told her.

I looked down the row at who was being searched. It didn't escape my attention that no one from our group was against the wall.

I saw people I knew. Max and Tuck were standing side by side. Tuck seemed to whisper to Max what was going on. Across from them, I saw Jermaine. He looked bored. Two students down from him, I saw Selena, which I thought was strange. Dale was a couple down from her.

The last person in that row was Loxley.

His vest hung open as he stood with his hands on the wall. He turned his head and before our eyes met, I looked away. I couldn't meet his eyes or anyone else's. I was allowed to walk freely while the law was being used to harass people just so my boyfriend could make a point.

Brent landed another kiss on the side of my mouth. "I'll talk to you tomorrow."

"Okay," I replied.

As I walked, I watched Miss Chen frisk Scarlet. Her expression was one of pity. Scarlet was shaking slightly and chewing on her lower lip. She looked like she was fighting not to cry.

"She's clean," Miss Chen informed the deputy.

"You sure?"

"Yes, I'm sure."

"Search her again."

"She doesn't have anything. I'm not going to keep patting her down until something magically appears. We'd be here until I retire. I'm telling you, she has nothing on her."

The deputy gave them both one more glare and moved down to the next person.

"AND THAT WAS THAT." I informed my parents.

Mom shook her head. "I can't believe that's legal."

"Why not?" Dad asked.

"To randomly search students? It sounds like they just picked people going down the halls."

"They had to have some kind of reason, a tip or something."

Mom grumbled to herself.

What bothered me the most wasn't the search but who was searched and Brent all but admitting he set it up.

"Did they catch anybody?" Dad asked.

"A few guys with pocketknives and I think one with some pot, but no guns."

"Who got caught with the knives?"

"I didn't know them. But that was the first time I've even heard about a blade since I started school."

"When I was a kid, all the boys carried pocketknives. Of course, we also used to lock our rifles in our trucks and as soon as the bell rang, we'd be headed to the woods to hunt."

"You drove? I thought you walked five miles barefoot through three feet of snow uphill both ways."

"Hilarious."

"We got anything going on Saturday night?" I asked both of them.

"No," Mom asked. "Why?"

"There's a party and Brent invited me."

"When do we get to meet him, anyway? You two have been going out for a few weeks now. Is it getting serious?"

"Not yet."

"Are you still... taking your medicine?"

Dad's way of being practical was making sure I had access to and knew how to use a shotgun. Mom's way was to put me on the Pill since I was thirteen. Catholic or not, Mom was paranoid about me turning up like one of her patients.

"Yes, ma'am," I replied. "And before you get too in-depth with your questioning, I'm expecting my regular visitor either tomorrow or the day after."

"I didn't need to know that," Dad grumbled.

We went back to eating and I thought of something. "Dad, you remember the crew I asked you to check out?"

He swallowed his bite of food and nodded.

"You know how many of them were caught?"

"How many?"

"Zero. None of them were holding anything."

"It makes you wonder, doesn't it?"

"It does."

"You two talking about the boy Marian told you about? That one they called Hood?" Mom asked.

"That's the one."

"I would love to hear that story."

"Why's that?"

"Just looking at it on the surface, I can't help but think there's so much no one is seeing. I would love to know what's missing."

"Why, Mom?"

She shrugged. "I just... I don't know. I think about that boy who lost his parents at such an early age and takes care of his blind grandfather, and I can't help but wonder what makes him tick. Is he really a criminal? Did he just do that one bad act and has reformed? Is it something in between?"

"Speaking of criminals," Dad said proudly, "another agent caught the guy. So he's being held without bond until trial. This might be an easier nut to crack than I thought."

"That's great, Dad!"

Cowboy thumped his tail from his spot at my feet.

"Your curfew is the same Saturday night as always, Marian," Mom said.

"Yes ma'am. It's not a problem."

Chapter 19

THESE PEOPLE KNEW HOW to throw a party.

It seemed like there were at least a hundred cars parked in a field off the main road. In the distance, I could hear music and see enough lights to illuminate a small stadium.

The moon was full and the air had a good nip to it. It wasn't cold enough to see my breath, but it was close. In the distance, I saw a roaring bonfire. I thought there were more kids here than at the Rebel's home football games.

I stepped into the lights and started looking around. I didn't see Brent. Cory Boxer was across from me, sitting on a cooler with a beer in his hand, talking to a couple of other guys. Further down, I saw Jermaine smoking something.

"Hi, Marian!"

I turned to see Selena bouncing up to me. She hugged me quickly, and I returned the gesture. It was nice to deal with someone who wasn't constantly stirring stuff up.

"Hey, Selena. Where is everybody?"

"I haven't seen any of the girls yet, but the boys are

hauling beer up. They've got a keg set up already."

This was going to be a big party.

"I wonder if Brent can dance."

She pondered. "I don't know. I've never seen him do it. Why?"

"That sucks," I grumbled. "I want to dance and no one knows how."

"Sorry. Maybe if you asked, someone could."

"I doubt it."

"You're probably right," she agreed.

"Probably right about what?" Asked a voice from behind me.

We both turned and I saw Selena blush.

Loxley stood there with his hands in his pockets, grinning. Beside him were Dale and Scarlet.

"Dance," Selena babbled. "Marian was asking if I knew anyone that knew how and I don't and she said it was probably for the best because she could out-dance anyone and..."

"Take a breath, Selena," I muttered.

"I can," Loxley declared.

"Can what?"

"Dance."

I snorted. "No, you can't."

"I swear I can. And probably better than you."

"Oh," I said confidently. "I doubt that."

"Sounds like a challenge to me."

"I think you just want to make Brent mad."

"No, I just like seeing you look surprised when I can do something you don't think I should be able to."

For some reason, I liked that answer. I did not know why and I probably shouldn't have. But I did.

"We doing this, or are you willing to admit you can't keep up with me?"

"Marian!"

Uh-oh...

I turned around to find Brent approaching. He had a red plastic cup in his hand. I braced myself for his eruption, one that I figured would be epic.

It wasn't. "What are we talking about?"

"Dancing. I learned how to two-step between walking and running," I explained.

Brent looked at Loxley. "What about you?"

He shrugged. "My mom taught me when I was little."

While Brent wasn't slurring his words too much, his eyes looked a little glassy in the firelight. I wondered if the alcohol had mellowed him.

"I need some water," I announced.

"We got beer," Brent offered.

"Maybe later. Come on. Find me a drink and you can show me your moves."

"Cool."

I took Brent's hand and he led me towards a spot behind a pile of wood.

"So, is this where you get mad at me?"

He dug out a bottle of water. "Why would I do that?"

I shrugged and took it from him. "Because I was talking to your worst enemy? I was talking to Selena and he just walked up. I know you're mad, but..."

"I don't care."

I was more than a bit surprised. "You don't?"

He picked up the nozzle from the keg and refilled his cup. "Not really. He probably did that just to piss me off. But you were right. If I let him get to me, he will. So I don't let him. Besides, you're my date tonight. Right?"

I smiled. "Right."

I chugged down half the water before I lowered it. Brent was still smiling. He stood next to me and I felt his hand slide down so it was in my back pocket.

That was probably a little further than I wanted him to go, but I gave him a pass. He could've gotten angry, but he didn't. Maybe he was learning?

As the night wore on, Brent and I got closer together. The temperature started to drop and I was grateful for the body heat. I lost sight of Loxley and crew — not that I was looking for them.

Brent was both sorts of affectionate — good and bad. I got kissed more that night than the entire time we dated. I got to be close to him and that was okay. But his hands tended to wander a bit, mostly to my backside. I let it slide since it made it clear he wanted me and I thought that was what I wanted.

"I'm ready for another beer. You want one?"

"No, thank you," I replied. "I'm not drinking tonight."

"Come on, Marian... just one? I got this for you."

He'd seen me drink one beer, so he got a keg for me?

"Okay," I relented. "One and one only. I'm going to have to head home in about an hour."

"Cool."

I moved back to the fire as Brent went to get the drinks. It was still roaring and it helped ward off the cold. I stuffed my hands in my pockets and swayed gently to the music.

"Hey!"

I looked the direction Brent had left to see him about a step from me. He was also looking for the source of the yelling.

"Hey! I'm talking to you, punk!"

My head whipped around to see Loxley storming in our direction. He yanked his cut off without breaking stride. Unlike the last time, he didn't hold it out for anyone to grab. He just let it drop to the ground.

I'd only seen it once, but I knew what happened when Loxley took that vest off.

Loxley stormed past me and without warning, slapped the beer out of Brent's hand. Most of it went flying off to my right, but some of it sprinkled against my jacket. Loxley then got nose-to-nose with Brent.

"You want to run that mouth now?"

The music had stopped. People were forming up around us. Brent looked confused.

"I ain't said shit, Hood."

Loxley brought his head forward an inch to bump into Brent's. Brent automatically slid his back just to give him room. I saw Jody as he stepped forward. That caused someone else I hadn't seen tonight to come out of the crowd — Little John.

"Bullshit. You got something to say. Let's hear it."

"You want to back up. Right now."

"You want to quit talking shit while you can still talk, bitch!"

This was the first time I'd ever heard Loxley sound so angry.

"I'm warning you right now," Brent said. His voice was still a low growl. "Back out of my face. Otherwise, you won't be safe anywhere in this county."

"It won't matter. You won't be around to see it."

"Back... away... now."

I guessed Loxley finally wrapped his head around the fact Brent could make his life miserable because he took a step back. He looked at Scarlet who nodded back. Loxley's eyes then glanced in my direction.

I was fuming. He'd spilled beer on me. Not only that, but I finally got a good dose of reality. Punching Jody, I could at least understand, but Brent hadn't been talking about him. In fact, he'd done his best to avoid a confrontation tonight.

He must not have liked what he saw because his head snapped away to turn and look at his crew behind him. During our stare-down, Scarlet had moved to join the boys. Dale had picked up Loxley's cut and was holding it beside his leg. Loxley seemed to deflate slightly.

"Let's get out of here."

The crowd parted as they left. Loxley walked away first, followed by Little John, Scarlet, Max, and Dale. Only the sound of crackling flames accompanied their departure from the ring of light and into the dark.

“I’M REALLY SORRY ABOUT that,” I told Brent.

We were standing beside my car, and I was telling him my goodbyes. He’d told me he was staying to supervise the clean-up.

“Don’t worry about it,” he assured me.

But I worried about it. I was angry at myself for even considering the fact Loxley was anything but the animal he’d shown himself to be tonight. I felt stupid. The last thing I needed was to have let my guard down around him.

Brent kissed me and I went with it. His body came forward and crushed me against the door of my car. His hands on my hips gripped me tightly and I could feel him hard through his jeans.

This was turning into George all over again. He broke from my mouth and went for my neck and I got on the offensive.

“Easy there,” I coaxed.

“Damn, Baby. I’ve been thinking about this for weeks.”

He accented his words with a shift of his hips. His fingertips gripped the hem of my shirt and he pulled it up. If he didn’t ease up on my neck soon, he was going to leave a mark I didn’t want to have to explain to Dad.

I slid my hands around so they were against his chest. “Brent, slow down.”

“I can’t,” he replied, his breathing becoming ragged. “I want you so bad right now.”

Did I want him? I didn't know. On the one hand, I thought he was a cool guy. He wasn't perfect, but no one was, especially in freaking Barnsdale County. Every girl at this school would consider him a catch.

But I'd learned my lesson the hard way. I wanted something besides a quickie in the back of a car, or even worse, on the hood of my old Beatle.

"Let go, Brent."

He didn't stop. I felt his teeth nip my neck, and I shuddered, but not because I was enjoying myself.

"Seriously... ease up."

"Don't be like that," he coaxed. "You know you want me, Marian."

I felt his hand go to my jeans and the top button come free. His hand went to my zipper and my hand shot down to grab his wrist.

"Stop," I said firmly, my nails digging into his skin for emphasis.

His head finally came around to look at me and I could tell this was probably going to get ugly. He was tipsy when I'd talked to Loxley and he'd been drinking steadily ever since. I didn't know if he could be reasonable.

"Don't be a tease, Marian."

"Move your hand."

He did — to slide the zipper down even with me holding his wrist. He was still stronger than I was.

He licked his lips. "You know, those nails are kind of a turn-on."

"This isn't happening."

"I beg to differ."

I didn't like his tone. "No, it isn't. Let me go. I'm leaving."

"You're staying."

I thought quickly. "You don't want to do this."

"Oh, yeah. I do."

His hand came up slightly and I felt it graze the lace edging of my underwear.

"Not this week, you don't."

"What are you talking about?"

Was I going to have to draw him a picture? "It means I've got a visitor this week."

Realization crossed his features. "You mean..."

"Yeah."

That got him to move his hand. "Well, shit!"

I let my hands drop to my jeans so I could zip them up. "Sorry."

"No, you're not!" He snapped. "You've been a tease all night. Don't lie. You wanted me all hot just so you could turn me down."

"I don't play that way."

"Bullshit!"

I kept calm. "I'm sorry you feel that way."

"Sorry isn't going to cut it."

I finished with my zipper. "What are you talking about?"

"I'm your boyfriend. I want more."

"Not this week."

He reached for his belt and started undoing it.

"What are you doing?"

"Getting what's mine."

I reached into my purse and brought out my keys. He didn't stop me as I unlocked the door.

"I'm leaving," I announced.

"Not until you get on your knees."

Was he crazy? "Not tonight, Brent."

Not any night.

"Yeah, you are. That's all bitches like you are good for."

I pulled a Loxley. I slapped him with everything I had.

It was enough to spin his head around. I put all I could muster into that slap and my hand cracked loudly when it collided with his cheek. Before he could turn, I hopped back, snatched my car door open, and slammed it into him. It was enough to knock him over and I dove inside.

He didn't get up as I fumbled with the keys. I got the right one in the ignition and turned it. The Beatle started and without buckling up, I threw it in reverse and spun sod backing out.

My headlights caught Brent's profile, still trying to stagger to his feet as I whipped the car around. Tires barked as I hit asphalt and I dropped the hammer to get me out of there. I was shaking with anger. I'd sworn I'd never be treated like that again and I meant it.

This would not be good.

As far as the aftermath went, school was about to become a battleground. The friends I had were linked to Brent. There was no way they would side with me. In fact, what if Brent decided to lie? In his state of mind, I wouldn't put anything past him.

Taking a deep breath and seeing I wasn't being followed, I forced myself to slow down to the speed limit. The road was deserted, so I relaxed just a little.

Short-term, I had to get past Dad. I pulled over at a crossroads and turned on the interior light. My neck was a little red, but I didn't see any hickeys. I grabbed a brush out of my cheerleading bag, ran it quickly through my hair, and draped it over my shoulders. That covered that. Raising my hips, I tucked my shirt back into my jeans and buttoned them.

I swore silently as I realized my jacket still smelled like beer.

"Hey, Dad," I said. "I'm home... and before you say anything about..."

"Why do you smell like beer?"

I held up my hands. "Someone spilled it on me. I swear I drank nothing but water. If you've got a breathalyzer, I'll consent."

"I believe you."

"Thanks. Mom home?"

"She's on tonight and off tomorrow."

I remembered then. "How was your day?"

It must've been bad because Dad didn't notice that I was obviously nervous. "My witness is dead."

"What?"

He shook his head and went to the kitchen table. I followed him.

"The sheriff's department found him in a trailer near

the interstate. Someone tied him up and put two bullets in the back of his head. The guy he fingered got out this morning."

"I thought he was going to be remanded."

"The judge let him out for some reason."

Dad looked physically ill. I reached over and put my hand on top of his.

"You okay?"

"No, Kitten, I'm not. This stinks."

"It is pretty bad."

"No," he corrected. "This doesn't make sense. He shouldn't have been allowed out of jail. That's almost an automatic for someone skipping on a felony warrant."

"You're thinking this was an inside job?"

"I'm thinking someone with some pull made it happen."

I sighed. "What's the next step?"

Dad shook his head. "I've got nothing."

"Don't give up."

Dad grunted. "I got some good news, sort of."

"What?"

"Another body turned up earlier tonight. Heck, I've only been home half an hour or so."

"How is that good?"

Dad slumped back in his chair. "It was the guy my witness fingered. He also had some interesting stuff with him."

"Like what?"

"The car the deceased was driving was his and was seen on the road the same night as Junior's log truck. We found a homemade club with Junior's blood type on it. We're betting the DNA matches. There were some specks on this guy's boots too. You could argue that was set up, but we also found the victim's fingerprints on the driver's side mirror, the dash, and the inside of the door handle of Junior's truck. That can't really be faked."

"Translation," I summed up, "it looks like this person killed Mr. Boxer?"

He nodded.

"So it is kind of good. The question is, who killed him?"

"I don't know, but he's going into my fastest growing pile."

"What do you mean?"

"He took an arrow to the chest."

My throat suddenly felt dry. "So... the vigilantes, huh?"

"It looks that way. Now we have to look at who would want this guy dead."

"The family?"

"They have alibis."

Something tickled the back of my brain. Cory, obviously angry at his father's untimely death, was begging Robert Loxley to do something. Loxley's crew promised him it would happen, but they had to be smart and sure — and cold. An arrow to the chest sounded cold to me.

But that was insane. They were hoodlums, but they were my age. It was one thing for a teenager to commit a random act of violence. But to plot out a murder? That was too farfetched even for Loxley's reputation. Never mind the obvious. I'd seen him earlier.

"How was the party?" Dad asked.

I shrugged. "It was okay. I don't think Brent and I will be seeing anymore of each other."

"What happened?"

I decided to hit the highlights. "He's got a sense of entitlement and grabby hands. So if someone calls you about me slapping someone..."

"I'll tell them where to go and what to do when they get there."

"Thanks, Dad."

"You're welcome, Kitten. Do I need to go have a talk with Mr. Dean and explain to him the proper way to treat a lady?"

"No, sir. Like I said, I handled it. Just expect me to be home more on nights and weekends."

"Every father's dream."

"I'm going to put some laundry on, go wash the smell of beer off me, and go to bed. The Cowboys have the matinee game tomorrow."

"Get your laundry going and go let Cowboy out. I heard him whining earlier."

"Yes, sir."

I hopped up, leaned over, and kissed him on the top of his head before I hugged him tightly. He patted my arm before I released him.

There wasn't any dirty laundry for me to do, so I picked up the basket of clean clothes that were mine before returning to the kitchen.

Dad had already gone upstairs. Balancing my load between my right arm and body, I shut off the lights, slipped out the back door, and locked it before heading up to my quarters.

I guessed Brent wasn't going to apologize this time. Not that it mattered. I'd let too much go and it was time to put my foot down. Brent thought he was above the rules. I should've known that when he set things up so all those kids were searched.

It didn't change my opinion of Loxley, though. I still thought that violent streak he'd shown was proof that he was dangerous. Brent was the second person I'd seen him strike.

I opened the door and slipped through. Without turning on the light, I put the basket on the table. Pivoting, I closed the door and locked it before I flipped the switch. I turned back away from the door and froze. My body completely locked up, and I felt a scream start in my chest and work its way up to my throat.

Robert Loxley was sitting at my kitchen table.

Chapter 20

"PLEASE DON'T SCREAM," HE said softly.

The fact he said it so calmly did it. Every serial killer I'd ever seen on TV sounded like that.

"Sic him, Cowboy!"

It was then that I noticed my dog was lying on the floor next to Loxley's chair. My guest had his left hand dangling down and was rubbing Cowboy's head. My dog thumped his tail and gave a puzzled look at my command.

"Traitor."

His tail kept thumping.

"What are you doing here, Loxley?"

"I just want to talk."

Slowly, I began circling around the table. "You promised me you wouldn't break into my house again."

He didn't seem to care that I was moving. "I know, and I'm sorry for that. But it's important."

I made it a point not to look at the bedroom doorway. "I don't consider this important enough to break your word."

"I do."

He replied about the time I got within arm's reach of my door and I sprinted through, making a beeline for my closet.

"It's not there..."

I snatched the closet door away from the wall and, sure enough, my shotgun was gone.

My head snapped around, and I braced myself, but Loxley was still sitting at the table. Even Cowboy hadn't moved.

"What did you do with it?"

He was still calm. "I hid it."

"Why?"

"Isn't that obvious?"

I stormed back into the kitchen area and went straight to my purse.

"What are you doing?"

"Calling Dad. I can promise you he'll make sure you never set foot in here again."

"Please don't."

I'd gotten Dad's contact info pulled up just as he responded. It gave me a pause. Why was he here if he didn't have any bad intentions?

I turned around, keeping the phone in my hand, and asked, "Why are you here, Loxley?"

"You smell like beer," he deflected.

"Yeah," I snapped. "Some jerk spilled it on me."

His chin dropped. "I'm sorry."

I stood there fuming while he sat there looking sorry.

Cowboy whined.

It was him that broke the silence. "Do you need to change shirts?"

I snorted. "With you sitting here? Fat chance."

"You could go into the other room?"

"I'd prefer you get out of my house."

"Let me say what I have to say, and I will. I promise."

"Just like you promised to not come in my house again?"

He sighed. "The agreement was only if I thought it was important. And I said I was sorry."

"It seems like all you boys around here do is apologize."

"I don't know about anyone else, just me."

I shook my head. "It seems to me you tend to know more about everyone else's business than anyone else."

"If you say so."

That answer struck me as odd. "You disagree?"

He only shrugged.

I snatched a clean t-shirt off the top of the pile in the basket. "Go in the other room."

"So you can go get your daddy?"

It was a good idea. Too bad I hadn't thought of it. "So I can change shirts."

"So go into your bedroom."

"This is my place, Loxley. I'll change wherever I want."

"I'm sorry, Marian." His voice was soft and just below sad. "But we've had this conversation. I won't go to jail."

"Then stop doing B and E jobs."

"I told you. I need to talk to you."

I sighed. "Will you at least turn around?"

Cowboy watched him as Loxley slowly stood. Just as I

asked, he turned and faced the door. His hands went to his pockets, and he settled into a relaxed pose.

I stripped the shirt off and realized my bra was wet, too. I didn't want to deal with that, but there was no way I was going without one in front of Loxley.

"Listen," I said. "Don't turn around, but you got beer on my bra, too. So I'm changing it."

He stiffened for a moment, but he didn't move.

I unclasped the front hook and shrugged the straps off my shoulders. Keeping my eyes on Loxley's back, I picked up a clean bra and slipped it on. He kept his rigid pose.

I was ready to cover up in case he tried to get an eyeful, but Loxley stood there patiently as I made the necessary adjustments, picked up my t-shirt, and got presentable.

"Okay," I announced. "I'm decent."

Despite the situation, I found it a bit funny how Loxley turned around. He did it slowly, with his body coming around first and his head following behind like he was afraid he might catch a peek of something that either he or I didn't want him to see.

"Now," he said calmly. "Can we please talk?"

I had two options: let him talk or get him arrested. I was tired and I was ready to take a shower and go to bed. If I called Dad in here, it would be an ugly scene, complete with a lot of flashing blue lights and me up for hours giving statements. It was just best to let him say what he wanted to say and get him out of here.

"Talk."

"I came to apologize. I didn't mean for you to get in the crossfire between Brent and me."

"You're a psycho, Loxley!"

He blinked in surprise. "No, I'm not. I did that because..."

"I don't care about your testosterone-fueled temper!" I snapped. "And I don't care about whatever beef you and Brent have. It's not my business."

"I did it for..."

"You did it because you two have some stupid grudge and you both need to get over it!"

"No, I..."

"Don't give me that crap!" I was on a roll. "You're a thug. Your default action is to hurt someone."

"That's not true..."

"Yes! It is!" I threw up my hands. "You're nothing more than the white trash everybody says you are!"

"You mean your preppy little friends?"

His voice had finally lost its serenity. That was fine with me. I was itching for a fight.

"My preppy little friends don't burn down houses, beat people up, steal, knock girls up and leave them or..."

"That is *not* true."

I took a breath. "Okay. Fine. You're not the father of Grace's baby. But who's to say there isn't another illegitimate Loxley running around?"

"You really have a poor opinion of me."

"You earned it, bud."

"And Dean didn't?"

"His reputation is spotless."

Loxley's arms crossed over his chest. "You believe that?"

"Okay," I corrected. "It might not be pure as the driven

snow, but it's cleaner than yours."

"That you know of."

This was getting old. "Look. Loxley. I don't know what you want. But I know what I want. I want you out of my house."

"I told you. I came to apologize and explain myself."

"You already did," I pointed out. "And I don't need an explanation."

"Yes, you do," he stressed. "Marian, I'm trying to tell you the reason I got in his face was..."

"I don't care, Loxley," I interrupted. "Read my lips: I. Don't. Care. You said you were sorry. Now leave."

"Is my apology accepted?"

That was a stupid question. "The deal was I heard it. I did."

"So it's not."

"No!" I snapped. "Because once again, here you sit in my house uninvited. And the reason you're in here trying to apologize is because once again you've shown yourself to be another violent, stupid, white-trash redneck. I don't want you around, Loxley. In fact, it would suit me fine if you just fell of the face of the Earth. You wanted to apologize? Mission accomplished. Now get the hell out of my house."

"You don't know anything about me."

"I know enough."

He sighed. "You're going to regret this."

"Are you threatening me?"

To my surprise, he shook his head. "No. I wouldn't threaten you, Marian."

"It sounds like a threat."

"I swear on my parents' graves I wouldn't dare harm you."

My heart betrayed me. While my body was in fight mode and my brain suspected he was just trying to throw that Loxley charm in my direction, my heart actually melted. Well, maybe not melted. But it did get a little gooey around the edges.

I sighed. "Get out, Loxley. Get out and never speak to me again. Never come in this house again. And I mean it. Next time you leave in handcuffs or in a body bag. I'm not screwing around."

Loxley slumped his shoulders, and I knew he was defeated. Reaching down, he patted Cowboy once more before coming back to full height and moving towards the door. I slid another step to my left, so I was out of arm's length.

"There's one more thing," he said before he reached for the knob.

I didn't speak as he turned around.

"What I did tonight, I did for you." He kept talking before I could snap at him again. "You don't know it yet, but I did. What I did will have repercussions for me. You remember when I said I owed you one?"

I nodded.

"We're even, Marian. You don't know it yet, but we're even. If you ever need something, you know how to find me."

Before I could say anything else, he was gone.

I stared stupidly at the door for a full minute after it closed. Only Cowboy's whining broke me out of my stupor. He probably needed to pee, but I didn't want to give Loxley the satisfaction of thinking I was going after him.

When I figured it was safe, I opened the door. "Go, traitor."

Cowboy slinked out and I heard him bound down the steps.

Tonight was over. I put my clothes away mechanically. I couldn't figure out the boys here in Barnsdale. Brent and Loxley both thought they were petty kings running around, doing whatever they wanted. It made me so mad I could've screamed.

As I moved to drop the now empty basket on the floor, I saw a folded in half piece of paper on the dresser that was out of place. I picked it up and opened it.

It's under the bed.

Underneath the message was the familiar drawing of a circle with two crossed arrows.

Dropping to my knees, I threw the ruffle back and sure enough, my shotgun was lying on the floor. I shook my head at Loxley's arrogance. It was official. He was nuts.

I pulled the gun out from under the bed and checked the load. Despite my anger, I couldn't help but smirk. He hadn't even unloaded it. I had to admit, Loxley had a set of brass ones. I returned it to its hiding place and heard Cowboy scratching at the door.

I crossed the small space quickly and opened up. The big lug slipped through with a doggy grin and a wagging tail.

How had Loxley gotten past him? Cowboy didn't like strangers. In fact, he really didn't like strangers, even to the point we had to put him up if we were expecting a package.

But he'd lain down at Loxley's feet just like he did with Dad.

"Traitor."

He kept wagging his tail.

Groaning, I locked up and turned out the light before I went to shower and get ready for bed. On my way to the bathroom, I stopped and looked around, expecting something to be different. But just like last time, except for the note and the moved shotgun, nothing was out of place. Loxley had come and gone like a ghost.

I'd had enough for today. I grabbed a towel and went to finally get that shower. Even with the change of shirt and bra, I still smelled like beer.

"MARIAN!" A VOICE YELLED. "Marian, wake up!"

It was dad, and I shot up in bed. He began pounding on the door, which got Cowboy barking.

"Marian!"

I bailed out of bed and threw the door open before Dad could start banging again. He stood there mid-knock with the phone up to his other ear.

"You could've just come in, Dad," I grumbled.

He held the phone out. "You mother wants to talk to you."

"Mom?"

"Marian, do you know someone named Selena Duncan?"

I immediately got a bad feeling. "Yes, ma'am. She's a sophomore and an acquaintance of mine."

"But not a friend?"

"We're friendly, but I wouldn't say we were friends. Why?"

"Because she needs one right now."

I bit my thumbnail.

"Are you there?"

"Yes, ma'am."

"Do you know who she's friends with?"

"Not really. I mean, I can't say I've ever seen her hang out with anybody but us. She's like me. She moved her right before school started. She's a year younger, so she just sort of... tags along, I guess you could say."

"I see."

"Mom. What's going on?"

"She's in my ER. Her parents are out of town and... well, I can't say a whole lot over the phone. But she really needs a friend right now."

Dad was looking at me expectantly. I scrubbed my face with my hands. It went without saying that I had my own problems. But if Mom was calling me...

"Let me get dressed."

"Thank you, Marian."

We hung up, and I handed Dad his phone. "Why didn't she call me?"

"She did, but you didn't answer. It's close to ten o'clock, you know?"

No wonder I had a headache.

"Come on in," I offered.

Dad followed me into the sleeping area and looked around. "At least you keep this cleaner than your old room."

"Ha, ha, ha."

His eyes fell on the dresser. "Other than some trash there."

Dad stepped to get whatever he was seeing and I had a panic moment when I realized it was Loxley's note from last night.

"I got it!" I squeaked, beating him to it.

"You okay, Kitten?"

I crumpled the note in my fist. "I'm good, Dad. I'm just... nervous. Any idea what's wrong with Selena?"

Dad shrugged. "I have no clue. But your mom is staying over for her. She should've been home three hours ago. That tells me it's something serious."

He had a point. I went to my closet and found some jeans.

"You want a ride?" Dad asked.

"I'll drive," I called. "I guess we're going to have to cancel football."

Chapter 21

NOTTINGHAM GENERAL HOSPITAL WAS tiny by Dallas standards. It was an older three-story building on Highway 92, only a few miles from the house. A slow, chilly rain had begun to fall as I made my way inside.

I ignored the main entrance and parked next to Mom's car. The ambulance bay doors had a keypad, so I went through registration.

"May I help you?" asked a plump older black lady who I could've sworn was wearing a wig.

"I'm here to see Dr. Fitzwalter."

She gave me a fake smile. "Just sign in here."

I then realized how I sounded. "Oh! Sorry! I'm not a patient. I'm her daughter."

"Oh! Of course, Sugar. Come with me."

She got up and waddled towards the door behind her, and I followed.

The receptionist led me down the hall and waved to the two nurses doing paperwork. The two rooms reserved for trauma — I'd been in enough ERs in my life — were empty, and I sighed with relief.

The receptionist knocked softly on a door marked "Doctor's Lounge".

Mom opened it a crack, saw me, and threw it open.

She pulled me into a tight hug. "Thank you, Ernestine."

"You're welcome, Dr. Fitzwalter. You have a beautiful little girl."

Mom didn't seem to hear her. Her pale face made the bags under her eyes look more pronounced than usual. It told me all I wanted to know.

Whatever happened to Selena, it was serious.

"Excuse us," Mom told Ernestine.

Before she could say anything else, Mom pulled me inside and closed the door.

"Thank you for coming."

"What's going on, Mom?"

She took a breath as if to steel herself. "Selena doesn't know I called you. She's asked me not to call anyone, not even her parents. I have to, of course, but I was hoping I could give her some time before I did. What I'm trying to say is that what I'm going to tell you is in the strictest of confidence. I could get fired for it. Selena might talk to you. I hope she does. But she might not, in which case you need to keep what you know to yourself."

I nodded. "I promise, Mom."

"Selena showed up here around four a.m. reeking of beer. She wouldn't tell the triage nurse what was wrong, just that she needed help. We thought she was just drunk and needed some help to get sobered up. When I examined her, she said she blacked out at a party and woke up in that condition. Her blood alcohol was about 0.02 which isn't nearly enough to be drunk even for a fifteen-year-old. Her physical exam showed… God." She stopped.

"Mom?"

"She has bruises all over her. She has evidence of… forced copulation. There's bruising on her wrists consistent with restraint."

My blood ran cold. "You're saying…"

"I'm saying someone did something terrible to her."

My hand went to my mouth as a slight gasp escaped. Mom's conflicted face looked ready to cry and kill at the same time.

"What do you want me to do, Mom?"

She put a hand on my shoulder. "Selena needs a friend right now. Later, she will need to call her parents and make a report with the police. She's been slim on details when I ask her."

"Do you think maybe we should call Dad?"

"It's not exactly his specialty."

"Yeah, but… from what I'm hearing, law enforcement around here kind of sucks."

"Let's try to get her to open up first."

"Okay."

We went past the nurse's station and rounded a corner. She didn't stop until we reached a room with glass windows covered by blinds. Mom gave the door a soft rap before opening it. I followed her inside.

Selena was in a hospital bed, wearing a gown. The covers were pulled up to the middle of her chest. There was an

IV in her arm with a yellowish liquid hanging beside her. Her head was bowed and her hair was covering most of her face.

"Selena? Selena, Marian is here."

"Hey, Selena," I said, stepping up on the opposite side of the bed. I reached down and gave her hand a gentle squeeze. "You're okay. You're safe now."

She didn't squeeze back.

"Selena," Mom said. "I called Marian because you need to talk to someone, okay? We're going to have to call your parents, but I thought I'd see if you wanted a friend with you right now." She waited a moment. "Do you want a friend here?"

There was a long pause before Selena slowly nodded.

"Is it okay if Marian sits with you for a bit?"

She nodded again.

"Okay, Sweetie. I'll check in on you in a little while."

There was no response as Mom left the room. I released Selena's hand and pulled a chair up next to the bed. I settled there and looked her over.

The normally bubbly Selena was statue-still. The gloom radiating from her was almost palatable in the air. My eyes fell onto the bruises on her arms. Not having any experience with this, I didn't know where to start.

"Selena? You know you're safe now, right?"

She didn't respond.

"Selena? Listen, it's just us in here, okay? It's just you and me. You know that, right? Look around. There's no one here but us."

Selena did raise her head slightly. It didn't move back

and forth, but I saw her right eye cut around the room. I held back a gasp as I saw the bruises around her neck.

"See? It's just us. Mom... Dr. Fitzwalter... said you needed a friend, didn't she?"

Selena gave another jerky nod.

"I'm your friend. Right, Selena?"

Another nod.

"You can talk to me. Anything you say will be between us. You know I don't talk, right? I'm not like Tina."

Selena burst into tears.

I jumped up and wrapped my arms around her shoulders as she blubbered against me. I shushed her gently, rubbing her back, trying to soothe her.

I held her until she stopped bawling and began whimpering. My eyes fell back to the bruises on her neck. I smoothed out her hair and did my best to comfort her. She sniffed and leaned heavily against my chest.

"Talk to me," I whispered into her hair.

"I shouldn't have let this happen," she whispered back.

I pulled her back and looked at her curiously. Her eyes avoided mine.

"Why would you say that?"

"Look at what happened to me."

"What did happen?"

She stared at her lap. "The party was starting to get boring, so I went for a walk around the edge of the woods. I figured maybe someone had a 'J' they wouldn't mind sharing."

I kept quiet and let her talk.

"I saw two people making out in the woods. I didn't

know them, so I just... left them alone."

I nodded along to encourage her to keep talking.

"I saw Corbin... well, his back. He was taking a wiz on a tree."

Again I nodded.

"I then saw Hood and his crew in a circle, talking."

I knew how she felt about Loxley. I interrupted there.

"Did you go talk to him finally?"

She gave a shy smile. "Yeah. I just walked right up to them and said hi.'"

"You did?"

"Uh-huh. I'd had a couple beers, so I guess I was just feeling brave."

If she couldn't handle her alcohol, she might not have realized she was walking into a lion's den.

"Did you just say hi or did you actually talk to them?"

Her face squinted like she was concentrating. "Yeah... I talked to him."

"About what?"

"Just... stuff. I asked him if he was okay since, you know, him and Brent had just went at it."

"Who was with him?"

"All his friends: Little John, Max, Scarlet, and Dale."

"Tuck?"

She shook her head.

"What did Loxley say?"

"He said he was fine. He told me not to worry about it."

"How'd he sound?"

She pondered the question. "Fine, I guess. But he's always been sweet to me. Not what you would expect from someone called 'Hood,' you know?"

I knew. "What about the others?"

"Well, I remember Max didn't talk, but he never does. Scarlet looked a bit miffed about something, but from what I've seen, that's normal for her. Little John was quiet, but he's always quiet. Dale? He's usually a talker, but he didn't have much to say."

Alarm bells were going off in my head. "Then what?"

"It was kind of awkward." I could tell she was thinking really hard. "Hood and I were the only ones that were talking. Like I said, he told me not to worry about it, but I could tell it bothered him."

This didn't sound like it was heading in a good direction. "Then what happened, Selena?"

"Nothing."

"What do you mean?"

"I mean nothing. Since they weren't in a talking mood, I made as graceful an exit as I could."

I mulled her answer over.

"I went back to the others," she went on. "Jody and Brent were talking, so I went to get me a beer. Jody pumped the keg and Brent worked the nozzle."

"That was your third?"

She nodded. "I don't drink much, but I figured I could handle one more."

"Do you remember what happened next?"

"Yeah. Hope came up and then we started talking while I drank. The boys went off somewhere. We talked for a few minutes and I needed to pee, so I told Hope I'd be right back. That's all I remember until I woke up."

It sounded to me like Selena was a lightweight. Three beers would've had me stumbling. The fact she remembered nothing meant she ran into the wrong person… or people… and they took advantage of the situation.

It made my heart drop into my stomach.

"What happened when you woke up?"

Tears flowed. "I woke up wrapped in a dirty sleeping bag a ways from where the fire had been. I didn't have any pants or underwear on. I went to get out and I felt the inside of the bag was wet. I… I reached my hand in there and when I brought it out, it was bloody. It was still dark, but the moon was bright, remember?"

I nodded.

She gasped and kept talking. "And I hurt. God, I hurt Marian. I screamed and no one came to help me. I screamed and screamed and no one came!"

The last part came out as a shriek and I quickly put my arms around her again to quiet her. Her body shook violently as she cried against me.

"Mrs.… Dr.… Fitzwalter… put a bunch of stitches… down there. I can't even sit down. It hurts so much. What did they do to me, Marian?"

"I don't know Selena. I don't know."

"Will God forgive me?"

That question struck me by surprise. "What do you mean?"

"I… I was… the whole… purity… thing."

I pulled her away just enough I could look into her eyes. "There's nothing to forgive, Selena. Someone did something bad to you. This isn't your fault."

"But... but..."

"No buts. You didn't ask for this. No one asks for this. And whoever did this to you has to be caught."

She didn't respond.

"If you don't say anything," I pressed, "they'll do it again."

I began rubbing soothing circles against her back again, wanting her calm. I didn't like the thoughts that were going through my mind.

She'd seen Hood and his crew. He'd been polite. They'd been awkward. She left, got a beer, talked to Hope, and going to the bathroom was the last thing she remembered.

Would Hood do this? He was a criminal. They all were. I thought Hood had left, and I'd bet everyone at that party thought the same thing.

I could eliminate Brent, Jody, or Hope. They weren't anywhere alone with Selena and I couldn't imagine a woman doing this to another woman, especially one she treated like a friend. Tina, I might have believed, but not Hope. Of course, Selena also said she saw Scarlet.

"Do you have any clue who did this to you?"

Selena shook her head.

"Would you tell me if you did?"

She nodded.

"Was there anything else weird you can think of?"

She cried softly again. "It's all I've been thinking about. The only thing I can think of was something I did — talking to Hood. That, and the last beer tasted a little funny. In fact, I think I remember Jody saying something about the kegs from that truck stop by the interstate have an aftertaste sometimes since they're not usually as fresh."

That wasn't a lot of help.

"Do you remember seeing anyone else?"

"It was mostly white kids left. Jermaine's crew had left about an hour before. I think I passed Alonzo Tuck. That kid whose dad just died..."

"Cory Boxer?"

"Yeah... him. I saw him. He was pretty trashed."

"Did you talk to him?"

She shook her head. "Someone... one of his cousins, I think... was helping him to their truck."

That would probably put him in the 'not guilty' category.

"Selena? We need to call your parents."

She stiffened.

"I know you don't want to. But my mom is going to have to. It's the law. They're also going to have to call the police."

"I don't want to." It came out as 'wanna.'

"I know," I soothed. "But like I said, if you don't report this, they're going to get away with it and might do it again. We need to stop them."

"I don't want people to know."

I bent down and brushed her hair out of her face so I could look into her eyes. "Selena? The only thing worse than people knowing is if no one knows. Because that will mean they'll get away with it and be free to hurt someone else."

She looked away and didn't answer.

"Hey," I said, brushing her hair out of her face again.

"You want me to call my dad? He's a pretty good cop and he's got contacts at the state level."

"Would you?"

"I would," I said with a soft smile, glad to do something that would actually be helpful. Whether Dad could do anything was another matter, but I had to at least try.

"Okay."

"I'll call him now," I said, getting up.

She went back to gazing at her lap.

"I'm going to tell my mom you want to see her. She's going to want to talk about calling your parents and the police, so be prepared."

She nodded and continued to stare.

I slipped out of the room and walked down the hall towards the doctor's lounge. As I rounded the corner, I saw Mom standing at the nurse's station, writing on a chart.

"Mom?"

She raised her head as I approached.

"She's ready to talk," I said in a low voice. "And she's ready for you to get in contact with her parents and the police."

"I'll call her folks and the sheriff's department right now."

I opened my mouth to thank her when I spotted something behind her. Through the glass, I saw into the reception area. Standing at the desk, I saw a familiar figure talking to Ernestine — Loxley.

"Excuse me," I said quickly before I brushed past.

Chapter 22

Loxley and Ernestine stopped mid conversation as I pushed through the door.

"You! Me! Outside!"

He and the obviously nervous receptionist shared a look before he gave a nonchalant shrug. To my annoyance, he opened the door and held it for me.

I stormed through it and, without giving him a chance, made a beeline through the waiting room and shoved through the exit onto the sidewalk. The rain was coming down at a respectable drizzle. I stopped under the overhang as Loxley joined me.

"Can I help you with something?"

Why did he have to sound so damn polite? "What are you doing here?"

He shrugged. "Visiting someone."

I shivered from the chill. "Who?"

"I didn't realize it was any of your business," he replied. Then he looked me over. "Are you cold? Do you want my jacket?"

What was it with him? "I'm fine. And I want to know what you and Ernestine were talking about."

"Catching up. She's an old family friend."

"I don't believe you."

He just shrugged his shoulders again as if to say, *"Yeah, so?"*

I took my shot. "You're here about Selena, aren't you?"

"She's here?"

"Cut the crap, Hood. You know she is."

For the first time, his expression changed. The cool demeanor vanished, and I saw... pain. But it wasn't at my confirmation that Selena was here. He already knew that. It was because I called him 'Hood' instead of 'Loxley.'

"Has she said anything?"

"Why?"

"Why what?"

"Why do you want to know?"

"Has she said anything?"

My eyes narrowed. "Answer my question. Why do you want to know?"

"I need to know."

"Why?"

"That's my business."

I was getting a bad feeling here.

"A little. She needed a friend and Mom called me."

Loxley nodded. "Good."

"There's nothing good about this... Hood."

Once again, I caught a brief glimpse of a chink in his armor. "I mean, it's good that you're here. She probably needs a friend right now."

The questions started flooding my brain hard and fast again. Most revolved around what he knew.

"Yeah, well, it's not like she could talk to Tina about this."

Loxley nodded in agreement. He then took a couple of steps to his left. Not wanting him any closer to me, I shifted to keep him in front of me.

"Did you see her last night?" I questioned.

"Yeah, she came over and talked to me and my crew for a minute."

"I thought you'd left."

"We had stopped to plot our next move before we got on our bikes. She came up on us and we chatted."

He took a couple more steps and I shifted with him. "She asked you about Brent?"

He nodded once.

"Where'd you go after that?"

"Home."

"What about the rest of them?"

"Max went home..."

"How do you know?"

The question obviously puzzled him. "Because I know Max and he had to get up early to help his dad. Are you asking about alibis?"

I ignored his question. "What about the rest?"

"Little John went home. He was going to get up early and give our tree stands one more check before bow season starts. His mom and two sisters will vouch for that. Dale said he was going to his dad's shop for a little while. No telling how many people were there on a Saturday night. Scarlet was with me, waiting in the alley while I talked to you. She then followed me back to the farm."

That struck me as odd. "She did?"

Loxley must've read my facial expression. "She did. If you knew Scarlet, you'd know that's not the least bit uncommon."

"Why is she staying with you?"

"That's personal."

Was it my business if Loxley was friends with benefits with a half sibling? Not really. My problem was she was an alibi I'd have to discredit.

"So Scarlet was with you all night..."

"...and Grandpa. Why are you asking me this?"

"I think you know, Hood."

For a third time, his eyes betrayed him. "You always think the worst of us, don't you?"

"You keep giving me reason to.

He sighed and ran his fingers through his damp hair. Being wet, it laid down for him, slicking back and making him look like a movie gangster — one of the suave ones, not one of the beefy 'yous guys' ones.

"I think it's just your nature."

"I think you're full of it!" I stepped forward and pointed my finger at his chest. "You've not only got a reputation, but I've seen how you act. Someone did something horrible to Selena and I think it was you. You're pretending you don't know what happened, but you do. You've got it in you. You were one of the last people she remembers seeing. You announced you were leaving the party, yet you hung around. I swear to God if it was you…"

"You'll what?"

"I'll see you're punished."

Loxley shook his head. "The cops won't catch these people."

"How do you know it was more than one person?"

"I pay attention."

That answer didn't make any sense to me. "Maybe because you saw it… because you were there?"

"No."

"You're friends with who did this?"

"Not a chance in hell," he replied through gritted teeth.

I realized something as he gave his short, clipped answers. When he'd moved, it was in a circle so we ended up in the same place the other started. From his position, I was completely dry, and he'd subtly put himself where his back was getting wet.

Very gentlemanly, but I wasn't in the mood to appreciate it. "You know who did this?"

"Maybe. I'm starting to think so."

"Who?"

He shook his head.

"So you're protecting them."

"No," he corrected. "I'm protecting Selena… and you."

"I don't follow."

"Did you ever think that if the people that did this knew Selena could identify them, or told someone who they were, that they might be in danger?"

"The cops are coming."

"Barnsdale Sheriff's Department couldn't find their asses with both hands and a flashlight, even if they wanted to catch who did this."

"You don't think they want to catch who did this?"

Loxley sighed. "Mark my words, Marian. They'll come in here, ask some questions, and won't get anywhere. They'll make her think she brought this on herself. They'll tell her that there's no case and tell her to forget it and get on with her life."

"That's not fair! She's the victim!"

"I agree. That's not my opinion. That's a prediction and an accurate one, I'm betting. I've got to go, Marian. Thank you for talking to me, even if it was to spew venom in my direction. I know after last night, it took a lot for you to do so."

He turned to walk away, and I said to his back. "Hey. How do you know what's going to happen?"

He answered over his shoulder, "I've been around, Marian."

"It's happened before?"

He didn't respond, and he didn't turn around.

"How do we stop it?"

He halted but didn't look back at me. "You don't. Someone is going to have to figure out for sure who did this and put an end to it. The law isn't going to help her."

"Who is?"

Loxley started walking again. As he stepped into the rain, I saw him reach underneath the neck of his jacket and pull his hood up without breaking stride.

"Unbelievable!" Mom exclaimed.

We were sitting at the kitchen table. Mom was on her third glass of wine. The wings Dad picked up for us to enjoy this afternoon were sitting on the stove untouched.

"I don't know what to tell you," Dad said slowly.

After Loxley left me standing, I went to the chapel. I didn't have my rosary, but I still said a prayer for Selena. I also used the time to think. As usual, Loxley had left me with more questions than answers. My parents used to hire this babysitter that liked trashy romance novels and I'd read a couple when no one was looking. They used to make dark and mysterious men sound so intriguing. Now they were just annoying.

Once I finished, I found Mom and followed her home. She had called Dad and he was going to do his best to butt into the investigation. Selena's parents had made it, but I didn't talk to them. Her mom looked like someone had died and her dad looked ready to make it so.

"You're telling me those... oafs... upset her?"

"It's a delicate situation," Dad said sadly. "And unfortunately, few people know how to handle it. They screwed up. No excuses. You... you know what I mean."

"It's sickening..."

Dad sighed. "But they have a point, Ellie. Unless we find a witness, someone confesses, or she remembers something, there is no case."

"They made her cry?" I gawked.

Mom snorted behind her wine glass. "No, them telling her she should've been more careful did."

Now I was mad. "What?"

"Kitten," Dad explained. "You know how I make you carry Mace in your purse and how I always tell you to listen to your gut and be aware of your surroundings and to always be in control of yourself?"

"Yes, sir?"

"This is why."

That got me from angry to hornet mad. "Are you saying this is her fault?"

He held up a hand. "No, I'm not. Nobody deserves this. Bad people look for opportunities to do bad things. In a perfect world, precaution wouldn't be necessary. But this isn't a perfect world. It's far from it. That's why I would carry a gun even if I wasn't a cop. It's also why we have Cowboy..."

I snorted, remembering how my dog didn't even posture at Loxley. Dad either paid no attention to me or had his mind preoccupied.

"...to try to head trouble off at the pass. This isn't Selena's fault. She was an opportunity for some bad people to do some bad things. The last thing I want you to think is that I'm blaming her."

"What are you going to do about it?" Mom asked.

"The only thing I can do — shake the bushes and see what I can flush out."

"That's it?" I asked.

"Rape is notoriously hard to convict on, Kitten." He looked at Mom. "You know that."

I snapped. "Why? Her injuries are more than enough to see someone abused her."

"Because it is," Dad snapped back. Now he was getting angry. "First off, we have to get a suspect." He looked at Mom. "You did a rape kit, right?"

She nodded.

"Unless it comes back to a known perp, which is unlikely since it was a high school party, we've got an unsub. So I have to build a case. I have to find suspects, put them at the party, show they had motive and opportunity, blow holes in any alibi they put up, hopefully find a witness or two, and get a reason to get DNA samples from them that will hold up in court."

Mom sat stone-faced.

"Then," he went on. "I have to be right. The DNA has to match. But that's when the difficulty goes up ten degrees. If they fight it, which they will, then Selena is on trial. They'll mention the fact she had alcohol in her system..."

"It wasn't much," Mom mumbled.

"It's enough," Dad continued. "Plus, you tested her hours after the attack. The defense would argue it was much higher when this happened. Did you do a drug screen?"

"She tested positive for marijuana as well."

"Anything that could classify as a date rape drug? GHB? Roofies?"

"We don't have the means to test for those, just the more common street drugs."

"So we've got a teenage girl who was at a party. She

had booze and pot in her system. The defense is going to question her..."

"She would have to testify?" I asked.

"She's the victim. She would have to tell the jury what she remembers. Plus, the law says the defendant has the right to face his accuser." He shook his head. "And it's the defense attorney's job to discredit witnesses, including Selena. So they'd drag up her sexual history..."

"She was a virgin!"

Dad held up his hand again. "Can they bring it up? It depends on how strong an argument they make that it's relevant. And she only said she's never had sex. Her word doesn't make it fact."

"Now you're calling her a liar!"

"Marian!" Dad said with more sharpness in his voice. "I'm laying out what a defense attorney would argue. Think worst-case scenario. What if it's someone with money and/or connections? They will not have some public defender that's going to try to plead them out. They'll hire someone good at what they do."

"So she will never sleep at night?"

Dad sighed. "I don't know. I hate it when we have to get lucky, but..."

I pushed away from the table. "This sucks!"

"I'm sorry," Dad said. You could already hear the defeat in his voice. "I wish there was more I could do. But even if I chose to cross a line, I wouldn't know where to start."

Loxley would.

He'd already told me he suspected who it was. For one brief moment, I considered finding out where he lived, driving out to that shanty, and begging him to deliver vengeance.

What would it cost me? Would he want money? Would he want my dad to owe him? Would he want a... favor... from me?

Was he even telling me the truth? For all I knew, he was the one that did this. He was there and he had a violent streak. He could very well have been the one that did this to Selena.

My brain told me he was on the suspect list. My heart said he wasn't.' While I'd seen Loxley punch Jody and slap a beer out of Brent's hand, I'd never seen him react unprovoked. I'd also never seen him even speak to a woman with anything but respect, even teachers. Dad said trust my gut, and my gut said Loxley didn't do this.

But my brain made it clear it wasn't letting him off that easy.

"Is there anything I can do for Selena?" I asked Mom.

"Not right now. She'll need some time to heal. I wouldn't expect her back at school for a while."

"Kitten?"

I looked at Dad.

"How mad are you?"

"Seriously?"

"Yes. Answer me. How mad are you?"

"I want whoever did this to pay for it."

"Then keep your eyes and ears open. You hear anything? Bring it to me. I want these people as badly as you do." His eyes got hard. "The way I see it, it could've been you."

"If I hear anything, Dad, you'll be the first to know."

Chapter 23

THE BATTLE DIDN'T START until lunchtime.

Everyone ignored me. Brent pretended I didn't exist and Loxley had nothing to say to me. I didn't have the brainpower to worry about it.

I couldn't get my mind off Selena.

I walked into the lunchroom alone and looked around. Everything appeared normal. Jermaine and his crew were in their corner. Grace and the other pregnant girl were at their table. Cory and his friends were at their usual spot, as were Loxley and company.

With nowhere else to go, I went to my clique. Brent was on one end of the table, so I took the other end beside Hope.

"You ready for Homecoming?" She asked me before my butt even settled.

"I guess," I mumbled.

"Anybody heard about Selena?" Mallory asked.

Tina had, of course. "Yeah, I heard she finally got more

than she could handle."

My eyes narrowed.

"She enjoyed the party, huh?" Jody asked.

"Oh, yeah," Tina agreed. "Word is she took on four guys at once."

"What?" Hope asked. "I don't believe that bullshit for a second!"

"You know how she is."

I finally spoke up. "No, Tina. How is she?"

Tina must've caught the tone of my voice because she didn't answer. But Brent did.

"You know 'Slut-lina.' She's made more men out of the sophomore class than the Army ever will."

"That's not true!" I snapped.

He shrugged. "That's her rep. And we can't seem to help our reps, can we, Marian?"

"What's that supposed to mean?"

"You know, kind of like you have the rep of being a cock tease that walks around here like she's got a corncob shoved up her ass."

"Excuse me," I said, picking up my lunch bag and standing.

"What's the matter, Maid Marian?" Brent taunted. "You jealous you couldn't find a group of these rednecks to make a woman out of you?"

The entire lunchroom went pin-drop quiet. Even the lunch ladies had stopped serving.

"Maybe I..."

"Maybe you just get off on being so cold ice cubes won't melt in your box?"

I turned to walk off, not wanting this to get any uglier. I saw Loxley standing up.

"Yeah, walk away, bitch. I'm done with you anyway. Go back to your slut friend. You can turn 'em on and they can run a train on her!"

The sound that broke the silence was a chair scraping as Loxley came charging around his table with vengeance in his eyes. Little John grabbed him by the shoulders and Dale quickly tried to step in front of him. It didn't even slow him down. Loxley's arms flew back behind him as he sidestepped Dale, sliding free and leaving his leather vest hanging in Little John's hands.

Oh, shit!

He blew past me with his eyes radar-locked on Brent. I heard more chairs scraping as people stood to get a better view.

Loxley stepped right in Brent's face. "You ever disrespect her again, I swear before God I will end you."

The Loxley from Saturday night, yelling at Brent, was scary. The Loxley here now, with a voice just above a whisper, was a notch above terrifying.

The lunchroom got even quieter, if that was possible. Tombs had more sound. People that had raised cans to their mouths didn't even swallow. Most of the students weren't even breathing. Including me.

"You ever threaten me again," Brent warned, "and I'll make sure you never take another breath."

Loxley smirked. "Your people have threatened my family for seven generations. Yet here we are."

"Is that a fact?"

"Oh, yeah. And if I ever see or hear of you so much as looking at her again, it will be a painful one."

Now it was Brent who smirked. "You think she wants you speaking for her? She's so far out of your league she wouldn't touch you with a biohazard suit. I know for a fact she wouldn't if she knew about Fat Lighter Hollow."

"What about your brother's truck stop?"

Obviously, that didn't bother him. Brent rolled his eyes like he couldn't care less.

"Or what about Saint Florence, Brent?"

That got Brent's attention. "How... how do you know about that?"

"Yeah, rich boy. We all got secrets, don't we?"

Brent's face had lost all color.

Loxley's eyes narrowed. "No more warnings. You look at her funny... you speak to her... you even make her feel uncomfortable being in the same zip code... they'll never find your body."

"That so?"

Brent didn't sound nearly as tough as he did a minute ago. Fear was visible in his eyes.

"Guaranteed. I'll paint this goddamn cafeteria with your blood!"

"Hey!" Mr. Culpeper shouted from the door. "Hey! Both of you! Break it up! Now!"

Loxley gave one last glare, turned, and stormed out.

Conversation began again at an inaudible murmur. Brent glanced at me, snorted, and sat back down like he hadn't been the least bit ruffled. Tina frowned. Jody started whispering in Brent's ear. Jermaine shook his head in disbelief.

I took the opportunity to turn and hurry out of the cafeteria. As I passed, I noticed Little John, Scarlet, Dale, and Max all watching me as I left.

I got a dozen steps into the hall and the bell rang. I never had a chance to open my lunch. Sighing, I made my way to Miss Chen's class.

Loxley was already in his seat. He was so angry, he was vibrating.

I didn't know if I wanted to talk to him or not. I wanted to thank him for the assist, but I didn't know the reason behind it.

Thankfully, he didn't try to speak to me either. He stared straight ahead with his arms folded. Miss Chen was looking at him with concern. I think in that moment even she might have been afraid of Loxley.

"Oh, my God," Miss Chen said, her hands going to cover her mouth.

I told her everything, starting with the party, covering Sunday with Selena, and finishing with what happened today.

"That poor girl. I have her second period."

"I knew that. Miss Chen, would you mind if I ate my lunch? I didn't get to."

"Please do."

I felt another headache coming on. Breakfast had been a

lost cause too and if I didn't get something on my stomach, I knew I was looking at a raging migraine in my near future.

"Do we know who did this?"

"Honestly? I wanted to ask you about that."

"Me?"

I nodded. "Yes, ma'am. You know more about what's going on in this county than I do."

"I honestly don't know of anyone who could've done this."

"Have there been others?"

She pondered. "Even if the answer was 'yes,' Marian, I couldn't betray someone's confidence like that."

"I don't want names. I just need a yes or no."

"One that I know of."

"How long ago?"

"Around Spring Break last year."

"Was it reported?"

"Yes."

I chewed thoughtfully. "If you'd give me a name, I could get Dad to pull some strings. Maybe he could connect the cases."

Miss Chen shook her head. "I won't do it. However, I will talk to her and see if she would talk to you."

"She's... here? In this school?"

She nodded once.

"Did she name any suspects that you know of?"

"Not to me. As far as the police go, I couldn't say."

I took a shot in the dark. "She mention Loxley?"

"Why would she mention Robert?"

"He was one of the last people Selena saw before she

blacked out. Plus, he has a criminal record."

"I don't buy that."

"Of course you don't. You're Hood's number one fan."

She snorted. "While I am grateful for what he's done, and continues to do for this community, I can assure you I'm not numero uno. There are plenty of people who think the world of Robert Loxley."

"But it's better that I don't know, huh?"

Miss Chen sighed and nodded. "Marian, if you knew, it would mean you had to know. If you had to know it meant something happened to you that you'd rather not happen."

"How can me knowing be so dangerous?"

"Because it's just a need-to-know basis. Had Robert and John not stepped in to help me once, I wouldn't be privy to anything. But they've learned they can trust me."

"You people are annoying!"

She sighed again. "I can see why you'd think that. But, Marian, we are products of our environment."

I chewed, swallowed, and pointed my fork at her. "And people can't change?"

"Robert did."

"How?"

Miss Chen didn't answer, but her look made me think she was considering my question. I took the pause to get another bite.

She finally spoke. "Do you know who my favorite writer is?"

"Not a clue."

She sat down. "Aristotle."

"Why?"

"I tend to agree with a lot of his philosophies. Not all of them, but a lot. I also find some of his quotes to be relevant."

"Such as?"

She took a deep breath. "Anger is a gift."

"It is?"

Miss Chen nodded. "Aristotle said that anybody can become angry. That's easy. But to be angry with the right person to the right degree and at the right time and for the right purpose, and in the right way — that is not within everyone's power. And it's not easy."

"What are you saying?"

"I'm saying that Robert learned from his mistake. Before he was arrested, he was just angry. Now he's learned that anger is a gift if it's acted upon the right way."

"Robert Loxley is a criminal, Miss Chen. You can color him with pretty words all you want. He's no better than a common street thug."

"Marian," she replied patiently. "If he is what you say he is, why do you talk to him?"

Good question. "I find myself in conversation with him whether I chose to be or not."

"That's B.S."

"Really?" I challenged. "So why do you think I talk to him?"

"Because you see something. Despite his exterior and the surrounding rumors, you're the type of person who makes up their own mind. And I get the sense your heart hasn't decided just yet."

"My heart has nothing to do with this because my mind is made up."

"Has it?"

I both loved and hated it when people pushed me to think. Dad said I got my critical thinking from Mom and I normally enjoyed a challenge. But I hated it when it was on something abstract, like feelings-- things that weren't always black and white.

"I tend to look for the good in people," I admitted. "So... yeah, I tried to see it in Loxley. But I keep seeing bad around every corner."

"Was he bad today?"

She had a point. "No. But it makes me wonder why he stood up for me."

"I know you don't want to hear this, but it's been my experience that Robert's intentions tend to be noble. He might not always do good things, but I believe they're for the right reasons. And I think if you asked the right people, they would tell you the same thing."

That made me think of a question. "Has Robert Loxley ever asked you for anything?"

"Yes."

"And?"

"And what?"

"Did you give it to him?"

She smiled softly. "Every time. Mainly because when he asked for it, whatever he wanted was something I would've given anyway."

"What was it?"

She shook her head.

"Why?"

"Secrets."

"I wish I could be in on these secrets."

"You think you do. I assure you Marian, you don't."

"Miss Chen, with all due respect, you're full of it."

"What do you mean?"

"You keep telling me that nothing is what it seems. And you keep saying that I'm judging Loxley and that I know nothing about him. Did you ever think, just maybe, you don't know anything about me either?"

"I know enough."

"So you think."

"I know that you're a good girl from a good family. I know that you're not from Barnsdale County. I know that if you avoid trouble, you will soon leave this misery, never return, and have the life fitting a woman of your station."

"Did you know I was the type to sit with a girl I'm only casually friends with who'd been raped just because she had nobody else and my heart broke for her? Did you know I caught Loxley breaking into my house to find something that belonged to a poor widow and I didn't turn him in? Did you know I'm unhappy here because everyone is out for themselves and this community is rotten to the core? Did you know my 'friends' abandoned me because I wouldn't get on my knees in the dirt for Brent?"

She rested her chin on her hands and listened to me as I made my confession.

"I want to believe Loxley is a good person," I took a breath and swallowed. "There are enough people that seem to believe it. But every time I start to think the same, something blows up in my face. He tried to pick a fight at the party. He was one of the last people Selena remembers seeing. He just threatened to kill Brent. Not beat up. Kill. He wasn't being figurative and I dare you to even try to argue he was. Combine that with some of the other stuff I hear and his criminal record and how can I see him as good?"

"You're confusing 'moral' and 'lawful'. When you wrap your head around the difference, you'll understand Robert Loxley."

"Do you think he'd actually do it? Kill Brent if he hurt me?"

"I can't say. But it's been my experience that if Robert says he'll do something..."

Chapter 24

HOMECOMING AT BARNSDALE HIGH School was a simpler ordeal than it was back home.

In Dallas, it was a week-long celebration. There'd been obvious excitement for a week beforehand, with special t-shirts for sale and a different dress-up theme every day leading up to Friday. School let out right after lunch, followed by a parade, and the dance itself was formal.

In Barnsdale County, there wasn't a theme week. There weren't any t-shirts. School did let out after lunch, but there wasn't a parade, which struck me as really odd. From what I was told, people would come straight from the football game to the dance.

I stayed after the final horn to clean up our sideline mess, and by the time I got to the dance it was in full swing.

I didn't want to be there, but they expected the cheerleaders to show up. Considering the Rebel's lost 42-0, I was hoping no one would be in a celebratory mood and I could get away with slipping out early. To top it off, I'd forgotten my sports bra and my straps were digging into my shoulders.

Black and red crepe paper adorned the gym, which was packed to the gills, and the heat was turned up way too high. I looked for somewhere to shuck my jacket off but had no luck. Someone organized a table with refreshments. I didn't see a punch bowl, but there were canned sodas and bottled waters.

"Marian?"

I turned around to find Hope standing there. She was biting her lower lip nervously.

"Can I... talk to you for a minute?"

I didn't need this crap tonight. "Sure."

We made our way to a corner of the gym. Hope was bouncing from foot-to-foot, nervous about something.

"What's up?"

"I need to ask you something."

"Okay... go ahead."

She took a deep breath. "I'm pretty much a shoo-in to be captain next year. You know that, right?"

"It's no secret."

"Well, I've got a problem. Tina called me last night. The rules are there must be cause for someone to be kicked off the squad and there has to be a vote, which isn't going to happen. But she's pressing for you to not be invited back."

I just shrugged. I was too down to care.

She went on, "Tina is slated to be my co-captain next year, so I'm sort of in a bind."

"You're asking me not to come out next year?"

She bit her lip again. "Not quite."

"So... what are you asking?"

"I like you, Marian. Lots of people do. You're smart and your ideas for routines are good. And I need a favor."

"Hope... just spit it out, okay?"

"I'm going to ask you to come back on one condition: you take co-captain. You agree and I won't care what Tina does. You say no, then... yeah, I'm going to ask you to not come back because it would eventually get pretty nasty."

"You want me to be your co-captain?"

"Yeah. Will you do it?"

"Why are you willing to side with me over your friend?"

"Let's get something straight," she snapped. "That bitch is not my friend! We hang out because our families either do business or socialize and I'm afraid if I don't, her parents and her friends' parents will make trouble for my daddy. If you asked around our lunch table, you'd find out I'm not the only one. She is a horrible person and words can't describe how much I hate her."

I hadn't known Hope long, but that was the first time I had seen any harshness from her.

"But you're willing to go against her now?"

"That's because, unlike Tina, I can honestly see us being friends. You're not fake like she is, and you're obviously more trustworthy."

"But what about your family ties?"

"Tina isn't the only one that can politic over the summer. All I have to do is tell the other girls the truth. With your dance and gymnastics experience, you'd be a bigger asset than anyone else that's going to try out. Plus, unlike Tina, we don't have to worry if you're going to stab us in the back. If there's a solid majority vote, she can't do shit about it."

"Can I think about it?"

She nodded. "You've got plenty of time. I just wanted to give you a heads up. For real, I meant everything I just said."

"Okay. I'll consider it."

She hopped forward and hugged me. "Thank you. And for what it's worth, Brent was out of line."

That made me feel a little better. Maybe everybody in this sorry place wasn't as bad as I thought they were.

I rejoined the crowd and began surveying the room. Just about everybody was there except the two men giving me an ulcer. I pulled at the hem of my jacket, trying to alleviate the stifling heat, and glanced around in search of a teacher who might be willing to adjust the temperature or at least let some fresh air in.

The opening notes of a slow song began and I saw Cory Boxer standing against the wall. He was wearing jeans, a blue shirt, and a striped tie. The mixture of country boy and snappy dress gave me a smile. I decide to approach him.

"Hey, Cory."

His eyelids blinked rapidly, as if he was surprised that I had spoken to him. "Hi...um... Marian."

"You by yourself?"

He nodded.

"You want to dance?"

Cory's Adam's apple bobbed and he nodded again.

"Be a gentleman, okay?"

"Okay."

I led him to the dance floor. He put both hands modestly on my waist and kept space between us. I let my hands land on his shoulders. He was just an inch or two taller than I was. He was smooth enough he didn't step on my feet, but he was obviously more of the shuffle-type slow dancer.

I didn't mind. "I never got the chance to tell you I'm sorry about your dad."

Cory nodded. "Thank you."

"The police have any leads?"

"His killer's been handled."

I faltered for a second, but I thought I recovered before he noticed. "Really?"

"Yeah, word is there was plenty of evidence that guy that got waxed was who killed my dad."

"Any clue who did it?"

He shrugged. "Who cares?"

Cory's words and his tone didn't match. While he might have said he didn't care, the way he spoke said the opposite— that he approved.

I changed the subject. "How's your mom holding up?"

"She's okay. She's sort of taking it day by day."

"I can't imagine."

Then it was he who jumped topics. "You had any more trouble with Brent?"

"No," I replied. "He hasn't said a word."

Cory smirked. "Hood scared him off."

"Maybe."

"That whole situation was weird."

"How do you figure?"

He shrugged. "Hood rarely gets involved in high school drama."

My mouth ran again before my brain could engage. "He just prefers the adult criminal acts?"

To my surprise, Cory grinned.

"Why do you think he did it?"

"I think he likes you."

I huffed. "I doubt it. He probably saw a chance to stick it to Brent and took it."

"I don't think so."

"Why?"

"Hood is a cool customer. He's always in control. I saw some girl last year get in his face yelling that he thought he was too good to date her. You know, just being a drama queen. Hood never lost it. Scarlet did… but not Hood."

"He punched Jody for calling your dad a 'piece of shit.'"

"He did?"

I nodded. "Yeah, the morning after he died. You weren't at school. But that doesn't mean he likes me, Cory. Brent and Loxley have this deep-seated hatred. I think they look for ways to one-up each other."

He didn't say anything. The song concluded and he hugged me gently. I returned the sentiment.

"Thanks," he said sincerely.

"Thank you," I replied. "You have fun."

We separated and I wiped my forehead. The cuff of my jacket came away damp. I pulled my hair up in a ponytail. Spying the refreshment table, I figured I could get a drink. I made the turn and ran into Brent.

"There you are."

I stopped dead. "Here I am."

"I've been looking for you."

"Why?"

"I need to talk to you."

"No, you don't."

"Yeah… I do."

"I don't want any trouble."

"There won't be any," he assured me. "Hood isn't here."

I glanced around, but not to confirm what he just told me. I wanted to make sure we were visible.

"What do you want?"

"I wanted to apologize."

"Fine. You did."

He blew out a long breath. "No, I really mean it. I was drunk and stupid."

"I can agree with that."

Brent gazed down at me. "Look, I'm not going to lie. You're a good-looking woman and… well, I had too much to drink. I've been hot for you since we first met and I let my mouth get away from me."

"A drunk man's words are a sober man's thoughts."

"Oh, and I'm being honest here, I had some thoughts like that. Like I said, Marian, you're pretty damn hot. But you're also a lady and the way I acted was no way to treat a lady."

"You weren't drunk in the cafeteria."

He winced. "No, I wasn't. I fucked up and let myself stew about it the rest of the weekend. Temper got the best of me. I should've just kept my damn mouth shut till I'd calmed down."

I could agree with that.

"Forgive me?"

"I don't know if I can," I admitted, "at least not yet."

"I understand."

Just like any other time, he sounded as sincere as your average politician — like he was pacifying me. But Barnsdale was making me jaded.

"Can we at least be friends? Seriously, I won't ask you out or talk about you or anything. I just don't want you mad at me."

"I'm still mad."

He kept pressing. "And you have a right to be. But I know I need to work my way back into your good graces. Just... let me at least try?"

I felt conflicted. He wasn't asking me for anything. He was trying to clear the air and see if he could make amends. On the other hand, he sounded so damn rehearsed. Not only that, but he waited a week to apologize and had blasted me in front of the entire school in the meantime.

"You look hot."

My eyes narrowed at him.

"I mean," he corrected. "You're sweating."

"Yeah, well, it's hot in here."

"Can I get you a drink?"

"I was on my way there when you stopped me."

"I'm trying to make amends. The least you can do is let me get you a drink."

I sighed. "Fine."

"Water?"

"Yeah."

"Okay. I'll be right back."

He walked away and my eyes followed him. He maneuvered around Jody and they passed a quick, low hand slap without Brent stopping. Jody turned away before I could make eye contact with him.

I wondered what that was all about. It was a low-five, nothing more. Maybe Jody was congratulating his bro that he'd gotten me to talk to him. This place had made me paranoid. Giving up, I shrugged off my jacket and tied it around my waist. I was cooler in just my cheerleading uniform, but not by much.

It was then that I noticed Dale Alan walking across the gym away from me. I lost him in the crowd and I started scanning faces. If one outlaw was around, it was likely there were more.

In the corner, sitting on the top bleacher, was Tuck. He had his arms propped on his knees with his hands folded, talking with a girl I had Anatomy with but whose name I couldn't remember. He didn't seem to notice me either.

Brent was taking so long that I was ready to go get the water myself. I huffed and started waving my hand in front of my face again, trying to generate some kind of breeze.

"Here you go," he said from behind me.

I took it and quickly twisted the top off. It came easily. I got three swallows down before I even tasted it.

I made a face. "This tastes kind of weird."

"Yeah, they didn't have any cold at the table. What they had was at least room temperature. I poured one out and filled it from the fountain."

It did have an aftertaste, but at least it was cold. I chugged down a few more swallows.

"So, you want to dance or something?"

He was trying to play nice, so I went along with it. "Maybe later. Let me cool off first."

"Okay."

"I just saw Dale Alan," I said after getting another swallow.

Brent shrugged.

"If Loxley is here, is there going to be a problem?"

He shook his head. "Just don't tell him I'm bothering you. I think he'll be okay."

That was good enough for me. I finished the water and started looking for a trash can. Brent held out his hand and I passed the empty bottle to him. He stuck it in the pocket of his khakis.

"Now, how about that dance?"

I shrugged. "Okay."

He took my hand and led me back to the floor. We passed a trash can full of bottles and he threw mine away. We got to the edge and he turned to face me.

"You're on probation," I warned.

Like Cory, his hands went to my waist but in the appropriate spots. "Alan is leaving."

I turned my head and glanced over. Sure enough, I caught Dale's leather-covered back as he walked out the door.

"See," he assured me. "No problem."

I shrugged and we went back to dancing.

"Thanks for giving me a second chance," Brent said as

we moved.

"It's not really a second chance. I mean, it is, but we're not back to where we were. You're going to have to earn your way back to even being considered okay much less going out with."

He nodded once. "Alright."

Despite shedding my jacket, I felt warm again. I was also feeling dizzy. I shook my head like a horse trying to shoo a fly. It only made my head swim worse.

"You okay?"

I nodded. "Yeah, the heat is just getting to me, I think."

My mouth had gone dry again and I tried to swallow but failed. My vision got a little blurry. I chalked that up to getting sweat in my eyes. The song ended and Brent gazed down at me.

"Marian?"

"I think I'm going to head home, Brent. I'm not feeling well."

"Okay..."

Before he could say something to reinforce his previous apology, I turned and walked off.

My stomach flip-flopped and I hurried towards the door, afraid I was going to throw up. I couldn't remember ever feeling that nauseous. A blast of cold air greeted outside. I shivered as it hit my sweat-soaked skin.

I started walking towards my car, rubbing my eyes. The streetlights were blurred. I coughed and it felt like the water was coming back up. I hoped to get home before it happened. I untied my jacket from my waist and fumbled with my keys before finally grasping them and retying my jacket around my waist.

I got to the Beatle and stopped to lean against the front fender when my world began to tilt on its axis. I shifted my weight to keep from falling, over-corrected, and felt myself tumbling towards the hood.

That was the last thing I remembered.

Chapter 25

Consciousness took its sweet time returning. I woke up in the dark in an uncomfortable position, half lying and half sitting. Everything sounded like I was hearing it from the next room. I was groggy and disoriented. The only thing audible was the faint sound of shuffling coming from above me.

"Glad that worked. Had to use less since the water wouldn't help mask the taste."

"You got the cuffs?"

"Oh, yeah..."

I felt my arms being pulled over my head and heard the ratcheting sound every person who's got a cop in their family knows. My head was pounding and my limbs felt like they weighed a ton each.

"I'm going first."

"Screw that. I'm the one that set this shit up!"

I shivered as I felt the skirt of my uniform being pulled up to my waist. There was more tugging as my bloomers were yanked down my legs and forced over my tennis shoes.

"Aw," a voice said mockingly. "Maid Marian wears white. Isn't that all chaste and shit?"

I knew that voice...

"Who cares? Get 'em off!"

Rough hands grabbed and yanked my underwear down. I couldn't tell how many- more than one, at least. I whimpered as my panties were torn the rest of the way instead of pulled off.

"Would you look at that?"

"Looks like a Hitler moustache!"

"I figured she'd wax all that shit off."

"You gonna turn that down?"

"Hell naw!"

My brain caught up enough for the realization to hit me. I didn't know how I got there, where 'there' was, or who was responsible. I just knew I was in trouble.

With everything I had, I took a deep breath, opened my mouth, and let loose a blood-curdling scream that was cut off by a hand clamping over my mouth. They released it for a split second, but before I could take another breath, warm and cloth was shoved into my mouth, muffling my cries. I tried to shout again and was rewarded with pain as someone cuffed me harshly in the face.

"Shut her up!"

"I like it when they fight," another said. "Ba-ZING!"

I knew that voice too. I couldn't place it, but I knew it.

Something, a finger, I thought, was shoved roughly inside me. Tears welled up in my eyes as I tried to wiggle away.

"Looks like wearing white is a front, dude," one of them said. "Maid Marian's cherry's already been popped."

"Damn, I was looking forward to watching her face when..."

I tried to cry out over the gag as someone grabbed the front of my blouse and yanked it up.

"She even matches. Ain't that special?"

Hands slid around my back, following the line of my bra strap. With the realization that there was no hook, I was violently snatched forward as the hands ripped to tear it off. I shrieked around the cloth in my mouth as I felt cold metal against my torso when my bra was cut away, freeing my breasts.

With my chest now exposed, I shivered even harder. I kept trying to scream, but I could barely breathe with whatever was jammed in my mouth. I quit trying when someone slapped me again for my trouble, reducing my cries to whimpers.

"Shut up!"

Somebody said something in a low voice — I couldn't make it out. Then came a metallic screeching sound and a blast of cold air. Whatever I was lying on or in rocking back and forth slightly.

"Come on. We can do her at the same time."

"Wait outside and keep watch."

"Man, I hate sloppy seconds!"

"Go!"

I heard grumbling and then the sound of metal screeching, cutting off the wind.

"Here we go."

I slammed my eyes shut against the darkness as I heard a zipper coming down. I knew what they wanted.

The realization gave me newfound strength. I tried to work the cloth out of my mouth, but it was so deep that it was choking me. My attacker grabbed my feet and tried to wrench my legs apart. I found the will to fight and started kicking. I cried as his fingernails dug into my inner thighs.

"Come on. You know you want it."

I'd only felt one other man between my legs before, but it's a sensation you don't forget.

Something warm and hard bumped against the scratches. A hand grabbed my right breast hard enough to make me squeal in pain. Out of nowhere, my head snapped back as I was struck harder than before. My muffled screams echoed through the confined space and I tasted blood.

He grabbed a handful of my hair and yanked my head back. I then felt something cold and sharp pressed under my chin.

"Stop!" he hissed.

I complied.

"You can be still," he warned. "Or I can fuck your face up. I'll be done with you anyway, so it don't make a shit to me."

I was sure I knew that voice...

Gloom flooded my system and mixed with resignation. I had nowhere to go. I couldn't run away and I couldn't fight. My only choice was to endure. But to survive, this not only meant him. I also had to survive whoever else was waiting outside.

There was no holding back the crying as he pulled my

legs apart again. My tears wet the blindfold as he kept torturing my breast like it might squirt out milk.

Please, God, please let someone see this! Please let someone stop this! Please... don't...

Something exploded and tiny, round-ish objects — hard pebbles but with sharp edges — rained down on my feet and bare legs, followed by that metallic screeching sound.

"What the fu—"

Before he could finish his curse, someone forcefully yanked him off of me and I heard what sounded like a struggle.

Whatever I was on rocked and I heard a dull 'thud' as something heavy bounced off it. I caught a solid smacking sound, what I assumed — and hoped — was someone's fist connecting with flesh. There were screams of pain. I heard more thuds. Then something slamming against metal before the final sound, like something heavy being dropped. And it got eerily quiet.

"Marian!"

Another voice I recognized, but couldn't place. My brain felt like it was only moving at half speed. Despite my inebriation, I registered the obvious concern in their voice. The speaker slid into the space I was occupying and pulled the cloth out of my mouth.

"Marian. Say something. Are you okay?"

Who was that?

"Help me!"

Someone pulled down my skirt and blouse to hide my nudity. The presence then vanished, and my head fell back against whatever was behind me. I was immediately panicked again, but he was only gone a moment Something clicked at my wrists, and they fell to my sides as the cuffs came undone. Lastly, he untied the blindfold.

I blinked stupidly as my brain tried to make sense of what I was seeing in the dim light. All I could see of my savior was his upper body as he hovered over me. He wore a dark hood that covered his head, and his face was hidden by a bandana from the bridge of his nose downward. The cloth didn't cover the sideburns flowing down past his ears.

Loxley?

"I've got to get you out of here," he mumbled as he slid out from above me. "Can you stand?"

"I'll try."

He lowered the bandana, slid off his jacket, and put it above me on the outside. I realized I'd been in the backseat of a car. He'd set his jacket on the roof. Loxley took my hands and guided me out. I stood, wobbled, and started to fall. He caught me and set me back down on the edge of the seat so my feet were on the asphalt.

"Here," he said gently, draping my jacket over my shoulders. He got my arms in the sleeves, paused, and then picked up the one he'd been wearing and layered it over me.

What was Loxley doing here? Who had just attacked me?

His jacket was heavy, warm, and smelled like expensive leather. I took a deep breath, inhaling the scent. It made me feel calmer.

"Slide your arms through."

I fumbled around and finally completed the task. As soon as I was wearing his jacket on top of mine, he picked me up like a child and carried me away.

It looked like we were behind the county maintenance shop on the back side of the school. I couldn't see my car. I could faintly hear music. The Homecoming dance was still going on.

We ended up at his bike, which was parked at the corner of the shop. Without saying a word, he lowered me onto the seat sideways. He then showed me my bloomers before he squatted down and worked them over my shoes, then up to my knees. He stopped there, took my wrists, and put my hands on his shoulders before he stood me up, grabbed my bottoms, and pulled them into place. Throughout the entire time, he purposefully avoided looking at anything he didn't feel privileged to see.

"I don't have my truck or a cell phone."

"Purse gone," I slurred. "Probably by car — wherever that is."

"Can you ride?"

"I... think so."

"You might want to cover your ears."

Slowly, I complied as he walked purposefully towards the car again. From his hip, came a Glock like Dad's. For a moment, I feared I was about to witness an execution. Instead, Loxley raised it, pointed at the car, and fired a shot that blew out the front tire on the driver's side. Adjusting his aim, he fired again and blew out the rear. Keeping the gun raised, he circled the car. I heard a third shot and finally a fourth. With the sound of air hissing out, I knew he'd flattened the car completely. I saw two bodies lying on the ground near the trunk, but my vision was still too blurry to make them out.

Loxley came back to me and tucked his gun into place before removing a full-face helmet from the backrest and sliding it over my head.

It was too big and I didn't like feeling closed in, but I held still. Loxley gently tilted my chin back and buckled it into place.

"Come on. Let's get out of here."

He helped me throw my leg to the other side so I could straddle the bike before gentle hands went to my hips and slid my body back far enough for him to sit in front of me.

"Hang on to me," he ordered as the bike roared to life.

IT WAS BOTH THE worst and the best ride of my life.

It was bumpy and cold. I was scared, groggy, and felt sick to my stomach. My thighs burned, my back ached, I could still taste blood in my mouth, and I knew my chest would be bruised. I felt limp as a dishrag. It was all I could do just to hold on to him.

And I was relieved. I clutched Loxley's waist like a life preserver. I felt safe. The jacket combined with the heat off the Harley's engine and Loxley's body made the cold bearable. I wiggled my hands around until I found his hoodie's front pocket and stuffed them in there to keep warm. If it bothered him, he made no sign. I had the feeling that despite the peril I'd just faced, never mind riding at night down a windy country highway, I was in no danger. He wouldn't let anything happen to me.

The Harley screamed towards our destination and I felt like we were the only two people in the world. The sky was clear and billions of stars set the backdrop of our journey. I turned my head and rested my cheek against his back as he kept driving. Time didn't seem to exist.

I felt the bike slow to a stop and heard a horn urgently blowing. It took everything I had to force my head up to see where we were.

He'd brought me home.

Lights popped on upstairs as Loxley put the bike on its kickstand. He eased himself off and carefully undid my helmet before removing it. Gently, a gloved hand pushed a piece of hair out of my face.

"Come on."

He swung one of my arms over his shoulder and helped me off the bike. My legs felt a little less wobbly, but I kept leaning on him. They weren't even close to good enough to do their job. Seeing I was still having trouble supporting myself, he scooped me up again and walked towards the house.

The porch light blinded me right before I heard, "What the hell's going on?!"

Loxley froze in place.

I could make out the silhouette of a person on the porch in a textbook defensive stance with a shotgun raised.

"What are you doing?!" Dad growled.

Loxley matched his tone. "Damn, man, lower that gun!"

"Marian!" Mom cried out.

She was immediately beside me, ignoring Loxley. He didn't move as her hands rested on my cheeks. She lifted my head up so she could look at me. Her face was slightly blurry.

"Bring her inside. Please."

Loxley carried me with Mom tagging beside him. I caught sight of Dad lowering his gun, an angry scowl on his face.

"On the couch," Mom ordered.

Loxley lowered me gently before taking a step back.

"Marian," Mom asked, kneeling beside me. "Did someone hurt you?"

My throat was so dry I could barely swallow, so I just nodded.

"You son-of-a-bitch!"

Dad came flying past Mom, throwing a wild punch. Loxley slipped it easily, causing Dad to stumble past and crash into the end table. Loxley stood there, feet shoulder width apart, hands down by his side.

"You don't want to do this," he warned.

"You're dead, Hood!" Dad snarled as he started coming up.

I could finally gather enough moisture to make noise. "No!"

All three heads turned to me.

I couldn't talk again, so I shook my head.

"He didn't do this?" Mom asked.

I nodded.

"Do you know who did?"

I shook my head to reply.

"You don't know, or you won't say?" Dad asked.

I croaked out, "I'm not sure."

He turned to Loxley. "Who?"

"It doesn't matter."

"The hell it doesn't!" Dad snapped. He stepped forward and jammed a finger in his face. "If you didn't do this, I want whoever did to pay."

"Marian?" Mom said. "You need to tell us what you remember."

Chapter 26

"YOU CAN COME BACK now," Mom called.

Dad and Loxley came in from the kitchen. Dad was still scowling. Loxley had a poker face.

"She has bruises and scratches on her thighs," Mom reported. "She's also got bruising on her right breast. I didn't see any internal trauma."

"I got there before that happened," Loxley assured her.

"A finger," I mumbled. "I think."

To this day, I wish I'd kept that bit of information to myself. The way Dad's face crumpled hurt worse than being slapped.

He went right back into cop mode. "What do you remember?"

I took another sip of water before answering. "I'd just said good night to Brent. He'd apologized for how he had been acting. We weren't going to get back together or anything, but we were going to be civil. I was feeling sick, so I went outside to head home. I was walking to the car.

That's it."

"What do you remember after that?"

"It was dark," I said, trying to think. "I heard voices. It felt like I was in a confined space, like the backseat of a car."

Loxley nodded.

"I'm pretty sure I remember two voices."

"Could you place either of them?" Mom asked.

"One of them I'd swear was Jody Robinson. I heard 'ba-zing' and Jody's the only one that says that. The other voice I thought I recognized sounded a lot like Brent." I paused. "He was the one that told me he was done with me anyway..."

"Did you see them?" Dad asked.

I shook my head. "I was blindfolded... and handcuffed... and gagged. I have no idea with what—something cloth." I frowned. "It was warm."

Loxley sighed and reached into his left thigh pocket. He came out with something white and silky and dropped them on the coffee table.

It had been my panties that had frayed where they'd been ripped off.

I blinked in surprise. "That's what they used?"

"That's what I pulled out of your mouth."

Mom got an ugly look on her face. She turned to Dad. "Call the Sheriff's Department."

Dad's expression changed and not for the better. Before, I saw anger. Righteous anger. It disappeared in a flash and I saw resignation.

Mom saw it too. "He can swear he saw what happened." She turned to Loxley. "You will, right?"

"If that's what you want."

There was something I was missing.

"Why wouldn't I want you to?" Mom was losing her temper. "I want these animals arrested!"

It was Dad who answered. "Because it's Marian and Hood's word against theirs."

Mom blew up. "So what? We've got two witnesses and her injuries! Call the Sheriff's department so we can get them documented!"

"You don't understand, Ellie," Dad explained. "Marian can't positively identify them. She never saw them. She can only say she thinks it was Jody Robinson or Brent Dean. We have nothing to give us DNA."

"We have his testimony," she pointed out, gesturing at Loxley.

"And you know as well as I do how that'll go. On one side, we have two kids whose parents are pillars of this community. On the other side, we've got Marian, who can't positively ID anyone and who they would treat like they did Selena, and Hood, who they're going to paint as a witness that isn't credible."

"So what do we do?"

Dad frowned. "If we go to the Sheriff, they're going to tell us with no witnesses, no DNA, and nothing else to go on that we have no case. There's no point in a rape kit since, thankfully, Hood stopped them. They'll question Marian about if she's had anything to drink..."

"Water," I interrupted.

"... but who's to say one of them or their friends wouldn't come forward and say she did drink tonight? Or that she willingly took whatever knocked her out?" He looked ready to collapse. "They'll make it sound like she chose this — just like they did with Selena."

Mom looked ready to kill someone.

"Then there's Hood. They could very well say that he did this. Marian can't identify anyone. It's no secret they have it out for him or that he's got it out for those boys and law enforcement in general. They'll say he's the one that drugged her, that he's the one that assaulted her..." He paused. "And let's be honest. I'm not convinced he wasn't."

"What?!"

Dad stood and squared his shoulders. "How do we know you didn't do this? I wouldn't put it past you to have set this up just because you can't stand the Dean..."

"Stop right there, Robert!"

I'd never heard Mom call Dad 'Robert.' Ever. Never once, regardless of how angry she was, had I heard her call him by his Christian name. I was so used to her and everyone else calling him 'Bob' that I'd forgotten he and Loxley shared the same first name.

"You will not be rude to him!"

Both Dad and Loxley looked surprised.

She turned to me. "He busted out a car window and took on two men. Then he freed you and brought you home. You can vouch for that much, correct?"

I nodded my head. "I'm also sure none of the voices in the car match his."

"How sure?"

"One hundred percent. Neither of those voices was

Loxley's."

Mom turned back to Dad, her eyes stern and her voice hardened. "As far as I'm concerned, he is welcome in this house any time. We owe him not only our gratitude, but our respect. And you damned well better give him both!"

I'd never heard my mom talk to my dad like that. I didn't know she had it in her. I knew she was smart. I knew she could be firm. But I'd never seen her be tough.

She looked at my rescuer. "What is your name?"

"Robert, ma'am. Robert Loxley."

She repeated it to herself. "How old are you, Robert Loxley?"

"Seventeen."

"You're a senior?"

He shook his head. "I'm a junior."

"Do you go by 'Robert'?"

"No, ma'am. My friends call me 'Robin'. Almost everybody else calls me that or Hood.'"

"Why Hood?"

He reached behind his head and tugged at the cloth sticking out. "This, I guess. It's about all I wear when it's cold. I guess it's a combination of that and some of my... hobbies."

"Why Robin?"

"It was my grandmother's nickname for me," he explained. "It's an old family name. She wanted my folks to name me that, but my parents thought it sounded too feminine. So they named me 'Robert.' But she always called me 'Robin.' So did all her friends. So many people heard them do it, they started doing it. She died when I was little, but it stuck. Only Grandpa and some of my teachers call me Robert."

"What did your parents call you?"

His chin dropped. "Earl called me 'Robert.' Mom used 'Robin.'"

"Would you be offended if I called you Robin?"

"No, ma'am."

She gave him a smile. "Robin, you call me Eleanor or Ellie, understand?"

"Yes, ma'am."

She didn't look as surprised at his manners as Dad did. In fact, I could've sworn she expected them.

"Well, Robin," she said as she stood.

She then stepped to him and hugged him tightly. She embraced him with fierceness, not like she was just being friendly. He hugged her back, though gentler than she was with him. He looked shocked.

Dad looked surprised too. I was too numb to look or feel anything but stoned.

She pulled away and said, "Any place I lay my head, you will always be welcome. Do you understand?"

I thought he was blushing underneath his beard. "Yes, ma'am."

"Now," she said. "I'm going to get Marian some more ice water. Is there anything I can get you?"

"That ride was pretty cold. I'd take some coffee if you've got some made."

Mom smiled. "I don't, but I'll have you a pot in a few minutes."

Mom brought me more water and Loxley, Dad, and herself some coffee. After giving Dad a warning glare to behave himself, she went to my room and brought me some clothes. With her help, I made it to the bathroom, used it, dressed in some warm pajamas, got on the couch, and propped up on some pillows with a blanket over my lap.

Loxley stood the entire time. When Mom and I returned, he was standing in the same place we'd left him — leaning against the entertainment center, a mug in his hand.

"Are you carrying a gun?" Dad asked.

"I'd rather you didn't ask me that."

"He blew their tires out so they couldn't follow us," I piped up.

Dad ignored me. "You're seventeen and on probation."

"That's enough, Bob," Mom said firmly.

Dad's jaw locked up, and he glowered at Loxley.

"So the police are out," Mom asked, "or did I misunderstand you?"

Dad sighed. "We can try. Unfortunately we're not going to get anywhere."

Mom looked at Loxley. "Do you know for sure who did this?"

"Yes ma'am."

"Tell me."

"I'd rather not."

"Why?"

"Because I don't want you to be a party to what I'm going to do."

"What do you mean?" Dad asked.

"I mean exactly what I said," Loxley replied simply.

"What are you going to do?"

"What the law won't."

"Robin," Mom said gently. "There's nothing you can do."

"I disagree ma'am."

Dad spoke up again. "She's right. We have to figure out how to do this legally."

Loxley raised an eyebrow. "So... what are you going to do?"

Dad didn't respond.

"Robin," Mom said. "Tell me what you're considering."

"What do you think I'm going to do,Mrs. Ellie?"

"I don't know."

"What would you do if you had them sitting here right now?"

Mom's expression darkened. "They wouldn't leave this room alive."

Then it was Loxley's turn to remain silent.

"Have you ever killed anyone, Hood...? I mean, Loxley?"

"I plead the Fifth."

That was probably the wrong answer because Dad's eyes went from Loxley's face to his hip.

"Who?"

"I plead the Fifth."

I finally got back into the conversation. "No, Loxley.

You're not going to kill anybody."

They all looked at me again.

"I want them to pay. But I don't want them dead. They didn't try to kill me."

"This isn't answering my question," Mom said. "What do we do?"

"I'll handle it," Loxley assured her.

"Promise me you won't kill anybody," I said. "I mean it, Loxley…"

My brain finally started working a little more and I remembered a few more details from the night.

"Before I left the dance," I said. "I was talking to Brent. He brought me some water. It tasted a little funny."

"He slipped something in it," Dad said. "Son-of-a-bitch!"

"He said he got it from the fountain since they didn't have any cold. That was how he explained the aftertaste. It was stifling hot in the gym and I was so thirsty I didn't think twice about it." Something else wormed its way into my brain. "Loxley? Can I ask you a question?"

He nodded.

I was intentionally vague since my parents were there. "You remember the first time we talked after the party?"

"I do."

"You remember what you told me?"

"I told you a lot, Marian."

"I was mad at you because you got beer on me when you knocked it out of Brent's hand. You remember that?"

He nodded.

"You remember what you told me now?"

"Remind me?"

"You said what I did tonight, I did for you."

"Yeah, I did."

"You also told me you don't know it yet, but we're even. Remember?"

"I do."

"Brent got that beer for me."

"I know."

"You knew, or at least suspected, he'd put something in it."

"Correct. I suspected. I was trying to tell you, but you wouldn't stop interrupting me."

"Selena told me that he and Jody poured her one before she blacked out. She said it tasted funny, but they told her sometimes the kegs from the truck stop are like that. They tried to do to me what they did to her, didn't they?"

"I thought you were the target. I didn't think they'd go after someone else. Hell, I didn't even know for sure it was them." Loxley sighed. "You remember the fight Brent and I had that Monday at lunch?"

I nodded.

"You remember when he said you wouldn't talk to me if he mentioned Fat Lighter Hollow and I mentioned both his brother's truck stop and Saint Florence?"

"Yeah."

"Fat Lighter Hollow isn't a secret. I'm guessing your dad has seen my rap sheet. It's where I burned down that meth lab. The secret of his brother's truck stop is how much time he spends there — a lot of weeknights and especially Friday nights after the game. He likes the company of the...

working girls… at his brother's place, if you get my drift."

No wonder he treated me like an appointment and hadn't always tried to find ways to spend time with me. He was getting his from truck stop hookers.

"What about Saint Florence?"

"Saint Florence is the private school Brent attended last year. He got kicked out for raping a girl in the boy's locker room."

"How do you know?" Dad asked.

"There are a lot more people in Barnsdale County that will talk to me than you."

"So we've got a pattern," Mom spoke up. "This might help."

"No, ma'am," Loxley explained. "She wouldn't press charges. The Deans agreed to withdraw him, so the school did nothing about it."

Dad smacked the arm of his chair. "And those bastards are going to get away with it!"

"How are you holding up?" Loxley asked me.

"I feel like I did last Thanksgiving when I had three glasses of wine before dinner."

"Go to sleep," Mom ordered. "You're safe now."

I settled back into my pillows as Mom pulled the blanket up to my chin. She leaned over and kissed my forehead. I gave her a weak smile and closed my eyes.

"You're going to do something, aren't you, Robin?"

"Yes, ma'am."

She didn't ask 'what' like I thought she would. Instead, she asked. "Why?"

"I doubt you'd understand."

I wanted to ask him to explain himself, but my eyelids had gotten heavy. I heard Mom's voice again, but I couldn't make out what she was saying. I didn't think I'd be able to sleep, but I was out before I realized it.

I WOKE WITH A start. Something, a dream perhaps, had disturbed me. I was still on the couch. The morning sun was coming through the window. Panic raced through my body and all I knew was I felt... something... all over me and I wanted it off.

"Marian?"

I didn't answer. Instead, I threw the covers off and stumbled to the kitchen. Mom was standing in front of the laundry room, shock written all over her face. I ignored her and bolted for the door.

"Marian!"

I ran up the steps to my apartment, grateful it was unlocked. The slamming of the door startled Cowboy. I shucked clothes as I went and was completely nude by the time I got to the bathroom. I pulled the shower door back, stepped inside, and turned it on before I even bothered to get the water warm. Ignoring the goose bumps popping up on my naked flesh, I grabbed my body wash and started scrubbing.

"Marian?"

"In here!"

I saw Mom over the shower door. She looked concerned

as I started scouring between my legs.

All I could think about was that finger…

"You okay?"

"I need to get clean."

Mom looked very distressed.

My hands slowed their scrubbing. "I… I had a bad dream, I think. I don't remember what, but I just… he touched me."

Mom stepped to the door and leaned on it, ignoring me being naked. "It's okay, Marian. You're safe now. This won't happen again."

"How do you know?"

Her head turned away.

"Mom?"

"I made your dad go to bed," she explained, "and I walked Robin out."

I stood there with both my hands at my crotch and just stared at her.

"It won't happen again," she repeated.

My hands began slowly moving again. "What's he going to do?"

"I don't know yet, but he promised me he wouldn't kill them."

My eyes fell to the finger-shaped bruises on my breast. "What did Dad say?"

"Dad doesn't know. The truth is, he's pretty upset. He feels powerless. Fathers are supposed to protect their little girls. But it will be handled."

I frowned. "Why?"

"Why what?"

"Why is Loxley going to handle this?"

"He has his own reasons."

"And what are they?"

She shrugged.

"You don't know or you're not going to tell me?"

"I'm not completely sure. All I know is that I was right."

"About what?"

"Remember when I told you I'd love to hear the rest of the story behind who Robin is? How I thought that he was more than a criminal? There is more."

"And he told you?"

"No, Marian. I feel it. You can see it in the way he walks and talks and acts. I've worked on more than my fair share of felons, thugs, hooligans, gangbangers and whatever other noun you want to use, and I've never seen a single one that acted like him. Honestly, he reminds me of someone I knew, and adored, a long time ago."

I was sick of Loxley's secrets.

He'd protected me from Brent, once when I didn't realize it and once when I did. There was more about him I needed to find out. I was going to answer this riddle once and for all.

"Mom? Where's Dad?"

"He went to the school to see if he could find anything."

"Where's my car?"

"Believe it or not, sitting in the driveway. You ran right past it. We were going to head to the school and see if we could find it, but when we came out, it was sitting there with the keys hanging from the lock. We're thinking maybe Robin and his friends brought it here. Why?"

"I... need it."

"Where are you going?"

"I need to talk to someone about this."

"That's good. Do you have someone in mind?"

"Yes, ma'am. Let me finish up here. Do you think you can find out where Mrs. Sadie lives?"

"Mrs. Sadie? You want to talk about this with Mrs. Sadie?"

"No, ma'am. But she'll know where to find who I do want to talk to."

Chapter 27

MRS. SADIE LIVED IN an old white clapboard house with light blue shutters and a large concrete porch. I pulled up in her dirt driveway and shut my engine off. I didn't have time to be nervous. I was on a mission.

My walk had a purpose as I mounted the steps, and I could feel the healing scratches on the inside of my thighs rubbing together. The front door was open and I saw two young kids sitting on the floor watching cartoons. They didn't notice me until I knocked.

The person I was hoping for answered. Alonzo Tuck.

He opened the screen door but didn't invite me in. Instead, he stepped out on the porch with me, closing the door behind him.

"You and I need to talk."

He pursed his lips and said nothing.

"I need some answers, Alonzo. You know I do."

"You need answers I can't give you."

"What? You told me if I needed answers to come see

you."

"That's right. But I didn't say I would be the one to give them to you."

"Then who can?"

"You mind taking a drive?"

"If it will get me the answers I need, yes."

"I'll be right back."

After telling Mrs. Sadie we were going somewhere, Tuck got into the passenger seat of my car and gave directions. We headed north towards the interstate.

"Where are we going?"

"We're going to get your answers."

"Okay, who's going to give them to me?"

His lips pursed, which I was beginning to associate with him thinking. "Someone that I think you'd believe. They'll tell you the straight, unfiltered truth. They're close enough to have the answers you want, but not so close they're right in the middle of it. I think you'd be more likely to believe them than me."

"I would believe you, Alonzo."

"You might not about this. Trust me. You'll understand when you meet this person."

"What questions should I ask?"

"Whatever you want to know. I would go with the obvious ones."

We ended up at another old house, this one white with a

black slate roof and a brick chimney. Behind it was a shed covering a tractor and some other large farm machinery I couldn't name. I pulled up in the yard and Tuck and I got out.

"Let me do the talking," Tuck said in a low voice.

We walked up on the porch, but before we could knock, the door opened. An old, wiry man wearing a pair of faded overalls, a button-up shirt, and a NASCAR cap stepped out.

"Can I help you?"

His tone wasn't unfriendly, merely businesslike. He was staring at Tuck.

To my surprise, someone I recognized came waddling out from behind him. She was wearing pajama pants and a Barnsdale High sweatshirt.

It was Grace.

"Pa," she said. "These two are friends."

"Since when do we have colored friends?"

His tone made me nervous, but Tuck kept smiling.

"Well, he's a friend of a friend."

"We ain't got no friends whose friends with nig-,"

"Robin Hood."

It stopped him cold. The man's head moved back and forth from Tuck to me with a penetrating gaze. Grace stood there calmly as his head kept bobbing between us.

"Miss?" He finally said to me.

"Yes, sir?"

"Be so kind as to pull your car under the pecan tree behind the shed? Then y'all can have a seat on the back porch."

"Yes, sir."

WE SAT ON THE screened-in back porch — Grace, Tuck, and me. 'Pa' turned out to be Grace's grandfather. Her grandmother was a textbook southern hostess. She brought us sweet tea, and unlike Mom's, it had enough sugar. She also served each of us a slice of pound cake.

"I'm sorry about Pa," she said to Tuck.

He shrugged. "Don't worry about it. You know as well as I do if I took you to Brownsville, you'd get the same reaction."

"So, why are you here?"

"Marian has questions. The kind I can't answer, but you can. Obviously you don't have to, but I'm hoping you will."

"You are?"

He gave a single nod. "When it all comes together, I think you'll be glad you did."

Grace turned to me. "Okay, Marian. Ask."

I glanced at Tuck, who gave me an encouraging nod. I was here about Loxley, not her. So I only saw one obvious question.

"So who's the father of your child?"

"I don't know. But I could give you a list of suspects."

Okay, this wasn't going well. I knew what I wanted to know, but I didn't think they were the obvious questions.

Grace bailed me out. "You see all those fields right

there?"

I tracked her eyes to the fallow acreage that stretched left, right, and straight back behind us as far as I could see.

"Yeah."

She picked up her tea glass. "That's my daddy's."

"Okay?"

"Tuck knew I'd be here though, didn't he? He didn't assume I was at home."

I hadn't thought of that. "Yeah?"

"You know why?"

"No."

"Because I live with Pa and Ma. My daddy called me a whore and kicked me out of the house."

Well, if she could only narrow her baby's daddy down to a list of potentials the shoe might fit, I thought.

She must've read it on my face. "I was like you, Marian. I was like you and Hope and Tina. I used to be part of that crowd. Not anymore. Do you have any clue why?"

"Because your dad kicked you out?"

She rested a hand on her stomach. "You want to know the full reason?"

I gave her a go-ahead nod.

"Spring Break last year, we all camped out on the river. We did all sorts of fun stuff: fishing, music, a bonfire, booze, weed..."

I took a sip of my tea.

She continued. "I blacked out the first night and woke up naked in my sleeping bag in the wee hours of the morning, a good piece from the rest of the group. I had bruises all over me. My... butt... hurt as well as the obvious place, if you know what I mean. I was also bleeding… from there. I found my clothes and left before anyone woke up."

She had my full attention.

"I went to my mama and daddy. Mama cried and Daddy threw me out. I came to Ma and Pa and they took me in. They took me to the Sheriff's office and…"

"Let me guess," I interrupted. "They made you feel like a slut, told you there was no case, and told you to be more careful next time?"

"Close. They told me to shut up and go away."

"What did you do?"

"We went to a lawyer. He pushed for charges to be pressed."

"You know who did it?"

"Brent and Jody had been giving me beer all night. Brent also gave me a tab he said was Mollie. My sleeping bag smelled like Jody's cologne."

"So, what did the lawyer do?"

Tuck spoke up. "He couldn't put enough pressure on them to stop them from covering it up. They told her they didn't have enough evidence to get a warrant for DNA, that it would be against their rights. They told her she should quit laying with strange men and lying about the good people of Barnsdale County."

"That can't be," I said, shocked. "I mean, the law is the law."

"When both their daddies are county commissioners, and they have the magistrate and the judges in their pockets, it can be."

"So what happened?"

"I was a pariah to your friends," Grace went on. "Rumors started flying, and because of that or pressure from people whose parents do business together, people shunned me. And the poor kids? Either I'd been such a bitch to them they thought I was getting what I deserved or they were afraid if they were nice to me, the people in power would come down on them."

I didn't know what to say.

Grace jutted her chin out. "I'm not a slut, Marian. I know that's what they say, but it ain't true."

I glanced at Tuck. "This doesn't clear anything up."

Tuck turned to Grace. "Tell her what happened next?"

She took another drink. "Pa went to Thomas Loxley. I don't know if you know this, but he's a retired lawyer. Pa wanted a second opinion."

"What did he say?"

She shook her head. "Mr. Thomas told us the powers that be were going to sweep this under the rug. It's not like a civil trial where all you have to do is sue somebody to get them in court. With this, they have to be arrested. They couldn't help me legally, but there were other ways."

"Other ways?"

"Other ways," she repeated. "Ma and Pa are retired. Pa still farms some but they can't afford me and a baby too, not with doctor bills and diapers and stuff."

I turned to Tuck. "The day of Junior Boxer's funeral when I saw you give Grace money?"

Tuck nodded.

"That's where I first heard the rumor Loxley was the father."

"Not even close."

I turned back to Grace. "I'm confused. Old Man Loxley is..."

"Don't you dare call him that!"

I recoiled at her fierceness. "Sorry. We were talking about what people at the lunch table had said and that's how Brent referred to him, so that's what popped into my head. Seriously, I don't know why I would say that."

Grace kept glaring at me. Disrespecting Thomas Loxley had obviously set her off.

"So I'm confused. Thomas Loxley is a retired lawyer and they own a bunch of land and they're giving you money, but they're poor?"

"Yes," she replied simply.

Not that simple for me. "How?"

"History, Marian," Tuck answered. "At one time the Loxleys were as rich as the rest of them. But several of these families tried to force the Loxleys to get into bed with them by doing something either immoral or illegal. And if you haven't figured it out yet, Robin doesn't take well to force. It's a family trait."

"So how can they afford to give Grace money?"

"It's not just me," Grace added. "I probably couldn't count how many people they've helped."

I remembered something. "Loxley paid for Junior Boxer's funeral, didn't he?"

Both nodded.

"But how?"

"They take it from those that took from others," Tuck said.

"I don't follow."

"You remember that hijacking the week school started?" Grace asked.

"The one full of car parts?"

"Stolen car parts," Grace corrected.

I wondered if Dad knew that. "Yeah?"

Grace and Tuck both were looking at me expectantly.

"Loxley did that?"

"Robin," Tuck replied, "as well as Dale, Scarlet, Little John, and Max. You saw that deal between Robin and Jermaine the next day?"

I remembered Jermaine slipped Robin a roll and Scarlet wrote something on a piece of paper and passed it to him. "Yeah?"

"Jermaine paid us and Scarlet gave him the location of where they hid the truck. They took the parts and fenced them for profit."

I slumped back in my chair, completely stunned.

"There's more," Grace added. "Pa had some tweakers set up shop on the back side of his property. He called the law but they didn't do anything, which led him to believe the Sheriff's department was in on it." She gave a tight smile. "The law wouldn't stop them, but Robin Hood did."

"Why do you call him that?" I asked. "I mean, Robin Hood?"

"Except for a couple of people, he gets called two things," she explained. "Ma and Pa know him as 'Robin.' They were friends with Mrs. Loxley before she passed and that's what his grandma called him..."

"She wanted his parents to name him that, but they

didn't."

"Correct. I consider him a friend. Actually, we're pretty close. So I call him 'Robin.' People that either don't like the Loxleys or know nothing but the rumors call him by the other name — 'Hood.' Sometime even people like me will use that if we're talking to someone and we don't want it known whose side they're on. Like I did in the grocery store." She shrugged. "I didn't know what you called him, so I used both names for your benefit."

"I call him 'Loxley.' What else has he done?"

"You trying to gather evidence?"

"I'm convinced Brent and Jody tried to rape me last night," I told her. "He stopped them."

She nodded. "They got Selena too, didn't they?"

"It looks that way."

Tuck exhaled a long breath.

"I passed out and woke handcuffed in the backseat of a car. Good thing Loxley showed up."

"I was watching from the bleachers," Tuck told us. "Dale slipped out to cover the back door. We saw you leave, but neither of us saw Brent or Jody give you anything."

"It was in the water bottle."

Tuck frowned. "I'm sorry. You were over by the table, so I thought you had gotten it yourself. We saw you leave, and Brent and Jody slipped out behind you. We didn't know exactly where they were going to do the deed, so Robin, Little John, and Scarlet covered all the roads away from the school, planning to follow them. Robin had the road by the shop. I can't believe they tried to attack you there. I'm really sorry, Marian."

"Forgiven, Alonzo. The fact y'all were even trying to help speaks volumes. But you're telling me that Loxley and crew are... vigilantes?"

"Among other things," Grace replied. "They help people in this county. Mrs. Kirkland's husband broke her arm and her jaw when she tried to leave him. They made it so he wouldn't do it again. Mr. Kershaw broke his hip when his tractor rolled on him. They got his crop in for him. For free. The youngest Baxter girl needed heart surgery in Mobile and the family needed five thousand dollars. They came up with it. Someone broke into Miss Neely's house. They caught who did it."

This was mind-boggling. Robert Loxley and his friends were... I couldn't even come up with a word.

"So you see, Marian," Grace said. "Robin isn't the devil you think he is."

"He uses violence, theft, and intimidation to get what he wants."

"What would you suggest?" Tuck asked.

I didn't have an answer. I was taught to respect the law. But there was no law, at least no legitimate law, in Barnsdale County.

"Any more questions?" Grace asked.

"Yeah. You're both okay with this?"

"I am," Grace said quickly.

Tuck shrugged. "Honestly? No. It bothers me this is the world we live in. But there's nothing to be done about it. It's either resist and be free or bow down and be slaves."

"Who are the Glorious Dead?"

Grace looked surprised by the question. "Who told you

about that?"

"I heard it at Junior Boxer's funeral. They were gathered around Earl and Joan's grave."

"More history. It goes without saying the corruption in this area has been around for a long time..."

"Loxley said the Deans had been trying to run his family out for seven generations," I interrupted.

"Since Reconstruction," Tuck confirmed.

She put her glass down. "Anyway, the Deans and their allies have tried to crush the Loxleys since the beginning and the Loxleys have resisted. Not only have the Loxleys resisted, but they've helped others to do the same."

I nodded along.

"The Loxleys, and the people allied with them, have always paid homage to those who dared stand up to those in power and paid for it in blood. They are honored as the Glorious Dead. I'm not sure of the whole story, but it was something the people around here that joined the Confederate Army did to honor their fallen comrades. Junior's brother owed some people money. They tried to make Junior pay the debt since they didn't think they'd get it from his brother, and Junior actually had a job. When he refused, they killed him. He resisted. That made him one of the Glorious Dead. It will be done for Ma and Pa's when the time comes."

"So Loxley and his gang are basically robbing from the rich and giving to the poor?" I asked.

Grace shook her head. "Not the rich. There are plenty of well-off people in Barnsdale County that only think Robin is some poor farm kid or only know about Hood because of the rumors. Hope, for one, and Nick and Brian too, I think." Their families didn't take from poor people to get rich or do immoral or illegal things to stay rich. But those that steal from innocent people? Yeah, they've felt his anger."

Anger is a gift.

I'd been wrong all along. Robert Loxley wasn't a street thug, much less a common one.

"Have I answered your questions?"

"You have," I replied. "And for that, I thank you."

"You do realize that if you ever talk, you won't have to fear them? *I'm* coming after you."

I raised an eyebrow, but I dropped it when I saw her expression. This wasn't an idle threat. Even pregnant, Grace looked ready, willing, and able to stomp a mud hole in me.

"Loxley saved me. If all I have to do to repay him is just not talk, I can do that."

"MOM? DAD? I'M HOME!"

I came into the living room to find Mom sitting on the couch. She smiled as I entered.

"You okay?"

"I am," I replied. "Well, not really. But I'm managing."

"You want to sleep in the house tonight?"

I shook my head. "I don't think so. I'm sure Cowboy won't mind snuggling with me."

She rolled her eyes. "What about Monday?"

"What about it?"

"Do you plan on going to school?"

"I haven't thought about it."

I really didn't want to face Brent and Jody. I also would've bet my bottom dollar word had already gotten out about what happened, at least some distorted version of it.

"I think you should go."

"You do?"

"I do."

"I don't want them to think I'm scared, Mom. But I am."

"No one at that school will hurt you, Marian."

"How do you know?"

"Robin will be there."

That was surprising. "You think he'll protect me?"

"He will."

"How do you know?"

"Because he's done it once. He will again."

"Did you ever stop and think he had other reasons?"

She leaned back on the couch. "I think he has several reasons."

"I really don't want to."

"Marian, you can't hide. Your Dad and I discussed it and we think you have to go. Now obviously we can't make you, unless we drive you and follow you around from class to class. But we agree you have to face your fear. And, like I said, no one is going to hurt you with Robin there."

Chapter 28

MONDAY CAME, AND I decided to go. I had to stop on the side of the road and throw up on the way.

My nerves felt completely shot. I had barely slept. I'd spent all day Sunday in my pajamas, curled up on the couch. Mom and Dad gave me space. I was showering four or five times a day. I kept Cowboy with me at all times. Even he sensed my apprehension.

Dad had gone back to the scene of the crime, hoping to find a clue. There was no evidence anywhere except for some broken auto glass. He'd believed that was his only chance of finding a way to implicate Brent or Jody but had struck out..

I pulled up to the school parking lot and immediately knew something was going on.

Cars were in their spaces, but no one was hanging around them. A large crowd had gathered by the fence around the basketball court. The only people not there were Loxley and his crew.

The wind was whipping pretty good, which made it colder. I stuffed my hands into my pockets. I couldn't see what was going on at the fence. Knowing I had to pass the bikers, I steeled my nerves and started walking.

I approached and their conversation stopped. All of them looked at me with blank expressions — except Loxley.

"Marian, how are you?"

"I'm fine, Loxley."

He turned to Little John and cocked his head. Little John nodded back, then motioned to the rest of them. He turned to leave, and they all followed in unison, leaving Loxley and me alone.

"Seriously," he said as soon as they were out of earshot. "Are you alright?"

Despite the wind whipping my hair sideways, I felt warmer being close to him.

"I still feel... on guard, "I admitted. "Plus, you know... the obvious worry."

"What's that?"

"That they'll try again... or they'll use their father's connections to get to me."

"Why would you expect their fathers to get involved?"

It was time to come clean. "I know what you are, Loxley."

"And what am I?"

"You're Robin Hood. I got an education Saturday on exactly what that means."

"Not what you expected, is it?"

"Not even close. Will you accept my apology?"

"You don't have to apologize to me, Marian."

"Yeah… I do. My gut told me you weren't what Brent's friends said you were. I should've listened."

"If you could tell what I was, my cover wouldn't be that good, would it?"

"Why do you do it?"

"That's a long story."

"I'd like to hear it."

"It's a story only my friends get to hear. Are you my friend, Marian?"

"Did you mean what you told my dad?"

"Which part?"

I swallowed. "That you've killed people?"

"I didn't say I killed anyone."

"You took the Fifth. If you'd never killed anyone, you would've just said 'no.'"

"Does it matter?"

"Murder is wrong."

"So is killing someone innocent and getting away with it. So is a mother crying because someone hooked their daughter on meth and is pimping her out. So is a father getting killed for someone else's debt."

"There are other ways."

He shook his head. "There should be other ways. I wish there were. But until those ways show themselves, I have work to do."

"But I can't be friends with a killer, Loxley."

His head dropped, and he sadly replied, "I understand."

My brain was congratulating me. My heart was kicking me for refusing to tell him it wanted to be his friend.

Especially since it felt at peace for the first time in... well, since it happened.

"What are you going to do about Brent and Jody?"

"It's already been done."

I shuddered. "Did you... kill them?"

He shook his head.

"Did you let someone else do it?"

"No, Marian. You said you didn't want them dead."

"What did you do?"

The corner of his mouth turned up into a grin. "Oh, you'll see."

I started to press him, but before I could, he slid off the bike.

"What about an ally?" he asked. "If we can't be friends, can we at least be allies?"

"I won't help you kill people, Loxley."

"I wouldn't ask you to. But now you know all the secrets. You're in whether you want to be or not."

"That sounds like a threat."

"I told you I'd never threaten you, Marian. I meant it."

I crossed my arms over my chest. "So, what are you doing?"

"I'm telling you the truth. You're in. I want you as an ally. That's it."

"So, what does that entail?"

"I want you to keep your eyes and ears open. I want you to observe. I want you to tell me if you see someone needs our help."

"I already do that for Dad."

"True," he admitted. "But like your situation, there are

things your dad can't do anything about. We can."

He was right, but I couldn't just jump into bed with him... figuratively speaking. However, I could do other things. I couldn't let someone's unborn child do without or let someone like Brent victimize people. If I could help, I would. I would just have to walk a fine line.

"I'll do it," I said finally.

"Thank you, Marian."

"But stay out of my house."

"Mrs. Ellie said I was welcome anytime."

I rolled my eyes. "Not in my room, then. Agreed?"

"I swear only if you invite me. Or I feel your life is in danger. Please, Marian, don't make me make a promise I can't keep."

I huffed. "Fine."

He stuck his hand out. Carefully, I stepped closer and took it. Just like the last time our hands touched, he was gentle.

Before I could say anything else, he turned and began ambling off. As he walked, he reached under his jacket and pulled his hood up over his head. I watched him as he moved to the left side of the crowd and disappeared.

Once I had my backpack and my lunch, I headed in the same direction. While I wasn't feeling social, curiosity killed the cat and all. Besides, if everyone was out there, that meant there were fewer people inside. I felt safer physically in a crowd-- more witnesses meant less of a chance of being attacked. But it made me nervous to be around a large group of people.

A large guy, taller and wider than even Little John, saw

me approach. He patted someone on the shoulder and they both looked at me. I blushed. They didn't speak. They just stood aside.

As they got out of the way, the people in front of them moved. People would tap whoever was in front of them, motion with their head, and the crowd would part. Half a dozen boys with what looked like paintball guns stopped dead in their tracks when they saw me. I walked with my head down, eyes on the ground, chewing on my bottom lip, not sure what I was about to see. Nothing could've prepared me.

Brent and Jody were handcuffed to the fence by their arms and legs, leaving them completely exposed. Both were wide-eyed and scared, both were gagged, and both were completely naked.

They'd been there for a while. Their skin was pale and their toes, fingers, noses, and ears were red with cold. To top it all off, both had their faces and genitalia painted a bright neon green.

Above their heads, someone had hung a homemade banner. The neat black letters on white butcher paper spelled out one word in three-foot letters: RAPISTS.

I stood there in open-mouthed shock as they squirmed against the unforgiving metal. Their cries were muffled and no one in the crowd moved to assist them.

"Aw," Grace said from near the front. "It looks like a grub worm wearing a turtleneck!"

Laughter broke out.

"They are some cute little nubbins!" someone else called out-- sounded like Hope.

The crowd laughed harder.

"Them boys have so much shrinkage they're going to have to stick a finger up their ass and yell 'snake' just to take a piss later!" Cory added.

The people laughed harder still.

Jermaine looked them up and down slowly before scornfully saying, "How you going to force yourself on somebody with them little things?"

That broke the crowd up. People were pointing and laughing. Phone cameras began popping up. Brent and Jody struggled harder, but they didn't have a prayer of escaping.

"Catch Jody!"

My head turned as Grace raised one of the paintball guns at him. She fired a burst of five. One missed, two struck him in the stomach and the final two hit him dead in the balls, splattering him with pink. He screamed in agony around his gag.

That got the others involved. Paintballs flew at them in every color. They squirmed, trying to avoid the shots, but they had nowhere to go. I saw Cory taking a shot... and Hope... and to my surprise, Selena was there blasting them with paint. It reminded me of the Middle Ages, when villagers would sentence someone to the stocks and throw rotting fruit at them.

I looked smugly at Brent and we made eye contact. There was no cockiness in his gaze. He was scared. He was humiliated. He was strung up and getting a serious dose of his own medicine. Both were.

This wasn't revenge — served cold, yes, but not revenge.

This was justice. They ruined people's lives and got away with it — until now.

I turned and walked away without a word. Nothing I could've done would have added to Loxley and company's act. No one stopped me, no one spoke to me, and no one sought my approval or asked for a signal to end it. I walked away, my head held high.

I might have been bent, but they'd been broken.

It wasn't over. Not by a long shot.

For Brent, it was. His parents, as well as Jody's, sent them to boarding schools on the other side of the country. They were too ashamed to show their faces in Barnsdale County ever again.

But my journey was just beginning. And it wasn't the end of my association with Robert Loxley, either. Despite my words to him, we became more than allies. In time, we became friends... and so much more besides.

"Not if, but when..."

As time went on, I did sort out my feelings for the man they called Robin Hood.

But that was another story.

FIRST OFF I'D LIKE to thank my friend David Badurina, a brilliant author himself, whose tireless patience with an amateur gave me the confidence and know-how to get HOOD finally published.

To my editor Timothy McKay: you absolutely rock! This man took on the task of guiding me through this arduous process and helped me turn my ramblings into a legit book.

Lastly, to Tonya and Jude: for tolerating my need for solitude at times to write, laughing along as I read aloud, providing inspiration when I was stuck, and stopping me from yeeting my laptop on occasion. Ya'll were a huge part of bringing HOOD to life.

To the reader: I hope you enjoyed this first installment. See you in the sequel!

T. Rogers is a new author bringing it from the Dirty South. T. is a husband, father, paramedic, meme addict, firearms enthusiast, and occasional shitposter. Fueled by caffeine and sarcasm, T. is drawn to anti-heroes, flawed protagonists, punchy dialog, and underdog stories. Any narrative, from urban and supernatural fantasy to crime and angst, are within his wheelhouse. No subject, no genre, no tale is off limits. T. lives with his family in small-town Alabama and when not writing is either cheering on the Crimson Tide or sitting in the corner with a drink in his hand, silently judging you.

www.ingramcontent.com/pod-product-compliance
Lightning Source LLC
Chambersburg PA
CBHW070242140726
47909CB00019B/2026

* 9 7 9 8 9 9 4 3 2 7 6 1 6 *